The death of a memory care patient leaves behind items assumed worthless. Yet an investigation with global dimensions proves they are worth a fortune.

The Improbable Collector

Another Suspense Novel by
ANDREW B. LOUIS

For information regarding permission, please write to:
info@barringerpublishing.com
Barringer Publishing, Naples, Florida
www.barringerpublishing.com

Cover, graphics, and layout by Linda S. Duider
Cape Coral, Florida

ISBN: 978-1-954396-54-8
Library of Congress Cataloging-in-Publication Data
The Improbable Collector / Andrew B. Louis

Printed in U.S.A.

To neighbors, friends and family members
who remain my best inspiration.

OTHER BOOKS BY THE AUTHOR

Other novels by Andrew B. Louis include:

Operation Kovesh, The Shadow Experts, Below the Surface,
The Crypto Trap, Escaping the Bear, Glitter and Smoke,
Trouble in the China Sea, Seven Miracles to Save the World,
A Crooked Few and *Tough Choices* available at Amazon.com.

www.AndrewBLouis.com

PREFACE

Though all the writing and errors are solely my own doing, a number of people contributed to the creation of the text. I would like to thank the numerous friends and family members, as well as my wife, who were kind enough to comment on various drafts and led me to make material changes for the better.

All the parties to this story are totally fictitious and if there was some resemblance with individuals or institutions, it would be purely coincidental.

SYNOPSIS

An old patient who has spent the last thirty odd years of his life in pre-assisted living and then in an assisted living community dies. Everything which was in his large two-bedroom apartment is placed on consignment in a nearby shop, with the mandate to get whatever they can for these 'worthless' items. Coincidentally, a couple who is looking for a pair of nice antique chairs walks into the shop. The husband, of distant French origins, sees a painting he likes and enquires about it. He is told it is a copy and used to belong to an old gentleman who had a small collection of such copies, all, apparently, works from the Impressionist era. Looking at the canvas more carefully, he discovers something which leads him to wonder whether the painting might not be mischaracterized as a copy. He and his wife further look around the shop and happen to like a couple of old Louis XVI chairs, which the shopkeeper hastens to describe as 19th century reproductions at best, possibly even more recent. The shopkeeper adds that these two small armchairs belonged to the same gentleman who owned the impressionist reproductions.

On the spur of the moment, the couple buys everything that came from that old man. In addition to the two chairs and twelve paintings, there was a nice desk with a carved desk chair, an antique secretary with a fold-down top, a large armoire, and an artist folder containing drawings and etchings. Painstakingly following a series of clues, a few discovered through skill and a few others through sheer luck, they are able to find out the provenance of the real collection which they had acquired for a song. Furthermore, they discover that the old man did not live a terribly happy life and died without knowing anything about all these treasures he inherited from his father. Yet, despite having lost most of his memory, the one thing he remembered was his father's last instructions: "do not sell any of this." Yet, he had forgotten the second part of the sentence which the duo found on a letter written by his father; it said: "Do not sell any of this *without asking for help from a proper auction house.*"

Discovering old letters, bills of sale and many other mementos, the couple is able to retrace the life of the old man's parents and grandparents, and to uncover at least a couple of crimes committed against the family, not least of which is the murder of a great-aunt. They tell that side of the story as well, taking the reader back to investigations carried out principally in Switzerland in the late 1940s and eventually uncovering the guilty party. Ultimately, they are delighted to have been able to uncover the old man's secrets and to preserve for him and his family a name and an identity in keeping with the station in life they deserved.

Prologue

SPRING 2001
NAPLES, FLORIDA

A U.S. couple, with a Franco-German ancestry was sitting in the Naples office of New York-based Jeff Baker, the impressionist specialist of Sotheby's, one of the top two or three auction houses in the world. A week earlier, they had brought down to the firm's Naples office a painting, part of a lot which they had recently bought. At that time, they assumed the painting was a good piece in the impressionist style of Claude Monet, the well-known French impressionist master, but most likely a reproduction and not a genuine work of the master.

In truth, the story was a bit more complex than as just stated here. The couple had indeed bought a number of artworks, paintings, furniture and even a couple of table-top bronze sculptures at a consignment shop in their neighborhood. They had made the purchase after one of the paintings prominently on display had attracted the husband's attention. It was being sold as a reproduction, but Mike, the husband, wondered whether it could in fact be genuine.

Growing up, when still living with his parents in a large apartment Rue de Rivoli in Paris, he had developed the habit of studying across the street, in the Musée de L'Orangerie, located in the Jardin des Tuileries. Rue de Rivoli was indeed quite a noisy artery in the center of Paris, running alongside the Louvre Palace and its garden. Despite the fact that the family's apartment looked at the large park, the Tuileries, and had double-glazed windows, Mike's room facing the front of the building and thus the street was not really quiet. In fact, it was downright noisy, particularly when the outside temperature was warmer than usual. At a time when air-conditioning was in its infancy and therefore not available in the vast majority of older residential buildings, it could be very hot when the windows remained shut in the late spring and summer, despite room fans. That was what had given him the idea to take his books across the street to the museum and study in the space reserved for the famous group of paintings by Monet representing water lilies. This was a suite of two oval rooms designed by the master himself to display his masterpieces. It offered the opportunity for Mike to sit on one of the numerous divans in the middle of the room, with his books on his lap or placed next to him, on the divan. What a luxury to be able to dive into school work occasionally lifting one's eyes from the books to admire these extraordinary paintings, and promptly to return to mathematics and physics, Mike's most favorite topics! Later, he would willingly admit that that this experience sensitized him to impressionists, adding that he could not count the number of visits he paid to all the various Paris museums where parts of the French impressionist collection was displayed, before it was mostly regrouped in the Musée d'Orsay. That is when his dream started one day to own one of Monet's paintings.

The painting which attracted Mike's attention in the shop on that day was surely not by Claude Monet. Yet, it seemed somewhat unusual: though it was in the general impressionist style, yet much more detailed than other comparable works, it represented a street scene in Paris, Boulevard Haussman as it turned out. It was depicted from a high vantage point, seemingly from the upper window of a building. It reminded Mike of work by Edouard Manet or Edgar Degas, though it had its own style. It did trigger something in his mind but, initially, he could not quite place what "it" was. Rather than admiring the picture from as far away as possible, as one should do when dealing with impresionist works, he came as close to the canvas as possible, and looked at every corner of the piece, ostensibly searching for a signature. Though most everything looked absolutely normal, the first thing he noticed was the fact that the paint in the lower left corner seemed just a bit different from the rest. The brush strokes were a bit longer, less loose; and the color surely looked more even, not displaying the subtle variations for which the artists in the Impressionist School were famous. He touched the painting on that spot and was surprised, and more than mildly embarrassed, to see a small paint chip detach. He followed its fall to the floor in front of him and saw it break down into so many pieces that any effort to pick them up and placing them back where they belonged would have been futile. Looking back at the painting, Mike saw that the chip that had detached revealed some black writing. Clearly, it was not a complete signature, but could it be a part of the signature he had not been able hitherto to locate? He could only read five letters: "*botte.*"

Jeff Baker, who had flown in specially from New York for this meeting in Sotheby's office in Naples, Florida, was quite categorical when, after the customary greetings and small talk, he affirmed:

"Mr. And Mrs. de Barral, you own a stunning water lilies painting. I know that this won't surprise you; you could surely see it yourselves. What makes it special, quite special in fact, is that I am virtually certain that it is genuine. It must have been painted by the master, Claude Monet."

Annabelle, Mike's wife, had immediately asked:

"Wait, wait, wait. What makes you so sure? "Virtually certain" is a pretty strong . . ."

"Well, Annabelle, if I can call you by your first name . . ."

"Please, go right ahead."

"Thank you. Please call me Jeff. Well, it's not only the quality of the work, but the many tests we carried out on the painting. As you know, it was brought to me in New York a week ago by Frank Smart from this office."

Annabelle and Michael nodded as they had not learned anything new. Yet, Jeff could clearly see that his short explanation was not going to be sufficient. They still needed more. Jeff further explained that the authentication process for any painting was always quite complex. In this particular instance, the fact that the canvas was signed made it considerably easier to attribute it, though it might still be a reproduction. To start, the style was clearly in line with the work of Monet. More to the point, he said:

"The subject is a variation on known works from the artist."

It represented the pond at Giverny, a French village where Monet had a home and whose garden he painted on numerous occasions. Additionally, the subject reflected other work by the artist: water lilies blooming on the water, a part of a green wooden bridge in the upper right-hand quadrant, a couple of weeping willow trees and numerous other flowers, probably bearded irises (there is an iris variety named 'Mme. Claude Monet'), azalea bushes, and rhododendron, on the bank of the lake, near to where one would know that the master's house was.

Jeff paused for a second and added in passing, almost as an afterthought:

"But that is not enough to allow us to answer the obvious question: is it genuine or a fake?"

He could clearly see that he had Mike's and Annabelle's attention, particularly given his last question, so he added:

"We know that Monet painted a series of canvases which we have all come to name the twelve Japanese bridges . . ."

"Really?"

"Yes, Mike. So, you could assume that this is a copy of one of them and be done with it. But I'm really not convinced."

"Why?"

"Well, Annabelle, for a start, it does not match directly with any of the twelve. See, I have here for you a picture of each of the twelve pieces which have so far been known and listed as a group. You can judge for yourself: your painting is not one of them. Now, if you were going to paint a reproduction, would you not copy an existing work rather than do something generally similar to it, in the same style, and yet sufficiently different?"

Annabelle nodded, though she added:

"Agreed. That would certainly be the sensible thing to do. But maybe."

She paused for a few seconds as if trying to search her memory bank and suddenly continued:

"I seem to remember an old movie, with Peter O'Toole and Audrey Hepburn. Audrey's father in the movie was a painting genius selling fake canvases, but he never copied existing work. He painted in the style of the artist he was imitating and signed that artist's name."

"I know what you're talking about. I think the movie was entitled *How to Steal a Million*. That's obviously a thought; it made for a great movie in fact. Yet, I've never heard of that in the real world. Here, the bridge is depicted with much less emphasis than in any of the other twelve paintings of the Japanese bridge in his garden. So, you could argue that the work in fact completes the series. Also, instead of being from a similar vantage point as the other twelve, it shows the familiar scene from a different angle."

Jeff paused for a second, and absorbed in his art history thoughts, added:

"It makes me wonder whether Monet had second thoughts."

Mike was about to interrupt but Jeff motioned him to wait with a wave of his right hand. He continued:

"He had ostensibly loved the point of view loosely used in the other twelve paintings. Otherwise, why would he have chosen it for the series? Yet, at some point afterwards, he may have thought that there might be a better angle, or maybe just another angle worth exploring. Thus, he may have painted your canvas to guide us to that different point of view. He may even have wanted to point us to the one representation among the twelve which he preferred. Another thought might be that there are other paintings in the Japanese Bridge series which like this one are still unknown."

Pointing to one of the pictures, he added:

"But back to the idea that this one is unique, and Monet wanted to suggest the one of the series of twelve he preferred. Look at this one. See, the colors he used are indeed quite close to yours. Interestingly, it would suggest that Monet may not have chosen the one which most critics did choose; you know, the one where the bridge dominates . . ."

Annabelle interrupted and still asked:

"I understand, but how do you know this is not a reproduction, maybe a good one, but a reproduction nevertheless?"

"Ah. This is where science comes in. Sorry for the jargon, but paints and even varnishes tend to develop fluorophores as they age."

"Fluorophores?"

"Yes. I'm sure you're not asking me for the chemical formula. You want to know how we would even trace them, correct?"

"Absolutely."

"Thank God, because I certainly don't know the formula; in fact, I seem to recall that there are several compounds, each with their own formula. But I know how our process works. The fluorescent chemical will show up when irradiated with long-wavelength ultraviolet lamps. I won't bore you with the details, but this allows us first to confirm the age of a painting and second to see places where the painting might have been repaired or just touched up."

"I hate to say it, but: so?"

Jeff could have noticed, but ostensibly did not, that Annabelle was smiling at me when she asked the question. Jeff was too far into his explanation to allow himself to be sidetracked. He continued:

"So, the age of the painting would fit with it having been painted by Monet. But there is more. People like me are trained to see whether the brush strokes correspond to those which we know are used by this or that artist. In this case, the ultimate proof would have to be a bill of sale or something equivalent to be absolutely certain."

"And if we don't have one?"

"Well, Annabelle, that makes things a bit more complicated. On the basis of the available evidence and conceding that I do not know everything and that my opinion could still be proven wrong, I am still pretty sure that this is a painting by Monet. The only interesting thing is that there was some residue of more recent paint near the signature. It looked like some had been washed off already, but there was still enough matter to date that extra paint: late 1930s; probably just before or during the Second World War."

Jeff paused for a second and concluded:

"So, from my point of view, scientific tools tell me that the time at which the painting was completed is consistent with the period during which Monet was active. The paint which we date in the late 1930s only applies to the area of the signature. It's almost as if someone had painted over the signature to hide the name of the artist."

Turning more directly toward Mike, he simply added:

"Now, do you have any evidence that the painting is not an original?"

Mike replied:

"No, not really. However, we don't have anything that gives us the provenance of the work. We bought this painting along with a few others from a consignment shop. They sold them to us as reproductions. The only thing we know is that they belonged to an older gentleman, a concert pianist we're told, who recently died without friend or family. The only other person that knew him, beside the personnel of the assisted living facility would be his banker; he provided him with the funds he needed to cover his expenses."

Jeff could only reply:

"That does not tell me a lot but let me give you a piece of advice: If I had to bet, and I don't like to do that, I would still bet this is a genuine painting, not a fake. What this means is either that your old man owned a hidden treasure . . ."

He paused for effect, but neither Mike nor Annabelle interrupted. He finished his thought:

"Or this is a stolen good. If I were in your shoes, I would not sell it before you've investigated this a lot more. Holding onto, concealing, and trading in stolen property is a serious offense. You might in fact need a thoughtful detective to do that work."

Mike laconically added:

"And a good lawyer!"

Chapter One

FALL 2001 - PRESENT
NAPLES, FLORIDA

My name is Michel de Barral. I recently almost retired from a business life which had taken my family and me around the world and back more than a few times. In fact, I remember, one year, clocking more air miles than a brother-in-law, who was then an airline pilot. I spent that life working as an investment manager. I moved to the U.S. in my early twenties to complete my studies in business, more specifically, in marketing and finance. A French national by birth, I became an American citizen by choice a dozen years ago or so; on the occasion, I changed the orthograph of my first name to Michael, which seems easier for Americans to pronounce, though most of my friends and business associates simply call me Mike.

Before coming to the U.S., I grew up in a home whose decoration emphasized period furniture, and fancy artwork on the walls and in display cabinets, as well as nice oriental area rugs on the floor. Our family tree could be traced back a number of centuries, to the 1100s in fact. However, the massive fortune which ancestors had at one time possessed in the sixteenth and seventeenth centuries when they sat at the Court of Louis XIV or Louis XV had surely diminished, and by one heck of a lot. Yet, I should honestly admit that I still lived a life of privilege; the last several generations of the family had been quite successful in their professional activities rather than resting on their aristocratic titles. This was a contrast to what several aristocrats, including members of our own family, had done in the eighteenth and early nineteenth centuries, which explained why the family's wealth then had melted like snow in the sun.

I met my wife, Annabelle, at Northwestern University, although she was studying humanities in general and languages in particular, and not business. Chance has a way of playing a role in all of our lives and mine was no expection. Annabelle was born in the U.S. although, two generations ago, her family came from Northern Germany, the Schleswig-Holstein province to be more specific. Her family background was thus German, Danish and even Swedish as the sovereignty over that province, which in fact originally was comprised of two states, Schleswig and Holstein, became a case for regional disputes between Prussia and the Scandinavian kingdoms from the fifteenth century onwards.

She grew up in Middle America and also in relative affluence, with her parents appreciating the fine things in life. In particular, they gave Annabelle and her siblings ample opportunities to tour the world, accompanied or by themselves, to see natural and artistic treasures and to complete a first-class education. Her parents had encouraged her natural talent to learn languages. Thus, she became fluent in English, German, Danish, some Swedish; additionally, French which she had picked during her time in high school, coincidentally had triggered her becoming a strong Francophile. Her French studies created the opportunity for us to meet, though our friends would say that we are now firmly Franco-Americans, as we intentionally straddle both cultures. I might even argue that she is more francophile than I.

Our home, in a gated community near Naples, Florida, was finished a few years ago. We built it as a place where we would spend a few short holidays, but not as a primary residence. Our move to make it our primary residence has required us to revisit both the layout and the decoration. For a start, we were going to jettison the typical "decorator" furniture which we bought when the house was just built. We had to find space for the more traditional, and in our opinion, more beautiful stylish décor which we had in our previous home in Greenwich, Connecticut. The necessity to expand the house, adding a couple of bedrooms, as well as a separate formal family room gave rise to the need to shop for additional furniture and decorative items, once the structural changes had been completed.

We wanted to remain consistent with the tastes we both learned from our parents: nice furniture and artwork, comfort, hospitality and discretion. My French aristocratic upbringing found a perfect echo in Annabelle's Midwestern roots. We both believed that what we actually had was nobody else's business and thus did not need to be on display, except when we enjoyed the items for their artistic beauty. Yet, even then, they would be displayed in an appropriate setting without undue emphasis being placed on any single item in view of its estimated current market value. In short, both sets of parents had taught us never to confuse price and value. Thus, visitors to our home could easily be excused for failing to appreciate the value of the home's decoration, which brought together beautiful pieces inherited from one side of the family or the other, and esoteric collectibles acquired during our various overseas postings or even more recently in New England.

On that day, in early November 2001, we had decided to go look for a couple of small armchairs for the newly re-decorated "sitting area" of our master bedroom. We were interested in period pieces from either the Louis XV or Louis XVI styles to be consistent with the room's current theme. We had quickly decided initially to eschew the fancy antique dealers which we could find both within Florida and even on the internet. We had indeed noted in our annual summer trips to France that antique furniture seemed to be falling out of fashion. Prices, which had remained quite elevated for the better part of a generation, seemed to be moving sideways to down while many other things saw prices moving up. Furniture fashion at that time appeared to be shifting toward art deco or even the Danish style which was one of the cheapest alternatives when we furnished our first apartment after our wedding. In our view, knowing of this trend gave us an opportunity to avoid chasing prices up. Nevertheless, at the same time, we found that licensed antique dealers in the U.S. had yet to reflect the price trends we had uncovered in France. There was nothing wrong with that, particularly in the eyes of someone who had spent a good part of his professional life looking for "price arbitrages." We concluded that it had to reflect supply and demand in a particular market. However, as shoppers in a broader market we knew enough to avoid overpaying.

Rather, we had elected to shop casually in a few of the many consignment shops that can be found literally throughout Southwest Florida. That is where we hoped to find nice things at a fair price, and, possibly, a significantly underpriced piece, for instance because it was mischaracterized. We had already visited at least three or four of these shops when we were hesitating whether to continue on our quest. As Annabelle had said:

"I hate to admit to it, but so far what I've seen is pure junk. I think most people confuse antiques with simply old stuff! Imagine, buying empty old bottles of olive oil? Where's the art in there? Can't fathom that."

I could not disagree but wanted to give our effort at least one other try: "You never know what you can find . . . Remember the two Louis XV Cabriolet chairs which we found in Darien, Connecticut, a number of years ago. They surely were not cheap, but we later discovered they were signed pieces and surely worth more than what we paid."

Annabelle exhaled in a deep sigh and agreed to one final stop, coincidentally not far from where we lived, adding:

"You make me think of Peter when he was looking at grapes on the kitchen counter at my parents' house. Remember how he used to say: "just one more, Gramma; just one more." Well, you make quite a good imitation of your oldest son, dear."

Our next step, therefore, was a shop in one of the ubiquitous strip malls found in Southwest Florida. It happened to be almost around the corner to an assisted living complex.

While Annabelle was looking for the two armchairs she had really come to find, I allowed myself to walk and browse around the shop, which was in fact quite large. Suddenly, I stopped in front of a painting, probably about two feet by three feet, maybe a bit more since it was framed. Though at the very moment I did not know why I was attracted to that painting rather than to any of the many others hanging nearby, the fact is that it seemed somewhat eerily familiar. Looking closer I saw the price tag and was even more surprised, silently noting in my mind: *I am not even sure that the price covers the cost of the frame.* Still, my curiosity piqued, I called a saleslady and asked a few questions about the canvas. Her replies were a complete surprise to me:

"This is part of a group of a dozen or so reproductions of paintings by French impressionist masters."

"Really? Where did you get them?"

"Oh. It's a long story. An older patient of the assisted living place next door just died. He had these reproductions and a few pieces of antique-style furniture in his two-bedroom apartment. I was told that there's no heir or contact. The only person the staff knew to contact if anything happened to him was his banker. Apparently, they did, and they asked us to sell everything for them, remitting the proceeds directly to the banker . . . As an anecdote, I hear that the old man also had a nice piano which the assisted living center decided to keep. They've placed it in room, off a corner of the lobby and named the room after the patient who was a concert pianist before his health declined a lot."

Had she been right near me at that time, Annabelle would have added that my subsequent behavior was "classical Michael." Indeed, we surely had no need for any of these paintings or even any of the gentleman's furniture, unless he had a couple of nice armchairs, which was what we were indeed looking for. Yet, I got into the game and asked the saleslady for a more complete list of what the old gentleman was thus posthumously selling. She went back to the front desk, took a piece of paper from one of the desk drawers and started rattling off:

"Twelve framed oil reproductions of impressionist masters, a large artist folder filled with assorted drawings, an antique-style desk with its armchair, an antique-style secretary with fold-down leaf upper front, two antique-style armchairs, a large armoire, a couple of bedframes with antique-style bedstands and two bronze statuettes."

I could only reply:

"Wow! Thanks. Let me take a second look at that earlier reproduction that caught my eye."

By then, I had called Annabelle and said:

"Look at this painting. Does it remind you of anything?"

Annabelle initially did not reply; she was staring at the painting and wondered what it was that she should be noticing. She punted:

"To me, it looks like a Manet. But I can't see any signature . . ."

"Maybe not a whole signature, dear; but look here. Five letters and a date!"

Suddenly, a lightbulb went on. I exclaimed, though in a hushed tone not to attract attention:

"I got it. I know. Must be Gustave Caillebotte. Do you remember the painting in my parent's sitting room, right next to the left window, near the door to the living room?"

"In truth, no. I don't. However, why is that relevant?"

"Well, dear, that painting was by Caillebotte. Dad had told me that he was not one of the major impressionists. At best, his reputation was made by being a supporter of the movement and a buyer of several of the group's paintings. As a painter, he was broadly ignored until the early 1970s, after I left France. While I was still living at home, I remember Dad joking that many people were focused on big name impressionists and paying fortunes for their works, and yet he could buy that painting for a song."

"Hate to say this, Mike but: SO?"

"People do not make copies of secondary painters . . ."

Her eyes widened and she smiled that beautiful smile I could not resist any more now than thirty years ago. She simply said:

"Now you're talking."

She paused for a second and added:

"Wait a tick. If this one is not a reproduction . . ."

"I know where you're going. My thought exactly. What about the others? Could they be genuine as well?"

We asked the saleslady if she could put a hold on the whole lot for a maximum of two hours. She agreed. We then drove back to our house and used our desktop computer to look for any information we could find. Wikipedia was still quite a novelty then and it was surely not nearly as developed as today. Yet, I whistled when the page came up. It gave me all the information we wanted: *"Caillebotte liked to paint reality as it existed (. . .), hoping to reduce the inherent theatricality of painting. (. . .) His style and technique vary considerably among his works, as if "borrowing" and experimenting, but not really sticking to any one style. (. . .) But may just as likely be derived from his intense interest in perspective effects. A large number of Caillebotte's work also employs a very high vantage point . . ."* Turning to Annabelle, I simply added:

"I guess that settles it. High vantage point?" A painting representing a Paris boulevard painted from an upper window of a building. Don't tell anyone, but if you ask me, I'll bet that this is a genuine Caillebotte and that someone has painted over the signature, possibly to hide it. My touching it led a chip to fall off earlier this afternoon."

"What do you mean?"

"I'll explain that later. What if the painting, and the others that came with it, had been surreptitiously brought to the U.S. with the signature hidden so that they would not be recognized?"

"By whom?"

"Who knows? Maybe the customs from the country where the paintings originally were, maybe U.S. customs, maybe even someone else . . ."

We drove straight back to the consignment shop, making sure that in my excitement I did not go through a red light or find myself speeding. We found the sales lady and casually asked her to show us a few of the other paintings. She obliged and I noted that they were all unsigned. Furthermore, there always was a kind of a smudge, a high-quality smudge but a smudge nevertheless, on each of them in the general area when I would have expected a signature. So I asked her whether she would be willing to sell the whole of the older gentleman's collection and if yes what would the total cost be. She initially looked surprised but offered with a knowing smile:

"You two needed to discuss that before making an offer. Right?"

"We simply smiled back."

Chapter Two

MARCH 1938 - 1978
PARIS, FRANCE & BOSTON, SKOKIE AND NAPLES, U.S.

The day was March 12th, 1938. Stephane Schneider, a well-respected physician in Paris returned home earlier than usual from the hospital where he worked and taught. He seemed agitated when his wife, Simone, greeted him in the hallway of their comfortable apartment near the Trocadero, on Avenue Kleber. He kissed her on the right cheek and invited her to have a seat in their living room with him. He then started a story which would eventually change their world.

He was with a patient, discussing the findings of a recent radiology exam, at the hospital, when one of his associates barged into his office with a very disturbing piece of news which he had just heard on the radio: Germany had annexed Austria in what it called the *"Anschluss."* Though tensions had been running high as Germany wanted to unify the Germanic populations in Europe under one regime, many had hoped that the sovereignty of Austria would be respected. Ostensibly, it was not to be.

For Stephane, the news of the day marked a crucial turning point. Both he, and his wife, about ten years his junior, were of

Jewish ancestry, though they did not attend religious services other than at the time of what they called the "high holidays." Similarly, they did not maintain a Kosher household, though they generally abstained from eating pork and had a *mezuzah* on the right side of their front door. Interestingly, they had placed it inside the door frame and not outside where it could be seen by others. Stephane saw Judaism as a tradition, not a religion. Thus, Judaism was surely part of who he and his wife were; he would not renege on it but in keeping with Jewish traditions he would also not proselytize.

So, to him, the *Anschluss* was the signal that Hitler, who had been elected the new German Chancellor on January 30, 1933, was not going to be stopped. His Nazi party, officially referred to as the Third Reich, had risen to power at the end of the Weimar Republic, a democracy established at the end of World War One. The Weimar Republic proved to be nothing short of an economic disaster with inflation running so high that Germans needed wheelbarrows full of Deutsche Mark notes to pay for a single loaf of bread. His ambition, succinctly summarized in published historical documents was *"territorial expansion, which was largely driven by his desire to reunify the German peoples and his pursuit of Lebensraum, "living space," that would enable Germans to become economically self-sufficient and militarily secure."* With Hitler's profound distaste for the British, the French, and the winners at the Treaty of Versailles which brought World War I to an end, there was little doubt where he would try to go next.

Like many of their friends and acquaintances in France, Stephane and Simone had heard of these dangers. They had kept monitoring them ever since Hitler had risen to power; yet they had felt until then that they could remain put. They had heard of a "concentration camp" being created in Dachau, but it seemed still somewhat far away. Plus, nobody really knew then what a concentration camp was or could eventually become. Antisemitic laws were not enacted in France until 1940 and 1941, and thus, on paper at least, Jews had the same rights as everyone else in 1938. Life was not totally secure, but then when had it ever been?

However, the *Anschluss* was telling Stephane that something was changing and that there was no way of knowing how far the potential danger could go. He concluded it would be much better to leave when he would be one of a very small group of emigrants rather than wait for things to get too visibly worse, and the desire for Jews to leave France too widespread. In his unhappy situation, Stephane knew that his family had experienced persecutions earlier before they settled in France. He knew that his father had fled Lithuania in 1890 to come to France.

Simone on her end did not have that history. Though of Jewish ancestry herself, her family had been established in France for several generations. She could not resist a good cry when Stephane told her of his decision. Yet, it was not terribly hard for Stephane to rekindle the kind of fears associated with memories of persecutions and of the only survivors being those who had had the courage to pick up stakes before it was too late. Deep down, she knew very well she could not resist what was going to take her away from friends and family. So, Simone quickly came to recognize that her husband was right. Additionally, as he explained to her:

"France and the old continent will only be a long boat ride away from America . . ."

Smiling meekly, while wiping tears away, Simone could only reply:

"Yes. I know. It's still nearly four weeks one-way. And it's so expensive."

Stephane knew better than to keep this discussion going. He had made his point. Simone had made hers. They both knew they were privileged enough that they could take the trip in relative comfort and that this was not one of those voyages from which there was no return. The death of his father six years earlier had reduced the connection Stephane felt he had to France, though his mother as well as his sister and her husband were still in Paris. They did not seem interested in leaving quite yet.

After having booked their crossing together with as much of their day-to-day goods as they could carry, they went through every room of their comfortable apartment, deciding what they wanted to take with them and what could be left in Paris. Indeed, they had originally decided that they should not sell their apartment, not so much because they fully intended to come back, but rather because they did not want to attract undue attention and did not want to take the time. However, it also allowed Stephane to retain some credibility when he told his mother, his sister and her husband, that their departure might not be final. The door was open for them to come back at one point. They were fortunate enough to have the means to start a new life across the Atlantic Ocean while keeping a suitable *pied-a-terre* in France. And the apartment on Avenue Kleber surely was a very nice *pied-a-terre*.

They quickly decided that they should only take with them the best of the artwork and only a few pieces of furniture, those which had the most sentimental value to them. Stephane and Simone had indeed agreed that they would like to have in their new apartment across the ocean at least one room that could remind them of what they left behind. They packed most of their clothing in the big, Provençal armoire which they definitely wanted to take with them, reserving for their suitcases only items which they would need to wear on the boat. Simone was surprised to see Stephane invite their good friend, Ferdinand, a local woodworker, to come to the apartment and help him with the packing. She did not fully understand why Ferdinand was going to help, but her job was to make sure that everything they took was clean and that their 5-year-old boy, Jacques, continued to be well taken care of. His sister, Caroline, who was ten years old, was old enough to take care of herself with limited help from her mother.

Their initial destination was Boston. Stephane was sadly well-aware that he would have to take anew all the various exams he had had to pass to get his doctorate when in Paris. He had first reacted forcefully when told that he would need to take his high school exam again, but, in the end, showing wisdom, he simply declared: *beggars can't be choosers.*

Stephane proceeded quickly through the retaking of a variety of exams, covering all of the topics he had to pass to obtain the right to practice medicine in Boston. Though his degree in France covered both general medicine and a specialty in radiology, he quickly decided that he did not want to take the time to suffer through another radiology residency. They surely had money and he could have managed to study some more rather than start practicing, but it was more a case of having had enough of the study and wanting to see patients again, in addition to a plain and simple desire not to spend too much of their reserves. He would practice general medicine and would be happy with it. While he was studying, Simone kept busying herself with the children and managing the household in a smaller apartment than the one they had left behind. They only had two bedrooms, with the children sharing a room, a nice L-shaped living room with the space for Stephane to have his "office", and a dining room and a kitchen, which, as it turned out, was in fact a bit larger than the one they had in Paris. Most French apartments tended not to allow as much room as their American counterparts for the kitchen.

Once he had taken his board exams in Massachusetts, Stephane started working at the local hospital. He had realized that he did not have the network he would have needed to start or join an independent practice. Plus, working in a hospital would allow him to meet colleagues and possibly at some later point to revisit his original decision to forego radiology.

He was lucky enough to meet someone at a conference who would change his medical life. The individual he met was Jewish as well. Though born in the U.S., his family had left the old continent a generation ago. He remembered what it was to live as a new immigrant, though he was still quite young when his parents moved to the U.S. from Austria. He listened to the tale of woe and success which characterized Stephane's move to the U.S. The success had to do with his ability to continue to practice medicine, but the woe was that he was only a general practitioner in a large city hospital rather than an x-ray specialist.

The friend, Maury Baumgardner, had created one of the first private hospitals in the U.S., in the Chicago area specifically, and offered Stephane a deal he could not turn down. Stephane was to come to the North Shore of Lake Michigan, to Skokie in Illinois, just outside and to the north of Chicago, and join the staff of Maury's hospital. He would have to pass the Illinois Board exam, but Maury told him that should be but a formality for him. Maury's proposal was particularly attractive as if would allow Stephane both to practice general medicine to earn his living and to spend time in the radiology department, doing what turned out to be a simplified residency. This made it possible for him to become a radiology specialist within five years, just one year more than it would have taken him had he studied full-time. Thus, while staying at the hospital, he would be able to expand his clientele substantially, keeping some general practice early on and gradually shifting to radiology. In fact, he was also able to carry out some research, following pioneering work by Dr. Karl Theodore Dussik from Austria who published the first paper on medical ultrasonics in 1942. That got Stephane on the publication bandwagon and enhanced his reputation, allowing him soon to be able to take a few teaching duties at Northwestern University in downtown Chicago.

Stephane would routinely comment to friends who wanted to listen that he enjoyed much more the general ambiance of the Midwest of the U.S. than the environment he had briefly encountered in New England. While people in the Midwest seemed more genuine, he had found New Englanders more "stuffy," less "friendly" and generally less welcoming to the stranger that he was. He thought this may simply reflect the more "mature" nature of society in New England, and the fact that groups were already created and thus harder to join by newcomers. The family enjoyed the life they were living and, after his mother died in 1941, Stephane and Simone made the decision to sell the apartment in Paris as soon as the war was over in 1945. They initially left all the remaining furnishings and the art collection he inherited from his mother in storage in Paris, fully intending eventually to bring everything over to the U.S.

Twenty years later, they had taken the additional step of purchasing a condominium near Fort Myers in Southwest Florida, an area which was only opening up, though it had had a number of famous homeowners such as Thomas Edison, Henry Ford, or further south, the Collier family to only name three. Eventually, the condominium was sold, and the family moved into a single-family home in the Port Royal section of Naples, way before it became the most opulent district it subsequently turned out to be. The beaches, tropical climate, landscape, and the definite midwestern atmosphere provided all the family needed. Naples eventually became the U.S. city with the largest number of golf courses per capita, making it easy for Stephane to practice a sport which he had picked up in Skokie. While golf was "stuffy" and limited to the wealthy in France, Stephane had found it easy and reasonably priced to start and then to enjoy in the U.S. Simone eventually showed some interest, though she never really picked up the sport in earnest. While he took that opportunity to bring back to the U.S. most of the furnishings he had left in storage in France, he still preferred not to move the art collection, other than the few paintings he had initially brought over, having noted that insurance costs in his newly adopted country could be considerably more expensive than what insured storage cost him in France.

Life was good, in fact very good, until tragedy struck in the late fall of 1968, when the family had flown to Naples to celebrate *Hanukkah* and the year-end holiday away from the frigid shores of Lake Michigan. The kept a spare automobile in Naples, a Buick Electra 225, which was so named because it was 225-inches long; eventually it had become known as the "Deuce and a Quarter." They had flown to Fort Myers airport and settled in their home in Port Royal for the two weeks the family intended to spend in Florida. By then, though nobody seemed to question the situation, neither of the children were married, though Caroline was 40 and Jacques, who by then had adopted Jack as a shorter if technically inaccurate version of his French name (should have been James or Jim) was 35. Caroline had been married when she was quite young, 20, but had ended up divorcing twelve years later with no descendant. Stephane and Simone had come to the conclusion that her infertility issue had to have played some role in the divorce, though they never discussed it with anyone outside of the family. Certain friends of the family were more direct arguing that it was the pressure from not being able to conceive which sounded the death knell of the marriage but would never say it too openly.

Jack was never married and did not ever seem to enjoy the company from either male or female friends too much. Today, certain people might wonder whether he suffered from autism, but this was not a topic which people discussed then, though his father certainly concerned himself with the situation and kept studying it in the published literature. Jack was totally committed to music, having studied piano and become quite a virtuoso. In fact, he had quite a few records to his name, both as a solo player and as a part of a quartet. Interestingly, he hardly ever deviated from pure classical music, and had never been more than occasionally tempted by the numerous blues or jazz clubs which are a well-known part of the landscape of Chicagoland!

Stephane and the family had decided to visit the John and Mable Ringling Museum of Art in Sarasota, less than one hundred miles north of Naples. He had exited the highway and was quietly driving on a country road, when a drunk driving a pickup truck much too fast collided with them at an intersection. Simone and her daughter Caroline were killed instantly. Stephane did not die on the spot but did not survive more than a few days after the accident.

Jack, the only remaining member of the family who was in the car with them was ejected and landed in a soft area. Jack suffered serious trauma to the head but survived the accident. Unfortunately, his mental capacities were partially impaired though he was totally physically functional. His major issues surrounded his ability to concentrate on anything other than music, together with memory problems. He maintained an ability to remember events having occurred prior to the accident yet seemed unable to remember much of anything recent. Today, people might suspect that the trauma might have amplified the condition which Jack seemed to have at the time, but it remained untreated.

Thankfully, Stephane had made plans should something happen to him or Simone or both, although, interestingly, he seemed to focus more on a plane crash than on a car accident. He left a letter of wishes which would allow Jack and Caroline to be well taken care of. The letter also mentioned a customary will, but we initially did not find it; at least, if it did exist, it was probably saved somewhere else than where we looked. Time would tell.

In the letter of wishes, he had asked that all real estate be sold and placed in a trust for the benefit of his two children, with his future grandchildren the remaindermen. He had mentioned that a charitable foundation ought to be created to receive whatever was left upon the death of his last surviving child if there were no grandchildren. No provision governed the trust if there were grandchildren who would then inherit its assets. All his financial assets were to be placed in the trust as well, which also was the beneficiary of the substantial insurance he had in his and Simone's lives. The children were to be given all art and furniture contained in the residences or in storage, adding that a letter to be opened by them only would inform them of anything they needed to know about these items. We did not find that letter either though we did later find a detailed inventory, which may well have been what Stephane meant. Until then, indeed, Stephane who had inherited everything that was available to him from his parents in France had focused his conversation with his children on the historical and artistic value of these objects rather than on their market prices. Again, this was his "value rather than price" focus.

With Jack the only survivor, Stephane's banker was charged with the task of finding appropriate accommodations for him. We found a letter which he sent to Jack in the central drawer of Jack's desk. He recounted the process he followed to fulfill Stephane's instructions. With no known family around with whom to discuss or debate any choice, he spent some good quality time with Jack. Stephane's banker realized that, in addition to the trauma-induced mental deficiencies, Jack probably suffered from some other social challenge, as he really did not appear to have any friend, nor did he seem to seek any; that part of the diagnosis was couched in extremely vague terms, and the foregoing represents our interpretation of what he meant, given other information we had. The banker went as far as having a few meetings with neighbors of the family in Port Royal and did not hear anything other than wonderful comments on Stephane and Simone, who appeared to be universally appreciated and loved. He did not record any comment on Caroline, though that was not surprising as, despite her divorce, she had remained an infrequent visitor to Naples. All comments which he heard on Jack were always focused on music: he was reported to spend countless hours practicing, which a few neighbors felt was wonderful while others were less fond of hearing scales and parts of pieces which he was rehearsing.

After having, as instructed, sold both the home in Port Royal and the house in Skokie, he eventually decided to buy for Jack a comfortable apartment in a gated community which also offered services which we would today call assisted living services. The banker's thoughts were that Jack might eventually need to move to the assisting living area if his health required it. He had made sure that the apartment was soundproofed as perfectly as possible, as he knew that Jack would inevitably want somewhere to locate his favorite Steinway grand piano. The apartment also had to be large enough that Jack could choose the furniture and art which he wanted to have in his new place and did not have to make too many heartbreaking choices; that may explain why Jack had a three-bedroom apartment, one room of which served as a music room. Not surprisingly, as Jack remembered his father once telling him not to sell anything that had come from France, as they were the family's treasure, he elected to keep all the items he could squeeze into the apartment (which looked more like a museum than a common apartment) while all the rest were kept in storage.

Chapter Three

2001
NAPLES, FLORIDA

The first thing which Annabelle and I did when we received the goods purchased from the consignment store was to place them in our garage. Though our house originally only had a two-car garage, the expansion we needed to accommodate our whole family with Naples becoming our primary residence allowed the construction of a second, two-car garage in a symmetrical position relative to the other on the front of the house. I know it may sound a bit trite, but both of us are sensitive to symmetry and the opportunity to recreate it as we expanded the house was too simple to be overlooked. We were indeed able to add one of the two bedrooms over the new garage and the other almost right behind it. That gave the house almost a two-wing look which made it look almost *"Aixoise,"* after an architectural style made famous in Aix-en-Provence.

Though we still had quite a bit of decorative work left in the house itself, the whole structure was by then completely inhabitable and fully air-conditioned. That included the second garage which already had its air-conditioning in place, though there was nothing else in it: a perfect spot for us to store temporarily at least our purchases, with plenty of space to spread them as needed. We had learned the hard way that air-conditioning was a very important and quite cheap addition to any southwest Floridian garage when we had needed to replace the top of my convertible; it had deteriorated because of the summer heat that damaged it in the first garage prior to our installing the air-conditioner there.

The space provided by the two bays within the new garage gave us ample opportunity to set up the various pieces we had acquired and thus begin in earnest our analysis of what it was we actually purchased. The only drawback was the cold, raw, concrete floor which forced us to be very careful whether we moved a piece of furniture or placed a painting down on it. Initially, our principal focus was on the paintings, as the recognition that the Caillebotte was quite probably genuine led us to check as carefully as we could the other eleven paintings and thus have a real inventory of what they were.

One thing kept nagging me. I could imagine that someone would have wanted to hide the origin of the paintings, or even their monetary value at some point. It was easy to believe that someone fleeing his home country with some of their most precious belongings would have wanted to hide their true value; that ought to have minimized the risk of theft and save on any potential custom duties, though we knew that artworks are typically exempt from import duties. At the same time, it was just as easy to imagine that someone who had stolen artworks would want to hide the signatures; they knew they had masterpieces but may not have wanted everyone to know it either. Yet, the thing that kept bothering me was: Why would the individual who brought them into the U.S. not unhide the signatures once in the U.S.?

In my mind, the question and the fact that I did not have a satisfactory fact-based answer made me fear that Annabelle and I might have happened on stolen art. That was the only almost reasonable explanation that came to mind at the time, though it was still totally unsatisfactory. Why would a thief not try to dispose of stolen goods? I know that there have been numerous stories written and films made of an art lover turning into a thief out of a desire to own a particular piece. Then, he or she might elect not to reveal the signatures he has hidden. But that sounded quite far-fetched when it involved twelve paintings . . .

Our first step when we had brought the paintings home had been to look more carefully at the painting which we had assumed was by Gustave Caillebotte. Annabelle took a damp cloth and applied it gently to the area where the paint chip had fallen off in the store. Initially, nothing much happened, except that she could see some paint leeching onto the cloth, albeit ever so slowly. Thank God; that had to mean that the paint was water-based and would eventually come off. She decided to alter her approach marginally. She calmly went to our bathroom, where she kept a supply of first aid stuff and over-the-counter surplus medication in one of her vanity drawers. She picked up a couple of gauze compresses, making sure that there were not of the pre-humidified kind; she did not want any sort of chemical to touch the painting. She dunked one of the compresses into distilled water. Coming back into the garage, she asked me to lay the painting flat on the floor. She then applied the compress to the area of the canvas where we could see some of the supposed signature. We gave the water a good fifteen minutes to work, although I must honestly confess that we kept lifting a corner of the compress every couple of minutes or so to gauge progress. We were driven as much by the curiosity of whether anything was happening as by the fear that we may be inflicting damage to the painting.

Eventually, the first signs of success began to appear: more and more paint was oozing onto the compress. Annabelle removed the compress and tried again to wipe the paint off. Success was not wildly more encouraging, yet there was some visible progress. Though we were beginning to see more and more of the letters in the signature, there remained a lot of paint where it should not be. Yet, we both noticed an important point, which was going to help us a lot in our detective work: water was not affecting the painting where the chip had fallen off; that area of the painting looked a bit clearer, but it was obvious, to our eyes at least, that, underneath the paint we were removing, we were looking at the sheen of varnish. That varnish would have been applied by the artist once the painting was completed, and thus below the layer meant to hide the signature. This encouraged us considerably as it meant that obviously for as long as we remained cautious, we could apply enough water to dilute the water-based paint that had been used to cover the signature without fearing that we would damage the work of art itself.

Long story short, we finally saw the signature appear: G. Caillebotte. On a hunch, time zones making it possible, I called my sister-in-law who had inherited the painting that was in our parents' apartment. She was surprised and kept asking questions, but I kept pushing back simply telling her to trust me. She went and looked at the painting on her living room wall and came back:

"On ours, there is a date as well. Right, under the signature, almost in the middle."

She paused and added:

"May not mean much, but, at least, that's the way ours is signed."

Annabelle worked her magic a bit more right under and virtually in the middle of the signature she had uncovered and, sure enough, she ended up revealing two digits: 78. We deduced that the painting had been completed in 1878. I ran to my laptop in my office to check Wikipedia. I was happy to see that this was indeed the way the master signed and dated his work. Annabelle kept on cleaning the whole area until no more paint seemed to be leeching onto the gauze, noting with a wry smile:

"No more paint, but still quite a bit of dirt. But I know I am not a restorer of old canvases. The dirt can wait."

We had a short laugh. We knew we had eleven more paintings on which to work and were anxious to see whether the Caillebotte was an exception, or all paintings were in fact genuine masterpieces. The next painting we attacked was relatively easy to select; it was the one which looked like a known work by Claude Monet. My love affair with Monet made that choice absolutely obvious, as I was thinking: . . . *what if I really had that Monet I've been dreaming of?* Looking down to the lower right or left corners of the canvas, we found an area on the lower left edge of the canvas with what we deemed some "suspect paint overcoat;" it surely shared many of the attributes we had seen on the Caillebotte. Annabelle applied her wet compress on the location, let it sit for long enough and finally revealed both the signature of the master and a full date to the right of the signature: 1899. I was beside myself with excitement; in fact, Annabelle told me to stop acting like a child opening a Christmas present. Our spur-of-the-moment purchase looked increasingly good. Annabelle calmed us both down:

"Don't forget that we may be looking at stolen goods."

We kept going on the remaining ten paintings, applying the water with admittedly less and less caution. Our efforts seemed to keep producing the same result: a signature which was very much in line with the artists we anticipated. What surprised us though we had noted it before we uncovered the signatures was that next to impressionists names such Manet, Monet, Renouard, or Van Gogh, we found a couple of paintings, one each by Paul Cezanne and Paul Gaugin. Though initially part of the impressionist family, they evolved away from it to become among the first in the post-impressionist era. This eventually led to Henri Matisse and André Derain starting the Fauve movement. A bigger surprise was that the list also included three less well-known names: Camille Pissarro, Berthe Morisot, and Alfred Sisley, along with a second painting by Caillebotte.

We cross referenced the dates and the signatures when we could and went as far as looking across as many art sites as possible to check whether any of them displayed any one of "our" paintings. I must confess that I was somewhat relieved not to see any of the paintings we had in the garage on any of those sites. While it did not rule out the possibility that we had stumbled on stolen art, it was reassuring that the art we had bought at least was not among the major or catalogued works of any of these artists if they were stolen goods.

Before closing, I have to admit that the work of hiding the signatures was in fact better executed than I might have initially led anyone to believe with my earlier comment. Nothing was absolutely obvious, and I can easily believe that many a non-suspecting soul would have ignored it, as I might have had I not clumsily led to a paint flake detaching from the Caillebotte and revealing some of the artist's signature.

Feeling that we had done just about as much as we could with the paintings at that point, we decided to bring them within the part of the house that was covered by our alarm system, which did not extend to either garage. It would be a twisted and perverse turn of event for thieves to come and steal from us goods that might have been stolen themselves. We were not ready to concede defeat on that front: the paintings might be stolen goods, but they might very well not be. With the paintings tucked away in a closet under the staircase to the second floor, we sat at the kitchen table and drew up a list of the "loot": Two paintings by Monet, two by Van Gogh, two by Caillebotte and one each by Manet, Morisot, Pissarro, Renouard, Gaugin and Cezanne. If these were genuine and not stolen, we would have stumbled on an absolute fortune. Any euphoria, however, was immediately damped by a nagging thought: could we really keep them?

On a hunch, I went straight back to the garage, to look at the Louis XVI desk we had bought along with all the rest. I looked in each of the three drawers on the front; they each had a lock, and the keys were in the locks. Interestingly, the locks and the keys did not look totally like those with which we were familiar. Typically, it is the male part of the key that enters into the lock, and the various serrations at the end of the key interact with the lock to allow it to open. Here, the key initially looked the same, but on closer inspection the male part of the key was in fact an empty cylinder rather than a solid piece of metal. The female part of the lock in fact had four protruding male parts which had to fit the exact contour of the cylinder to allow the key to penetrate all the way into the lock. Once there, the serrated part of the key played its usual role, and the lock could open. I had never seen anything like that but found it quite clever. I assumed that this was a more sophisticated setup, which suggested that the piece of furniture had been built by a master builder.

The desk had a central drawer, a bit shallower than the other two which were symmetrically arranged on the left and on the right. The middle contained a neatly arranged folder. I saw a few pictures, as well as several letters. I called Annabelle who came to join me in the garage. She suggested, and I wholeheartedly agreed, that we ought to sit down to peruse the contents and naturally pointed to the two cabriolet armchairs we had purchased. Speedreading the letters, they confirmed that the old man's name was Jack. He had to have been quite close to his parents, particularly his father: I did not see any letter written by his mother, though a few birthday cards proved she existed. We suspected that the letters from his father probably also mentioned her, but, at that point, we were not ready to pour into what was written in detail. We were on a mission, a mission to find anything which might shed light on the paintings we had just finished cleaning up sufficiently to reveal the artists' signatures.

The drawer on the right side had quite a number of letters and a few photos, also all in a folder; the one element which I thought was interesting, but which would require Annabelle's help, was that there were a few letters written in French, which would be no problem for me, and also in German, or at least something that seemed like German; they looked old, judging by the handwriting. However, there was nothing among these papers that was of direct relevance to our current pursuit: anything that told us who had bought the paintings, when, from whom and at what price. Certainly, there was no folder containing any information on any of these goods. I knew we would have plenty of time to look through those later, though I was still a bit ambivalent: was it right for us to peak into the gentleman's private stuff?

The drawer on the left was not as well-organized, but the subject matter explained it: it contained several newspaper clippings. One of them was terribly sad; in fact, it was not one, but two articles clipped together. The first reported on the car accident which had killed Jack's mother and sister, while the second dated less than a week later reported that his father who had been badly injured in the accident died as well. Among the other clippings, it was interesting to find articles which talked of Jack's performances as a concert pianist; he must really have been quite good. The folder also contained a receipt from a local storage company; it listed a number of items which had not been sold when Stephane died and made it clear that they were all Jack's property. We did not know if they had been separately sold by Stephane's banker when Jack died, although it did not make a lot of sense for that scenario to be real: why not entrust the whole of Jack's goods to the same shop? It was thus probably more logical to think that these stored goods were still in storage. In fact, since we had the receipt, we wondered whether we had bought these as well but were totally unsure. We would eventually need to see an attorney. I made a mental note that we would need to check on this.

Returning to the fact that I found nothing related to the paintings in the desk, I was thinking to myself that I could not or should not have been surprised: the desk had to be the first place anyone would look. Furthermore, if someone had found bills covering the purchase of even just one of these paintings, assuming that it proved the artwork was genuine, that someone would immediately embark on the kind of work which Annabelle and I had just carried out. They would have either found out the art was genuine or not. And we would not be asking the question ourselves as we could only have bought the lot if they had concluded the art was not genuine. Deep down, I knew that there were plenty of other places where "stuff" might be available, for instance in one of the other pieces of furniture, but I had neither the courage nor the inclination to look at that point. It was late and I was tired. Adrenaline can push someone to exceed their limits, but it does not eliminate them: mine were catching up with me, and I am pretty sure Annabelle's were as well.

Chapter Four

2001
NAPLES, FLORIDA

The following morning, Annabelle and I discussed our next move as we were having breakfast at the table in the kitchen. In some way, we knew that we had to have an expert take a look at the paintings, but we surely did not want to give away our whole game quite yet; we were not going to disclose the whole "collection." We thought we should pick one of the paintings and have an expert tell us first if it was genuine and if so, what its value might be. We could always expand the exercise to the rest of the canvases if the results on the first seemed to justify it.

We had in the past used Sotheby's to buy a few pieces of Japanese art to complete my father's *netsuke* collection which I had inherited, and even a nice cocktail ring which I had recently given Annabelle for her fiftieth birthday. We also had used other auction houses here or there, but we were never in a situation where the items we were considering each possibly represented the whole of our net worth, if not more. We quickly came to the conclusion that we should use Sotheby's, for a reason that might be quite stupid, but shows human frailties so well. Years earlier, when I had brought to the U.S. my father's *netsuke* collection, I had contacted both Sotheby's and their major competitor to take a look and tell me what was great, good or simply fair. I had felt that the competitor had not taken me seriously, while Sotheby's had pulled out all stops to help. Whether that was really what the competitor did or simply how I felt on that day did not matter; I selected Sotheby's then and had a truly first-class experience with them then. So, Sotheby's it was this time as well. Simple as that.

So, while the decision to show only one painting as a start was not terribly difficult, the question of which painting we were going to show was a lot more challenging. We went back and forth for a little while, not so much arguing about one or another of the pieces, but rather on how we should make the decision. We still kept in the back of our minds the reality that we did not know what we had. The paintings could all be reproductions, notwithstanding my belief that no one in his right mind would copy the work of Caillebotte. They could also all be genuine. If they were genuine, they could all be stolen. And, though less likely, there could be some mix of both. My juvenile "love affair" with Monet together with the fact that the painting "talked" to us led us to settle on the "Japanese Bridge," as we called it. It was our favorite and we let our hearts drive the decision, though I am not sure our brains would have come to a different outcome if let to operate on their own.

We knew that Monet had painted a series of paintings on that subject. In fact, it was one of his "trademarks," so to speak, that he would take a subject and paint it in numerous conditions; the examples of the Cathedral in Rouen, the famous haystacks, Venice, the poplars, the London House of Parliament, and most of all the Water Lilies immediately came to mind. These series were seen by Monet as a whole which, when all paintings were contemplated together, should capture what he was trying to represent. Each series had over time been carefully catalogued, with the Water Lilies by far the most prolific as it is said to contain more than two hundred and fifty oil paintings. Looking into details relevant to "our own painting," we learned that the "Japanese bridge" series contained twelve different canvases. For some reason I cannot explain we could not find pictures of all the paintings in the series; most likely it reflected the fact that Wikipedia was still in its infancy. So, we could for a while at least either believe that we had one of the originals in front of us, or sadly only a copy of one of them. However, even if we were looking at an original, had it been Jack's property or was it a stolen good, or both, i.e. first stolen and then inherited by Jack who had no idea that the painting might have been stolen?

We contacted the Naples office of Sotheby's and made an appointment for the following morning with Frank Smart who was quite welcoming and seemed genuinely interested in our piece. He asked us a few questions, the most important of which related to the bill of sale related to our purchase. We produced the hand-written bill which the consignment shop saleslady had filled out. His face changed as he was reading it, and he asked:

"It says twelve reproductions of impressionist paintings here . . . I assume this is one of them. I have to compliment the painter as this is a hell of a good copy, but what else can I tell you?"

That is when I had to open the kimono just one bit. I did not want to discuss the whole lot, as I did not want to encourage him to ask to see all the paintings at that point. So, I let go of a little white lie, all the while looking straight into Annabelle's eyes to make sure she understood the game I was playing. I said that I had no difficulty believing that all the paintings were reproductions, and that the truth was that we bought the lot simply because it contained two armchairs which we liked quite a bit, as well as a desk and its desk chair. I added that given the fact that the price being asked for the whole was not more than what we would have expected to pay for the armchairs and the desk, we simply bought the whole lot.

"Interesting, Mike, if I may call you by your first name, but why this one and not the others? And what do you want us to opine on?"

"Please . . . I was getting there, Frank. For reasons that I can discuss but which are not terribly important, I love the work of Monet, and frankly, I have always dreamt of owning one. I certainly never had the means to buy one. But as my wife and I were looking more closely at the painting, we noticed that the paint in the lower left-hand corner looked a bit different from the rest. More uniform color, longer brush strokes, something we could not explain. On a hunch, we decided to apply a wet gauze compress to the area, and, to cut a long story short, that superficial paint leeched onto the compress and revealed the signature . . ."

Frank Smart looked pensive. Even maybe a bit suspicious. He asked:

"Could it be a disguised stolen good?"

"Could. Certainly could. Wouldn't know how to find out though. In fact, why stop at the signature being covered up. Why not wonder whether the whole painting could be a reproduction of a real painting with a completely different subject? We uncovered a signature, but we certainly were not about to apply our wet compress treatment to the whole piece . . . Having said that, would you use a well-known subject by a Master to cover a stolen painting? And if so, why would you not sign that well-known subject as well?"

"I see. This makes a bit more sense now. Did you do the same thing on any of the other paintings?"

I lied as I said: "No. Not yet. We wanted to have a real expert take a look at our favorite one and then decide what our next steps were going to be. It did take us some time to reveal the signature on this one. Why spend the time on the others if this one turns out to be a fake?"

"You said that you bought pieces of furniture as well. Correct?"

"Absolutely."

"Have you looked at them in any detail?"

At that point, I had no difficulty sticking to the truth. I told the story of my inspection of the desk and of what I found in the drawers. Frank seemed interested, but the part that caught his attention the most predictably was the fact that there was no record of the "seller" having ever bought the items. He asked further:

"What other piece of furniture did you buy?"

Annabelle beat me to the punch:

"Well, the two Louis XVI-style armchairs, the desk and its desk chair, both Louis XVI-style as well, a fine woodwork secretary, which does look like it is in the same style, though it could be a tad older."

She stopped and immediately corrected herself:

"I don't mean older with respect to the piece of furniture, obviously. I mean older style, may be Transition, for instance."

Frank knew that the Transition period corresponded to the last of the three phases of the Louis XV style, running from 1750 to 1774. Then, the newness and Rococo extravagance of the Louis XV style gradually made way for a return to the classical inspiration, which one had seen earlier. Eventually, it became a hallmark of the Louis XVI-style and found its zenith in the Napoleonic Empire era.

He nodded, allowing Annabelle to continue:

"What else? Oh! A gorgeous armoire, actually it is quite tall. No wooden inlays, but beautifully carved front, both the doors and what I'll call the crown at the top; it even has carvings on the sides, in a bas-relief mode. It's in a dark brown wood; I'd guess walnut, but I'm no expert. The style looks older than Louis XVI, maybe Regence, but who knows? That there is no marquetry work suggests it could be from the provinces rather than Paris, but again who knows? We also bought an artist folder containing at least two dozen etchings or drawings; I did not see any that bore any signature. But then again, I did not look terribly carefully either; most artists do not sign their drawings in preparation of oil paintings, correct?"

She paused for a second and, without giving Frank a chance to answer her question, genuinely speculated:

"In fact, if you agree that the paintings are reproductions rather than genuine pieces, it could well be that the drawings were made by the faker to train his hand."

Turning to me she added:

"We should look at these more seriously, honey. That may be a clue."

I smiled and agreed with her. Frank was now seemingly a bit lost in his thoughts. He was obviously still hesitating between the belief that those were simple reproductions and the fear they were stolen goods. He asked whether it would make sense for him to come and visit us at the house and take a broader look at what we had. We replied that it would certainly make sense, though it did not seem to us to be a matter of extreme urgency. I offered our preference:

"Let's focus on this one and see what your specialists think of it. This will help us decide whether any next step is necessary. You have our absolute commitment that should we ever find that this is a stolen good we would immediately make it available to be returned to its rightful owner. We're prepared to put this in writing if that helps."

"Thanks. This does help, but I don't think we need anything written down."

Pausing for a second, he added:

"As for the painting, I'll have to have it shipped to New York. What kind of insurance do we want to take on it?"

I surely had not anticipated the question. I looked at Annabelle. She looked back at me with a blank stare which I interpreted to mean that she did not have any thought on the topic. So, I punted and simply said:

"Well, we're prepared to pay for FedEx shipment or anything equivalent. I think we should insure it as if it was a reproduction. We leave it up to you to advise on the return shipment when your experts have made up their minds. Am I making sense?"

"Sure are. Let me ask one final question: am I correct assuming that you are not considering selling it at this point?"

"Absolutely. First, we don't know what it is. Second, we surely would not want to sell it if we found out it was a stolen piece. Third, we have yet to examine in more detail the other pieces of furniture to see if there are any other papers that could shed light on what we have bought . . . And finally, if it is a real one, if it is not stolen and if we are allowed to keep it, I would most likely want to keep this one: a dream come true. But who knows about the others?"

"Quite sensible. You may already know this, as I believe you are of French origin, but antique secretary desks were often called secret desks because they had several secret compartments in which people used to hide things . . ."

I smiled and replied:

"I had completely forgotten, thank you. And yet, now, I remember as a child being called in my parents' bedroom out in our country house. The front of the antique secretary to the right of the door into their bedroom was folded down; don't ask me what period it was. I saw my dad go grab a small piece of something off the desk, no bigger than a matchbox. It was wrapped in brown paper. He threw it to me inviting me to catch it. I tried, but I dropped it. I had been surprised by its weight: a lot more than I expected. He picked it up from the carpet, smiling at the trick he had played on me and placed it back on the folded down desk of the secretary. He invited me to unwrap it. I walked right next to the desk and was stunned when he told me that I was looking at a gold ingot, weighing one kilo, a bit more than two pounds. That's when I also noticed that the right column of the right-most cubby hole inside the secretary was pulled out. He explained that it was a secret compartment. He placed the ingot back into its brown paper wrapping, slid it back in the secret drawer and pushed the front of the column just as you would a drawer. He did not seem to do anything else, and yet the drawer seemed to be locked back in place . . ."

"Excellent story. I can totally sympathize with it. I've been surprised by the ingenuity behind the location and locking mechanisms of these hiding places."

He paused for a couple of seconds and then, almost in passing added:

"But don't assume that secretary desks are the only place where there might be secret drawers or compartments. I have seen them in virtually any furniture . . ."

Annabelle had to ask:

"Including in armchairs?"

"I'll grant you that's quite rare, but it is possible. What makes it rare is that any intrusion into the seat or the back of a chair is bound to leave a trace; in fact, in the trade, we call it a "destructive search" by which we mean that the piece cannot be used as is without repairs after it has been searched: it would need to be reupholstered. So, it would only be a hiding place if you really only intended to retrieve the secret once. Say in the case of a massive emergency. Yet any furniture that has any form of cabinet or box-like structure within it is fair game. Your imagination is the only limit to your search."

Frank paused again and added:

"But you probably only want to embark on that kind of search if we find that this painting could well be genuine and is not stolen."

He paused a final time and corrected himself:

"Come to think of it, looking into these pieces of furniture may be the only way you could prove they were purchased and not stolen . . . So, check the cabinets but don't cut into the seats of your armchairs."

With a smile, he added:

"At least not yet!"

Chapter Five

2001 AND 1941
NAPLES, FLORIDA AND FRANCE AND SWITZERLAND

Earlier, after we had found letters and photos in our first examination of the desk, we decided to spend more time learning whatever we could from them. This was our first opportunity to build in our own minds as close as possible a picture of who Jack, the old gentleman, was at the time. Also, we could thus get to know his family, at least know it as much as the letters and diaries would allow us to. One letter particularly attracted our attention. Handwritten in French, it was addressed to Stephane, whom we believe was Jack's father, and was dated July 2nd, 1941. It said:

> *My dear brother,*
>
> *You were certainly more right than you ever thought you'd be when you decided to leave France when you did. Though there was no real worry for three years after your departure, the recent past has made up for it. Thank God, Mother did not get to see much of it. I am sure her heart would have been broken; may she*

rest in peace. By the way, I finally received a settlement from her father's company. I made sure it is safe where you knew Papa also kept things secure. I believe that what I received included your share as well, and thus the account is opened in both our names.

As you know, after the German blitzkrieg[1], France was divided into an occupied zone and a "zone libre." Paris unfortunately is in the occupied zone.

With the armistice signed on June 22, 1940, with Germany in the Compiègne forest, in the clearing of Rethondes, and two days later with Italy, France was divided into two zones. The unoccupied zone, or zone libre, comprised the southeastern two-fifths of the country, from the Swiss border near Geneva to a point 12 miles east of Tours and thence southwest to the Spanish frontier, 30 miles from the Bay of Biscay. Though the so-called "free zone" was typically administered by a French government based in Vichy, there were strict antisemitic laws and practices which made it both difficult and dangerous for Jews to travel freely.

The letter went on:

Late last week, we had a terrible visit at the apartment Avenue Paul Doumer. I am not sure if I should say thankfully or not; but I was not there when it happened. As it was a Thursday, Albert, our son, your only nephew, had come home from his boarding

---

[1] Literally "lightning-fast war."

school to visit us, as there is no class on Thursdays. A while after he arrived, I had to go do my daily shopping with a few trusted friends. We go shopping together with the ration tickets we receive from the authorities; there are many things in short supply because of the war, so everyone gets an allocation and must make do with it. Being together with these friends allows us to trade among ourselves, so that whoever has too much oil but not enough salt, or too much sugar but not enough butter, for instance, can find some balance with the help of her friends.

I do not believe that anyone other than a very small number of very close friends knew we were Jewish. So, I'm not sure we were targeted because of religion. I am pretty sure that the people in our building knew we were well off though, but so were they; so why pick on us? As you know, we never advertised the family's wealth. How someone found out, we'll never know. At any rate, the Germans came and pretty much went everywhere in the apartment as if they were looking for something. For instance, every painting had been taken off the wall and it seems that the intruders looked behind each of them, as if they expected us to be hiding things there. Anyway, I still don't know, and probably never will, why they came, but it had to be either because we are Jewish, and they wanted to arrest us, or because they knew we were wealthy and wanted to steal our stuff. Or, come to think, maybe a little bit of both. In the end, I could not find anything missing. If they were looking for valuables, I am sure glad we followed your advice and painted over the signature of the canvases which came from Papa. None of these were missing, including the two which were in the artist's folder with the drawings and etchings. Glad you took the other two folders.

However, the real bad news is that they took Jean and Albert away. Jean left a note scribbled on a piece of paper. I am sure he did not have much time to say anything much other than the fact that they were being taken away and that he would contact me when he could. A couple of extra words in the lower corner of the piece of paper told me that I should flee as quickly as I could and drive to the place you and I used to go on holiday, if I could make it.

I have no idea where they took Jean and Albert, but we know that, in the last several months, people taken away like that are rarely heard from again. My heart is broken and I'm not sure I want to live any more. What's left of my life isn't worth it. I promise I won't do anything drastic, at least not right away. I keep hoping that one day Jean will knock on the front door. But I want you to know my terrible fate, as I cannot stay in this apartment anymore.

You will note from the envelope that I did not mail this letter from Paris. I was too worried someone was watching me. I did not take the time to call you either, I was too frightened or could only think of one thing: fleeing as fast as I could. The first thing I did when I returned to the apartment and found it all upside down was to call Jules, our driver, and Marie, his wife, our cook and maid. I am sure you remember they live in a small apartment on the last floor of the building. You may or may not remember, but they are Jewish as well and I feel I can trust them fully: drawing the authorities' attention to us could not help but get them in the same hot soup as well. I asked Jules to take all the paintings in the apartment, remove them from their frames and place them in the trunk of the dark burgundy Citroën Traction Avant 15-6 which Jean had bought just before the start of the war, as it was first released. Don't ask me too many details, but I remember him telling me that it had a new stronger engine in a revised body; I also remember Jules complaining that the steering was much heavier than its smaller, less powerful predecessor, the 11, which Jean had before he bought that one. Thank God the gas tank was full, a big luxury these days as it is at times hard to find gas.

To save on space, Jules took all the paintings off from the chassis on which they were stretched and slid them flat into the underside of the wooden floor of the trunk. That wooden parcel shelf is covered in leather on its sides. The small incision which Jules made was patched up with glue and you would have to know exactly where to look to find it. A couple of the paintings were too big to fit flat into that space; Jules rolled them up into a cardboard tube and placed it below the floor of the trunk. Marie prepared in a hurry what food she could with what we had and the three of us piled into the car with whatever else we had space for.

I will not put in writing where we are going, first because I am not sure we are going there directly and second and more importantly as I don't want to run the risk of being found out. I know I just said I trust Jules and Marie, but there is no point giving them that information. They will find out when we get there, though they know the place as they have driven us there on holidays in the past. That way, even if either of them is captured and, God forbid, tortured, they cannot reveal anything they don't know. I know you know the place and I remember how much we loved being there when we were both kids. Also, the person I will contact when there is the individual whom our mother used to refer to as "her local friend," the one who had to handle the settlement from Mom's estate with respect to the silk business.

The envelope tells you what city we have reached already.[2] I hesitated a few times asking Jules to stop in one of the towns we drove through in the last few days, but something was telling me to keep going. After all, what we are trying to do is to get to the "zone libre" and the sooner the better. Please forgive me for the delay. Once there, we should not have too much difficulty reaching our hideaway. The key is getting there.

Edith's letter continued:

Jules has developed a routine. He drives for a while and drops Marie and me at a farm or a small hostel who will agree to take us. He then goes on scouting the area with the help of local people to decide on the best route for the next leg of the trip. We are using secondary roads and traveling in the early morning and late

---

[2] The envelope carried a postmark from Troyes.

evening, taking advantage of the cover provided by the relative darkness, and yet avoiding the night when we would need headlights that can be seen from afar.

Nonetheless, summer is beautiful this year, and the days are so long. I remember how you used to love seeing the forsythia in full bloom; their yellow flowers lit up the sides of the roads. Clearly, they are mostly if not totally faded now, but rapeseed fields have taken over; yellow as far as the eye can see, and soon sunflower fields will fill the void when the rapeseed bloom has dulled out. Moreover, you can still see a few blooming fruit trees here and there. It seems odd: nature is happy and smiling, and many of us, humans, are struggling and crying. Whenever we are close to a major road, we see hundreds of people walking south. I guess they must be a part of the millions trying like us to escape to the free zone ever since the Armistice was signed. It's hard not to feel that in our distress we are lucky: they are walking, and we are riding in a car.

Please kiss Simone and the children for me. I hope my next letter will carry good news.

Your sister, Edith.

Annabelle noticed that a second sheet of paper had been added to the original letter. In fact, Stephane must have stapled it to the first, as he had not kept the envelope. It read:

Something terrible just happened. It could be the end of the trip, and quite possibly the end of the three of us. We had decided to spend the night just outside of Troyes, at a farm on the edge of the Forêt d'Orient, at

Thennellière, a small town. Jules, as was his custom, borrowed a bicycle to ride into town and to ask a few questions. The problem is that he did not come back when he should have. Marie was crying for fear that she had lost him. I was not terribly far behind her, as I cannot drive and our plan to flee would be quite seriously in jeopardy. Coincidentally, the farmer had brought up a bowl of soup. Seeing the two of us in such sad shape, he asked after Jules. We found a way, all the while crying profusely, to tell him that we did not know where he was, that he had gone into town and not returned yet. He kindly offered to go into town and see if he could find anything out. I gave him a couple of gold coins just in case, but Marie and I certainly fear the worst for Jules, and for us should he talk and tell whoever is holding him where we are.

Though we surely knew that there was a lot more work needed before we were in the position to say we knew everything we needed to know with respect to the paintings, we had by then a good enough indication that they might well be genuine. That immediately raised the key issue of whether they were honestly owned by whoever was selling them or had in fact been stolen, somewhere along the line. Annabelle and I were initially scratching our heads, reluctant as we were to hire a private investigator, at least right away. Indeed, we were not prepared to shell out significant amounts of money hiring private detectives, at least until we had done everything we could by ourselves. We kept arguing that we would not want to spend more than what the whole thing had cost us to verify that what we owned was both valuable and legally acquired. At the same time, we were wondering how we could make any progress without a specialist, I must confess that we remained wary that we both were caught up in a process and were enjoying ourselves. The appeal of the novelty and the unusual could not be allowed to create the risk of us not doing what we should or delaying it so much that we might be accused of hiding stolen goods.

As we were talking of what the various options could be, a thought came to my mind. In fact, it was more sudden and violent than I am just implying; it blew the door open on its way into my mind. We knew that police organizations worldwide did look for stolen goods and frequently were able to trace them. I wondered whether there might not be some global database that could help us look into the issue. After all, I certainly had read of Interpol in both newspapers and crime novels—the International Criminal Police Organization that facilitates police cooperation and crime control across borders. Plus, it should appeal to my French roots, as it is headquartered, of all places, in Lyon, France. Searching the internet for clues, I discovered that Interpol maintains a "Stolen Works of Art database."

They describe it as their main tool to tackle the traffic in cultural properties. Looking for its site, I was immediately captivated. In particular, reading the official description of the database, it became quickly obvious both that the work would be doable, and that we should certainly start on our own before calling upon a specialist:

Our database of stolen works of art combines descriptions and pictures of more than 52,000 items. It is the only database at the international level with certified police information on stolen and missing objects of art.

Countries send us information about stolen and missing items, and our experts add this to the database. In accordance with our strict data processing rules, only information provided by authorized entities (INTERPOL National Central Bureaus and specific international partner organizations, such as UNESCO, and ICOM and ICCROM) can be inserted into the database. Only fully identifiable objects are entered in the database.

Anyone can apply to become an authorized user of the database, to check in real-time if an item is among the registered objects, using our Application form.

As well as classic data fields, users can complement their search by uploading a picture of any object of art and checking it with our image-matching software.

The database is also one of the international registers mentioned in the 1995 UNIDROIT Convention on Stolen or Illegally Exported Cultural Objects when outlining the concept of due diligence.

We quickly discovered that there were at least two levels at which we could operate: officially and unofficially. Though we were fully prepared to ask for the required permissions to access the database, we were reluctant, if we could get away with it, to disclose too much about us. We need not have worried as we found that getting permission to use the database was not cumbersome and did not require overly onerous disclosure. In fact, we were surprised how fast and painless it was for us to receive the authorization to peruse the database.

At that point, we had decided, for the sake of simplicity and as we could always come back later if we needed more, to focus solely on the twelve paintings and to ask totally in the open. We had not taken a good inventory of the various drawings other than noting that they looked to be contemporaneous with the paintings and were not all signed, though we did find a few which had either a signature or simply initials. Thinking of the furniture, we assumed that there would be less in the database first because furniture is harder to trace and because we knew of a trade, at least in France, where thieves stole pieces of period furniture, disassembled them, combined the pieces with newly fabricated ones and resold the lot as period furniture. A dishonest seller could always touch the one part of any piece that was genuine and declare to the unsuspecting buyer that "he was guaranteeing that this piece was genuine." If caught, he could always argue that he did not mean that the overall piece was genuine, but that he meant that the part he was touching was genuine and prove that it was indeed.

So, turning to the twelve paintings, we first took pictures. I remembered having seen my father do it, way before the advent of digital photography, as he wanted to document certain paintings he owned for insurance purposes. As he had asked me to assist, I recalled that he said that he had to make sure that the sources of light used to create the right illumination environment, in other words the flashes, had to be set at 45-degree angles on the right and the left of the paintings to avoid any reflection in the lens of the camera. I can still recollect the frustration which inevitably arose, as we got the film developed and the photos printed, usually a week later, when one or several paintings still had reflections on them, requiring a second take. I could not be sufficiently thankful for the beauty of digital photography: I was able to see each photo as it was taken and work on the setting or the light until we had a result that satisfied Annabelle and me.

Once the pictures were taken, we knew that we simply had to sign into the database, upload them and check them with what the database called their image-matching software. This is where the software would look into its files for pictures which would be close enough to the photo we were testing. At that point, it would have flagged us that the painting might be a stolen work of art. We both jumped up with a mixture of relief and satisfaction when the verdict came out: none of "our" paintings were on the Stolen Work of Art database. Always level-headed, Annabelle remarked that this was a solid first step, though she was sure that there was more that should be done. We discussed what we should do next, and we both immediately agreed that we should call our friend Frank Smart at Sotheby's to tell him both of our investigation and of the conclusion which our work with the Interpol database suggested.

He asked if he could conference Jeff Baker and I immediately agreed. I told them what we had done, and their initial reaction was one of great surprise, not because the paintings appeared not to be stolen goods. Rather, the big surprise for them was that we had not discussed the other paintings, other than when we showed the bill where we paid for the lot bought at the consignment shop. Jeff could not resist a quip:

"So now, you own twelve paintings, and you know that they are unlikely to have been stolen. You must feel considerably safer now that this risk has receded into the background."

Matter-of-factly, I replied:

"The key issue now has to be whether they are real or reproductions."

They seemed to agree and asked me to forward the pictures to them electronically and offered to have the other paintings reviewed by an expert. We nitpicked for a few seconds on the resolution of the photos as they wanted something as detailed as possible. I replied that my camera was a state-of-the-art Nikon I had just gotten as a present from my wife the prior Christmas and that the issue would therefore not be how good the photos were, but how many megabytes of electronic data our email connection could handle. We agreed that we should send one picture in each email, start at the highest quality level and keep trying with ever declining quality settings if the email could not go through. As it turned out, we were able to send everything with only one level of quality reduction.

Always the businessman, Frank asked whether we might be interested in selling any of them if they all proved genuine. I replied that we still did not know enough, to which Jeff added:

"Without a solid provenance, you would be leaving a lot of money on the table . . ."

I nodded and asked:

"How crucial do you think it is for us to have you all physically review and conduct a detailed examination of all these paintings?"

Jeff frankly remarked that there should probably be no hurry, other than the fact that an insurance company might require some "official sign-off" before agreeing to write a policy, which both he and Frank adamantly recommended that we buy as quickly as possible. I asked whether the work that had to be done required shipping everything to New York, or if it would be possible to fly the expert and his equipment given the number of pieces. Jeff was initially non-committal, but Frank's insistence finally won the day. The expert would travel, at Sotheby's expense, to our place. We only needed to commit that we would give the business to them if we ever sold something.

The following week, the verdict was in: the twelve paintings were judged highly likely to be genuine, and the recommendation was they should be insured as such.

In the meantime, we were given "our marching orders" to keep looking for any documentation that might link all of them or failing this at least a few of them to the seller. Frank added:

"At that time, you'll be able to decide what you do with them with much more confidence."

I did not miss the hint and simply thanked them both for their help.

Chapter Six

1941 - 2001
FRANCE AND SWITZERLAND

By then, Annabelle had become somewhat emotional reading Edith's letter. I know my wife and her empathy for Edith and what she, Jules and Marie were going through was getting to her. She had paused for a few minutes as the story of Jules not returning when he should have had triggered tears. She got herself a nice glass of cold sparkling water and dutifully returned to what was a supplement to Edith's first letter, or probably more correctly, Edith's second letter, though sent in the same envelope as the first:

> *As you can gather since you are receiving this addition to my letter, the Jules saga had a happy ending. Neither Marie nor I have been arrested, and the three of us are back together.*
>
> *Jules had indeed been arrested by the French police in Thennellière. They were loyal to the Vichy government, who had been constituted to work with the Germans. The officers must have seen something suspect, though Jules swore that he did not know what*

it possibly could be. They stopped him and asked for his papers. As an aside, I must tell you that we had decided to leave anything that could identify us as Jewish in Paris, even if it meant traveling without papers; Jules only had his driver's license. So, he calmly replied that he did not have any other government identity card than his driver's license, because he was fleeing, trying to reach the zone libre. Further, he had to concede he did not have his driver's license with him as he had left it with the car. Unfortunately, I had not given him the address of our destination, and he did not know where we would stop next. So, he could not give an address of where he was going.

The lack of papers, the fact that he was fleeing and that he did not know where he was going did it. The French wanted to keep him in prison. Jules, while he was captive in the police bureau even overheard them talking of releasing him to the Gestapo, the German police force founded as soon as Hitler came into power. It was known during the war for their ruthlessness and virtually unlimited power. Heinrich Himmler, their overall boss, was often quoted as being the second most powerful man in Germany, right after Hitler himself. Needless to say, overhearing that, Jules was even more frightened and later told us that he was at least as worried for Marie and me as he was for himself.

Apparently, our kind farmer who had gone into town and was looking for Jules without saying as much heard that someone had been caught by the French police the prior evening. He went straight to them. He explained to the local head, whom he apparently knew, but with whom he was not very friendly, that he knew Jules. Better yet, he vouched for him, saying that Jules's car was in fact parked at his farm. Given that the farmer only gave me back one of the two gold coins (which I asked him to keep to thank him), it would seem that he might have slipped a gold coin to the officer to get Jules released. He took Jules with him, threw the bicycle in the back of his van and drove back to the farm with him.

He told us that we had been lucky and that we needed some form of documentation. We were not about to tell him the full truth, so he had us stay another day hidden on the farm while he managed to have someone forge believable papers which would keep us free. The key was that the address on the papers would be south and east of where we were, so that we could say that we were trying to go back home. I shudder when I think that these false papers clearly did not have our pictures on them, but really pictures of people who were thought to look enough like us. I guess that the quality of all identity photos currently in use allowed people to think that the trick would work. I should add that we have not had to show the papers since; maybe it would be better for me to write "not yet."

Come to think of this and given the speed with which our farmer was able to help with the fake papers, I wonder whether he was not a member of the Resistance, or at least friendly with it. At the same time, even if he was, he must have had to be quite careful with the police: you imagine the tension between a police officer loyal to Vichy and a member of the Resistance sworn to defeat Vichy which he would have seen as a puppet regime for the Germans.

You can glean from that scary incident that the trip so far has not been easy. Until we get to the zone libre, there are many German patrols on the main roads. We must avoid them, and simultaneously avoid the French police as many of them are not on our side, as Jules's story demonstrated if needed. Plus, we have been told that Germans soldiers can be disguised as French police officers; so, you just don't know who your friends are. I've heard it said that as many as 1.8 million people are trying to move from the occupied part of France to the zone libre; so, we are not alone. At the same time, I am constantly fearful that someone or something will signal that we are Jews, at which point we would all be marched into prison or worse.

We can hardly drive more than sixty miles in a day, although it seems at times, we travel a lot more but with little forward progress. We are occasionally warned by locals not to continue on the road where we are because of German patrols in the area. I cannot tell you how many times we have had to turn back and retrace our steps to find another, usually smaller road that we could take. It's been a lot like two steps forward and one step back. I am thankful to Jean for having bought the whole set of Michelin maps and for the fact that he had placed it in the glove compartment of the Citroën.

I am grateful for having thought of sewing a number of gold coins into the clothing I wear, in addition to those I carry hidden in my purse. They allow us to buy food and lodging and more importantly gasoline.

I will contact you again as soon as it is safe. Hopefully, Jean and Albert will be with me. That's the hope that keeps me alive, though it eats at me that I have not had any news for four days. But then I realize that I could not have had any since I have been on the road. Jean will immediately guess where I am when he sees that Marie, Jules and I are no longer at the apartment. He will know how to contact me there. My friend, Rose, whose address is below, knows your address but does not know where I am going. She will contact you if I cannot and ask her to, and you can contact her yourself if you wish. She has a telephone land line, and I can go to a post office to call her if need be. I would never use our phone line at the holiday house to call anyone. However, make sure that you keep our family's secrets, including the address of where I am hoping to go for now. Other than Jean and your family, nobody else knows where it is.

For the second time, please kiss Simone and the children for me. I hope my next letter will carry good news.

Your sister, Edith."

Annabelle again had tears in her eyes as she finished reading the letter. She noted that the package of letters from Edith had a sizeable hiatus between the first two and the next letter. She assumed that this was because Edith was too busy fleeing to write anything. Yet even though she was not writing to her brother, Edith had maintained her own diary which Annabelle had found below the stack of letters. That made me worry that something must have happened to her at some point, otherwise why would her nephew have that diary? We will know more as we uncover more letters or diary entries. Annabelle is more optimistic than I, and she argues that it only suggests that Edith died before her brother. She did add with a bit of a sad smile that it probably also meant that Jean and Albert were also dead, otherwise one of them would likely have inherited Edith's stuff.

Using Edith's diary, Annabelle was able to piece together the trip which Edith, Jules and Marie had taken.

The big "surprise" was that it had taken them a couple of days to leave Paris proper. Ostensibly, that had to be the time at which their fears of being found or arrested were at their zenith. After all, the apartment had just been visited by the police. That would justify someone thinking that the officers would still be looking for them. The fact that they might even come back to the apartment explained their urge to leave. Yet, given the less than two miles which separated the apartment from the "*Bois de Boulogne*," she had expected that they would have gone faster. The "Bois" is the large public park located along the western edge of the 16th *arrondissement* of Paris, near the suburbs of Boulogne-Billancourt and Neuilly-sur-Seine. The land that runs to the west-southwest of the French capital was ceded to the city of Paris by the Emperor Napoleon III to be turned into a public park in 1852.

In fact, Edith's diary provided a very simple explanation. Jules had indeed elected to get out of Paris proper as soon as he could, and for that reason had driven through the Bois de Boulogne. However, once he had, he was on the "wrong" side of Paris given that Edith had simply said that they were going to the southeast of France. Now, they were on the southwest of the French capital. So, they first needed to weave their way back to the east, southeast of the capital. Looking at a map and given the locations mentioned by Edith, we understood that Jules' great idea was to use two other parks located one west-southwest, the other due south of Paris. He must have believed that they would provide hiding places.

The *Park Naturel de la Vallée de la Haute Chevreuse*, close enough to the exit of the *Bois de Boulogne*, was indeed crisscrossed by alleys and paved roads but seemed generally devoid of any German patrol. It took Jules nearly a day to cross it, as he would drive a mile or two on a narrow but paved road. As soon as he found an alley into the forest on the right or on the left, he would drive into it, continue for long enough so that he could park the car into the underbrush and stay there and observe the surroundings, without the car being visible from the paved road. He would walk away from the car, back toward what Edith called "the main road" and see whether he could see anything. If he felt that all was clear, he would drive back onto the paved road until the map showed he was close to the next major intersection. Before getting there, he would look for another side alley and repeat the maneuver, going on foot from his "temporary parking space" in the wooded area to inspect the road that they would need to cross. They would only proceed to that road and beyond if he came back to the car with the message that the coast seemed clear. We could easily imagine how long this process would take to travel 16 to 20 miles.

Leaving the park at Dourdan, Jules drove fifteen miles until he reached the famous *Forêt de Fontainebleau*, also known as the *Park Naturel du Gâtinais Français*. There he was able to follow similar tactics, although a significant change was needed. While there were more major roads within the park than in the earlier one, the big challenge came from the location of its famous castle. The Chateau of Fontainebleau was indeed occupied by the Germans from June 16, 1940, until November 10, 1940, and again from May to the end of October 1941. Thus, Jules knew that, in July 1941 as they were driving, there would be Germans not only in the castle area, but in fact probably also in outposts located through a large section of the park. To make things more challenging, the castle was in the southeast corner of the park, just where Jules would have wanted to pass. He therefore chose to stay on the west edge of the park, driving south into and out of the park, never penetrating more than a mile or two into it. Once he reached the limits of the southeast corner of the park, he drove due east and then southeast to reach Sens, often billed as the gateway to Burgundy, on the third day. They were able to spend the night in a small hostel whose owner nicely took them in, served them a healthy dinner and sold them some provisions for the next day; cynically, Edith noted that offering a gold coin in exchange for the service had found a way of overcoming the initial reluctance of the owner who wanted to avoid all kinds of possible trouble.

The next day, they drove to Troyes, fifty-six miles away and, once Edith had posted her first letter, found a hiding place in the nearby forest. It seemed they stayed there two nights, which fits with the story of Jules being arrested and released in the very early morning. Further, Edith's diary reveals that Jules did not want to leave the area without a full tank of gas, which his arrest and few hours in prison had made it impossible for him to attend to the first twenty-four hours. They finally were able to fill-up, leave, and drive seventy-five miles to Langres, near the place where the river Seine originates. Anecdotally, Edith did comment on the extortionist behavior of certain gas stations, noting "you'd believe they are not French, like we are."

The next letter Annabelle found added to the information she had gleaned from Edith diary. It demonstrated the difficulties associated with private travel during the war. Until Langres, Edith had primarily been driven east as Jules had been told that it was still safer there, at least for people who were trying to get to a point south of the Jura and north of the Alps. Yet, there, Jules veered to the south, and they made it to Dijon the following day. Jules had dropped Marie and Edith at the periphery, on a small farm which allowed its guest to sleep in the hay reserve above the stables, while the car was hidden behind a large haystack, with a dark green tarpaulin thrown on top of it. As he had done in previous circumstances, he borrowed a bicycle from the farmer and went into town. On his return, he reported that the town was crawling with German soldiers and stated point blank would surely not like to have to go back into it. He still felt he got a lot of information as to how to drive securely further on, though he had all the time been careful of the French who collaborated with the Germans.

Edith explained that Jules exercised great care and, for instance, invented at least a couple of possible destinations, and asked the same questions from several people. He was hoping both to confuse any potential traitor and to get valuable insights by cross-referencing the responses he received. He knew that, just south of Dijon, where the Burgundy area began, the family would finally reach the free zone. Having located a gas station where he knew there was gas available while on his bike trip, he returned to the farm, uncovered the car, and went back to the station to fill up the gas tank. Each time he filled up the car, he knew full well that he had overpaid for the fuel, as he should only have received but a small "ration." But Edith had been quite clear: the point was getting to the destination as quickly as possible, the details of which she had not shared with him quite yet and not saving money along the way.

That night, the family was awakened right after midnight. It was the farmer who had just heard through the grapevine that there were German soldiers less than a couple of miles away. He was not sure whether they had camped for the night or were on patrol. Yet, he told Jules to drive away as fast as possible, both for their and his own family's safety. Edith, Marie, and Jules quickly piled into the car, nicknamed by contemporary French people the "Queen of the Road" as it was both very comfortable and spacious inside, with a good engine. They travelled about twenty miles until they could find another farm which would take them, as Jules did not like the idea of driving at night. He had in fact driven those twenty miles without any headlights, thanking his lucky star for some good moonlight. It turned out that they had escaped real danger. Jules had heard from one of the farms where he had tried to continue their night that a farm less than five miles north had been visited by the Germans, in one of their initial incursions into the zone libre, which eventually was "reconquered" in November 1942, after the allied forces invaded North Africa, in what was then known as Operation Torch. It did not take much for them to assume from what was being told that this had to be the farm where they had stayed. Edith could not know whether the farmer and his family had escaped, but she worried for them, all the while praying that she had not left anything that could be used against him or his family.

The next day, they drove to Dole, a major town in the Jura department of France, but less than 35 miles away from where they were. There, the group was faced with a very difficult decision. Jules had followed his customary approach, asking people how best to keep driving toward the Swiss border, as Edith had concluded that she should be open at that point as once she had talked of Switzerland, she effectively allowed Jules to guess the destination. It was in her view safer for him to know than for him not to know and end up in the wrong place. The advice he had received was unequivocal; he should drive toward Champagnole, and from there use tertiary roads to reach the *Lac de Joux*, on the other side of the border. He had been told that the roads were not very good, but with a wink of the eye from the person who gave them the advice, the superb suspension of the car should make the way passable provided one did not drive too fast. That route, he had been told, was much more direct than the alternative which would have him drive further south and then veer east.

What he had not been told, unfortunately, was that the recommended route would require him to drive through a "forbidden zone" which had been declared by the Germans, and where refugees were prohibited from returning. Though the forbidden zone primarily comprised the East of France, a small sliver extended south, almost all the way to Geneva. Fearing that he was running low on fuel and would need to fill-up before crossing into Switzerland, Jules decided that they should spend the night in Mouthe, a small town whose fame would eventually be the result of having the lowest temperature recorded in France, in 1968. From there, he would only be a mere four to five miles away from the border.

He filled the car up with the help of a gold coin and they all went to sleep in a single room with beds that were more like cots than beds. Fortunately, for the second time, he was awakened in the middle of the night by the owner of the small hostel where they were staying. The owner told him to get up and retrace some of his most recent steps, because he had heard a report that German soldiers were patrolling the D389 road that they would need to take a few hours hence when they left at dawn. Given where the soldiers were reported to be, they could reach the hostel, if they chose to, in less than an hour, and even faster if they drove. There was no way of knowing whether the patrol would come all the way to Mouthe, but the risks were just too serious. Jules quickly woke Marie and Edith up and, within less than fifteen minutes, they were back in the car and headed in a southwesterly direction, aiming to get to Oyonnax, a town in the Ain department and unquestionably in the free zone. Unfortunately, this took them further away from their eventual destination and would add more than 100 miles to their trip. On the other hand, they were in the free zone which would likely make their forward progress somewhat easier.

Chapter Seven

2001
NAPLES, FLORIDA

The initial peeks we were getting into the family of our "seller" and the suggestions wisely offered by Jeff Baker and Frank Smart of Sotheby's were certainly sufficient encouragement for us to start in earnest our quest for "documents." Placing ourselves in the shoes of Jack's father, we assumed that, if there were relevant documents to be found, he would have hidden them in one of the secret compartments of the three main pieces of furniture which he must have enjoined his son not to sell: the secretary desk, the armoire, and the writing desk. Clearly, he might have elected not to hide them. He could simply have placed them in a folder and left them in plain view. However, something told us that this scenario was unlikely. First, we should have found the folder in plain view, say in a drawer, and we surely had not. Second, how could someone who had taken the time and effort to hide the signatures on all the paintings leave such sensitive documents for anybody to find? Indeed, although it would have allowed us to find them, anyone else could have found them as well. Why hide signatures if a document nearby tells the whole story: name of the artist and purchase price? At the same time, how could Jack behave the way he did if he had known that the canvases were originals; and he would have known that since he could himself have seen the contents of the folder.

In our minds, it was more than probable that we had to look for them in places that were not readily accessible. That thought naturally led us to look for them elsewhere than in the desk drawers. They had to be hidden and that had to mean that the key in our view had to be in a secret compartment in one of the three main pieces of furniture. We could have started further inspecting the desk; after all, it was still the most logical place. Somehow, I allowed the memories of my youth to dictate a different tactic. I had seen my dad deal with a secret compartment in a folding desk secretary, and we were therefore going to "attack" the secretary we had purchased as well.

The first step involved using a dolly to move the cabinet from the garage to the sitting-room extension of our bedroom which we had just completed. Annabelle had by now decided the room would have a Louis XVI theme, which she saw as a historical wink at the rest of the bedroom which was in a Louis XV style. The extension would therefore have a small love seat, the two cabriolet armchairs, the secretary desk along the lone windowless wall and next to it a modern piece of furniture that would house a hidden TV set, with the usual DVD paraphernalia under it.

As Annabelle and I were having a cup of coffee at the table in the kitchen, she asked:

"Before we start on the secretary, any idea where to start?"

"Truth is, I have none. I've told you that I remember, as a kid, having seen numerous hiding places in the several antique secretary desks my parents had at home, both in Paris and in the countryside. The only places I remember seeing hidden drawers were in the upper section, behind the folding desk."

Annabelle frowned. Somehow, she was disappointed that things would not be as simple as she had hoped.

We first inspected the outside of the piece. Its structure looked very familiar, very traditional in fact. A piece with a full-width drawer on top, a drop-leaf desk just below, and at the bottom a cabinet closed with two doors. The whole piece was finished in inlaid wood veneer, including the back, which was somewhat unusual as that part is usually facing a wall and treated in a much simpler fashion than the rest of the piece. The veneer had a simple diagonal diamond motif, repeated in each panel. The very top of the secretary was finished with a dark-green marble slab, with a bullnose edge curved around the top and bottom for an even finish. The simple drawer below the marble had a fascia that extended into the rounded corners of the front of the piece, forming a bit of a crown running all the way to the back. The diamond motif was there as well, though it was stretched quite a bit as the drawer was not very high. There was marquetry fluting along each of the four corners all the way down to the floor. This was pure Louis XVI style. The few gilded bronze accents, near the top, at the waist and at the feet signaled that the maker was a fine artisan, probably having worked in Paris, for the local aristocracy. This ought to have led us to look for the maker's signature, but neither of us thought about it at the time.

For some reason, we started our investigation with the cabinet at the bottom. We gently turned the key in the lock on the right door and marveled again at the quality of the design and the finish. Opening the two doors in full, the craftsmanship was stunning: we discovered that the whole of the space was filled with three recessed drawers. We smiled at each other noting that having drawers in that part of the piece was quite usual; yet what was unusual was that the drawers would be hidden behind two doors! We noted to each other that the design the woodworker had chosen was surely more elegant. In fact, I was frankly quite surprised to find a sheet of thick brown tanned leather dressing the inside of each of the two doors. On the spur of the moment, I wondered whether it was a way of protecting either the doors or the drawers if one attempted to shut the doors with one of the drawers not perfectly closed.

Focusing more sharply on what we found once both lower doors were opened, we immediately noticed that the three drawers were framed on each side by two rounded half classical columns, with a bronze crown and pedestal. There was no marquetry inside the cabinet. Everything was in well-polished high grade mahogany wood, with a few elements finely sculpted. The fluting on the two half columns on either side of the set of drawers, which echoed the fluting found on the four outside corners of the piece of furniture itself, was executed through real half cylindric grooves carved out of the wood, rather then, as on the outside, with marquetry.

I winked at Annabelle, as this was giving me a first opportunity to look for some secret hiding place, even though they would be in the lower rather than the upper section of the piece. I remembered, back at home when I was a child, similar columns that popped open when one found and pressed on a button or even just pushed back a bit on the column. I first tried pushing back on each column, executing a small up or down move, hoping this would trigger a hidden spring. It did not work. I went looking for a button that would trigger the opening mechanism. Looking around, the only place that made any sense was in one of shelves in which the drawers were located; the button, or a small cavity, would in my mind be recessed into the wood and small enough not to obstruct the drawers from sliding forward or back. So, we carefully removed all three drawers from their spaces and placed them on the carpet beside us, leaving the empty shelves for us to explore.

Next, I slid my hand into the space where each drawer had been, keeping it flat, with my fingers pointing first to the bottom of the space, second to the top and then to the sides. Starting with the top-drawer slot, I let my fingers look both on the right and on the left, seeking some button or cavity in which I might find a trigger which would pop the side columns open. Having run through the exercise for each drawer shelf and not found anything, I asked Annabelle to repeat the maneuver, hoping that her smaller hands and forearms might have more freedom of movement and thus get to locate something. Both efforts ended in complete failure.

I was truly surprised that we had no success as there undoubtedly was space on either side of the drawers, behind the columns. Why would anyone choose to waste space, on either side of the inside of the cabinet? To have columns only for the sake of decoration? I would certainly not portray myself as a very experienced connoisseur of French antique furniture, but I still have seen quite a few of these cabinets over the years. In fact, we currently have a couple of them, one each in two of the children's bedrooms. I had never seen a setup such as the one we saw in the lower half of this piece.

On a hunch, I asked Annabelle to lean the piece of furniture backward enough so that I use a flashlight to inspect the space between the bottom of the lower cabinet and the ground. The wooden slab down there was a bit darker, greyer than the rest of the piece, but this did not surprise me: it had ostensibly neither been varnished nor polished, nor was there any marquetry. A small mark attracted my eyes when my flashlight set its rays on it: was I looking at a stamp? Could it be the signature of the maker of the piece of furniture? I knew from personal experience that woodworker signatures were always hidden and often very hard to identify when some mark had been found. Here, the mark, somewhat worn by the passage of time, only comprised a couple of letters: A.G. I looked further to the right of the "G", hoping to find the rest of the signature. That search did not produce anything more, leading me to conclude that I was simply looking at initials. Unfortunately, at that time, search engines such as Google or sites such as Wikipedia were embryonic, and not sufficiently developed to answer my obvious query: what did A.G. mean? I went straight to my office which doubled as a library and searched my Encyclopedia Britannica. Unfortunately, I could not find anything which might clarify whether I was looking at something important or not. There was an article on what the French call "*estampille*" and which focused on the way woodworkers would sign their work. With the benefit of hindsight, I can only marvel at how much more efficient any of our searches can be now thanks to the Internet.

Yet, having read that maker stamps were often on the chassis of the piece of furniture, or even on its top when it was covered by a slab of decorative marble, I inspected the piece much more carefully, looking for any mark. There was none on the back of the furniture: that should not have surprised me since, as I have already indicated, it was covered with marquetry with the same design as the front and the sides of the piece. This was surely not a location where a woodworker would affix his signature. No woodworker would damage the marquetry with a signature, unless that signature was an exquisite work of art on its own, and that would be immediately visible. There was always the possibility that the signature was inside rather than outside, but we had not seen anything. With Annabelle's help, I removed the marble from the top of the furniture and, though delighted, faked being non-plussed as I simply remarked:

"Well guess what!"

On the back, left corner of the upper plateau was a signature, which looked that it was raised relative to the immediate surrounds. The story does not tell whether it was created in the same manner as the *Ukibori* technique which Japanese carvers discovered to create raised features or raised characters in *netsukes*: the well-known engineering principles behind it is that compressed wood returns to shape when wet. But that could easily be the technique used by the woodworker here, as it would be considerably easier an approach than carving the signature in low relief by removing wood around it; particularly here as it would have required the whole of the top of the piece being shaved down a couple of millimeters. The signature we discovered was not limited to initials, but clearly said: "Antoine Gosselin," and next to it there was a stamp which I did not recognize. Back to the encyclopedia, I quickly found that the gentleman was a very well-respected master who was born in 1731 and died in 1794. Reading the paragraph dedicated to him, I saw that he at times signed a piece twice, once with his full name and a guild stamp next to it, and another with a simpler stamp comprising solely his initials. Though I had just read that the presence of a signature was not a guarantee of authenticity, as the stamps of woodworkers were at times affixed posthumously or when during their lifetime without care as to whether the furniture had been made by him or not, I felt quite strongly that I was looking at the real thing. The coincidence of having exactly the three marks which Gosselin was known to use made me feel comfortable that the odds were in our favor that this was a real masterpiece. Turning to Annabelle, I could not hold back a dumb joke:

"That alone pays for everything which we bought at that consignment place."

She smiled but matter-of-factly added:

"Still, that doesn't tell us anything about the paintings and the rest. Does it?"

As usual, she was the practical soul, and I was the dreamer. I conceded her point, and went back to work, this time focusing on the upper half of the piece of furniture. We did not need to spend much time with the drawer at the very top of the piece: we promptly removed it from its shelf; Annabelle quickly ran her right hand through the space and confirmed that there was no asperity or cavity she could feel inside. Thus, if we were looking for something that might trigger the opening of a secret compartment, we had to look elsewhere.

Once the leaf desk was dropped down, the inside of the upper cabinet was revealed: it was breathtakingly beautiful. The artist had imagined a finely sculpted space entirely made of mahogany with a few bronze highlights. On either side of the space, the front third comprised the first four steps of two curved staircases which led to an upper gallery: the first steps of each staircase faced each other. The next step curved around thirty degrees, the third another thirty degrees, with the last one on each side curved a full ninety degree relative to the first one, so that it faced the back of the piece; it took three more steps for any imaginary midget who would have climbed these stairs to reach the gallery. Both staircases had a couple of chiseled bronze banisters running the full length of the stairs, one to the right hand and the other to the left hand, as one would typically see on the large, majestic staircases in the aristocratic residences of the time.

Between the two miniature staircases, there was a flat space, a sort of a backward extension of the desk that protruded from the front of the piece. Interestingly, looking at it more closely, I noticed that this flat space could be partially opened. There were two horizontal mahogany sliding panels which could alternatively completely cover the space, meeting in the center or sliding to the side to reveal a cavity with a depth that could not be more than three or four inches. The cavity was wider than its opening, as the "sliding panels" had to find space to be stored while opened; there was room to place a variety of small objects, folders, sheets of paper or even small books under the space which contained the sliding doors when they were opened. That cavity was effectively sitting on top of the cabinet which we had found when we looked at the lower half of the piece. Unfortunately, the compartment appeared empty, except for the dust which had accumulated over time. I did not take the time to inspect it with great care, as it was in plain sight: why would anyone hide the triggers for any secret drawer in a space anyone could see and access?

Allowing my eyes to return to the twin staircases, I directed my attention to the "gallery" that ran the whole width of the space; it was about three inches wide. At each end, there was a small bronze candlestick; though it did not comprise a real miniature wax candle, the candlestick was sculpted in a way such that one could imagine both the candlestick and a candle inserted into it. Along the gallery and on its back wall, one could see four cubbyholes separated by columns. I noted that the columns looked quite similar in design and execution if not in scale to the two we had found in the lower cabinet, though quite a bit smaller. In all, there were five of these columns: three half columns separating the four rectangular cubbyholes and two quarter columns at either end, in the back corners of the gallery. The corner columns looked to be a bit wider than the others, but their decoration was similar.

There was a mahogany balustrade running along the front of the gallery, a finely carved rail on top of low balusters; the picture was completed by a third candlestick midway along the full width of the gallery—it was affixed to the half column in the middle. The whole was so carefully designed and sculpted that it was very easy to imagine that one was looking at a real gallery inside a majestic home. Under the gallery and thus opening on the same level as the front of the desk, one could find four pigeonholes, mirroring the cubbyholes just above. In between the two center pigeonholes, and right under the central column with the candlestick in the gallery, we found another half column, very much the same as the three that we had seen above, in the gallery.

There was no doubt as to what we needed to do next. Where would the woodworker have hidden secret compartments? Logically, I assumed that the columns were the key. One question immediately popped into my mind: could the different materials used by the artist to create the piece be a clue to which features were those that contributed to opening the secret compartments? Turning to Annabelle, I could not help saying:

"There's got to be something with these columns. I know we haven't found anything down below, but there might be stuff here."

She smiled and added:

"Personally, I am not ready to give up on the cabinet below. There still might be a way we've missed."

"You and me both."

In our effort to find secret compartments in the upper cabinet, we first focused on the single column in the section under the gallery. After all, it was by itself. Could that be a clue? Remembering my youth and the "secret" mechanisms which my parents had shown to me, I first inserted my hand into each of the two pigeonholes on either side of that column, looking for a small cavity in which I was hoping to find a button which would trigger the spring-release of the column, which I assumed hid a vertical drawer behind it. My hopes were dashed as there was simply nothing I could find or touch. I extended my search to the two outer pigeonholes and came back with nothing to show for the effort. I could not believe that this incredibly fine and fancy piece of furniture would have no hidden secret compartment. Annabelle interrupted:

"Mike, I don't understand. You talked earlier of using the bronze features to try to find the secret and you've just done everything but that."

I looked a bit contrite, as I had to concede that I was allowing myself to follow steps which were set in memories of my youth. She was right. So, next, I started to fiddle directly with the column between the two center pigeonholes itself. I focused on the small bronze crown. I tried to move the crown first trying to rotate it and then attempting to move it slightly up or down. Nothing. I then turned to the pedestal, which similarly refused to rotate or budge up or down. Still no success.

Annabelle was by now getting impatient and let me know that she was. She noticed that the column had small vertical grooves running almost the full height within its wooden shaft, the delicate fluting we had earlier noticed. She gently pushed me aside and seized the column with the tips of her thumb and index finger using the grooves to get some grip. She then tried to move the main body of the column, first downward and then upward. The moment she moved it upwards, we heard a discreet "click" sound and the column popped forward, revealing a vertical drawer behind it. She removed it gently and placed it flat on the desktop. What a disappointment: we had found a secret drawer, but it was absolutely empty, save for accumulated dust!

Annabelle was not a happy camper. She surprised me as I knew her as a calm and gentle person. For some reason, these efforts were straining her nerves. Despite the disillusion and the tension which her demeanor caused, I decided that we had to keep going. I moved immediately to the columns along the back side of the gallery. Annabelle asked why I was being stubborn. I simply replied that I believe that all the furniture pieces I had seen in the past almost always had more than one secret compartment. She stepped away but let me do my thing. On a hunch, I first fiddled with the bronze candlestick on the middle half column, wondering whether it could be a simpler opening mechanism. It did not work! I reverted to the maneuver Annabelle had tried on the column below on the columns alongside the gallery. The center half-column, located right above the column where we had already had success, responded to the same attempt—a small upward push and they popped open.

It contained bundles of banknotes, all in French Francs; each column containing four bundles amounting to 1,000,000 French Francs each.

I could not resist saying:

"So much for my choosing the bronze as the material hiding the trigger mechanism!"

Annabelle who had by then regained her usual joyful demeanor smiled and jokingly replied:

"You were right, Mike. Except that the bronze told you where not to go!"

We took the bundle of banknotes to the kitchen table and decided to drink a good glass of sparkling water to which I had added a couple of drops of Pastis, a French anis-based liquor.

"Mike, how much do you think these are worth? That's four million Francs, isn't it?"

I replied that I was totally unsure whether there would be any market for banknotes that all seemed to be dated in the early 1930s. I knew indeed that France had moved to a "new Franc" in 1960 (one new Franc being worth the same as 100 old Francs). I also knew that France would introduce the Euro in the next twelve months and that, starting February 17, 2002, the Franc (new in this case) would stop being accepted for tender. We were looking at a lot of money which was soon to be worthless, unless a buyer was available in the U.S. Not very likely . . . But who knew for sure?

That is when I observed a change in behavior on the part of my dear wife. First, it was clear she was disappointed, but, in fairness, so was I. The first secret drawer contained nothing. The bundles of banknotes in the second might be worthless. In some ways, Annabelle had had it. She reminded me that we were looking for documents which would allow us to trace the provenance of "our" paintings. Not only had we not found any, but whatever we found was effectively worthless. That's where I should have kept my mouth shut and did not. I reminded her that we did not know for sure that these notes were worthless. I pointed to an optimistic scenario which would allow us to trade them in a bank, in which case I told her that we might get up to seven to eight thousand dollars, which would more than pay for everything we bought.

That did it. Annabelle told me that she could not care less about a few thousand dollars and that I seemed to be forgetting our goal to prove our paintings were genuine and not stolen. Again, I could have stopped right there, but did not. The spat that we had was totally unnecessary. In the end, I told her that I was going back to the bedroom to keep working on the piece. She mumbled something that was at best unclear and simply added:

"I'll be in the living room if you need me."

No smile. No nothing! I was in the doghouse.

I decided that I should nevertheless continue to work on the upper columns. After all, we had found a way to open two secret drawers, why not keep on going in the same area? I immediately moved to the column adjacent to the one we last opened. Repeating the same maneuver as a few minutes earlier, I was delighted to see it pop open. The content of the drawer behind the column was quite a bit different from the other two we had opened earlier. It contained six gold ingots, each about the size of a matchbox, therefore weighing probably one kilo each, or a bit more than two pounds. It also held a bunch of gold coins, a mix of Louis D'Or, Napoleon I, Napoleon III, and the famous Gold French Rooster. Interestingly, while the Roosters were all dated to before 1914, the two Napoleon coins bore dates ranging between 1910 and 1933. I could not resist running to the living room and triumphally displaying my discovery to my wife, who, I must admit, proved forgiving, welcoming the news.

Her face said it all: she had forgotten the earlier spat and then told me that she was happy that I kept going. Together, we proceeded to get to the other half columns. Interestingly, the three half columns popped out as we pressed upward, while, on the other hand, the corner columns required one to press downward rather than upward. I am happy to report that they all popped open and that behind them, we found treasures, and those would surely be marketable today: loose cut diamonds, loose colored gemstones, seemingly all rubies, emeralds, or sapphires, in various cuts.

We took the whole "loot" and sat in the leaving room with a treasure trove of items strewn on the glass-top coffee table. We had indeed decided to celebrate our discovery with a good glass of Sauvignon Blanc with sparkling water. Annabelle exclaimed:

"I just counted the gold coins, there are 210 of them! I can't believe it. Together with these gems, this whole thing must be worth a lot of money . . . Nearly 25 pounds of gold, plus all these precious stones . . ."

"I'm sure you're right, honey."

I paused for a few seconds, letting my mind wander, I added:

"I guess it makes sense. The people from whom our man got the furniture and presumably the paintings were probably worried that they could be apprehended and were hiding whatever they would need to start a new live elsewhere. It fits perfectly with what we have learned so far of the old man's family: they were Jewish and were fleeing persecution."

Totally in character, Annabelle observed:

"Travelling with such a piece of furniture could not possibly be simple."

"Grant you that. But I can think of two options. Either they could remove all the things we found from their hiding places and take these valuables with them to start over again. Alternatively, they could keep the loot in the furniture and hope that nobody would mess with it until they got it back on the "right" side of the Atlantic Ocean. In fact, we don't know whether the stuff was in the furniture when they fled. Maybe they took it with them and shipped the furniture separately."

"I can see that. Or, by the way, some combination of both. Back to my earlier point, I hate to say it, but it still doesn't help us with respect to the paintings."

"Can't argue with that. I want to take a closer look at the lower half of the cabinet. I am not ready to believe that the columns down there are just for decorative purposes. After all, we tried everything else, including the small space behind the top balustrade. That the only obvious next spot for us to investigate,"

The look on Annabelle's face was telling me that I was on thin ice. Unfortunately, I did not notice it. First, I was excited by everything we had found so far. Second, I was so convinced that there was something down below that, with the benefit of hindsight, nothing would have stopped me.

With that, I ran from the living room to the small sitting room and attempted the same maneuver as had been successful with the upper part of the cabinet. My logic, in my own mind, was impeccable: we had solved the riddle and it had to apply to every similar element in the piece of furniture. Well, though the logic might have been impeccable, it did not work. We could not move the columns, their bronze crowns, or their bronze pedestals. They seemed definitely set in place.

Looking straight into Annabelle's eyes, I could only say:

"Can't make it out. I'd be pretty sure that these columns hide something, but don't know how to get them to reveal their secret."

Her eyes and her voice then seemed to convey different messages. Her mouth, with some apparent calm I should add, said:

"Agreed. We'll have to take another look at the secretary. Could the trigger for the lower columns be somewhere in the upper part of the furniture?"

He eyes on the other hand were shooting darts at me. I think she really had had enough of that treasure hunt game. Her last words were however still somewhat encouraging:

"How about a button hidden in the cavity in the front middle? How about the bronze candlesticks? Don't they look like an unnecessary detail?"

She paused and without giving me a chance to reply, she added:

"We also need to look carefully at the Louis XVI writing desk. I remember that there was something that troubled you when you first looked at the three drawers. And what about the big armoire?"

Chapter Eight

1941 AND 2001
VERSOIX, SWITZERLAND, SKOKIE, ILLINOIS, AND
NAPLES, FLORIDA

Annabelle was still reconstructing the last leg of the family's trip from Edith's letters and diary. Though they had finally reached the zone libre, they still had to cross into Switzerland. The country, maintaining what it called an "armed neutrality" in the war, was prepared to help its neighbors to some extent, or more specifically to help refugees from its neighbors. At the same time, it could not be obvious about it, failing which Germany would have concluded that Switzerland was aligned against them. You cannot be neutral and help one side. Little did Edith and her companions know that her decision to flee to the Geneva region would be emulated by numerous Jews as well; eventually, the border between Geneva and France was closed in August of 1942.

Yet, in July 1941, they were the unwitting beneficiaries of the fact that they were among the first ones to make the decision to flee and to aim for Switzerland. When one knows why the timing and the destination were chosen, it is not hard to appreciate the amount of luck or lack thereof that determined the future for so many families. In Edith's case, the timing of their departure was dictated by the intrusion into the Paris apartment in the early summer of 1941 and thus, from their point of view, was totally driven by chance. The selection of Geneva was because the family had a home just outside Geneva, which again was something over which Edith had no control as the purchase had been made quite a bit earlier, by David Schneider, her father, and his wife.

Thus, though the border was technically open, Edith and Jules remained very cautious. They had in fact been told that there were occasional patrols which might not support their desire to cross. With some advice from people in the area, they had concluded that the safest route for them had to be to aim for the south shore of Lake Leman, effectively bypassing Geneva to the west and south and using mountain roads in Savoie to reach Switzerland. Despite the fears that gripped them, they found ways to enjoy travelling in these wooded areas, with deciduous trees proudly displaying their newer, lighter green leaves while all the evergreens provided the bulk of the dark-green color. Danger had not been eliminated. The route they had chosen would require them to drive through a zone where they might encounter Italian soldiers. In fact, the zone would become controlled by Italy in November 1942.

Jules was lucky to find a place in Archamps, almost due south of Geneva, but still in France, where they were going to spend the night. More importantly, he was delighted to meet a gentleman who was willing to give him precise instructions to get into Switzerland. He had required payment in gold coins, which Edith was quite happy to provide, though she thought at the time that his demand for three Louis gold coins was surely not cheap. Ostensibly, the gentleman must have had some secondary activity involving sneaking contraband goods into or out of Switzerland, and maybe certain people as well.

The gentleman offered two options. The first which would be by far the simplest would involve crossing into Geneva a few miles up the road, as there were three ways to enter Switzerland between Collonges-sous-Salève and Bossey, two villages near Archamps. Once across the border, they would find themselves almost immediately in the southern suburbs of Geneva, and from there would only need to cross over the Rhone River in the center of town and drive less than ten miles to Versoix. The gentleman, however, suggested that simpler did not mean safer. Indeed, he said that he had heard of people who had chosen that route and somehow did not make it. He explained to Jules:

"The route may be safe if you walk it. In fact, people who live in France and work in Geneva use it daily. They know the officials at the border, and the officials know them. However, that does not mean that the border police officers would react the same way if they saw strangers walk the same route. In your case, the difficulty increases drastically: you would be strangers, crossing the border in a car, with that car being registered in France, and needing to go through a formal border post. I don't like the odds."

After being briefed by Jules, Edith understood the implications and replied:

"What is the alternative?"

Jules explained that the gentleman offered an alternative that was quite a bit longer:

"Forty miles at least versus two."

Edith was clearly surprised, but Jules expanded on the gentleman's suggestion. He argued that the roads that he had recommended would involve going through at least three different mountain passes and would certainly twist and turn. Yet, he added that there was no reason the border police would venture into the area, though individual custom officers might. Jules attempted to quote the gentleman verbatim from memory:

"People around there know one another, and they don't make much of a difference as to whether they're Swiss or French. The alternative route I would recommend would get you to "emerge" in Switzerland at Morgins. From there you would follow the "Trois Torrents" River and eventually cross over the Rhone River at Colombey. You would surely have enough gas to drive to Ollon. By then, you would have crossed Canton du Valais and be in Canton de Vaud. You would be far enough into Switzerland that you would no longer need to worry. I'm sure you could find a decent hotel and some gas at Ollon."

Jules thanked the gentleman and paid him. Edith had agreed that it made sense to follow the gentleman's advice, though she asked if they could start driving toward Collonges-sur-Salève and make a final decision there. She was still of two minds as to whether they should really take the long road. As Jules was at a point where he could turn left onto a road that would drive him into Switzerland and Geneva, he spotted a patrol in the distance. Though he was pretty sure that the soldiers were not Germans, he immediately decided to follow the gentleman's advice and drive on.

Roads were so narrow that Jules was happy when he drove twenty miles an hour or so. Add to the narrowness the damage caused by the snowmelt which left loose gravels on the side of many curves, and you will have a full picture. All three of them were thankful that the snow season was over, though there remained a few greyish snowdrifts here and there to remind them both the time of the year and most importantly of the elevation of the roads they were using, particularly when they were facing northward.

Being knowledgeable on cars himself, Jules was bemoaning the fact that André *Citroën* had been forced to abandon his project of an automatic transmission and power steering when he first came out with the car. The weight of the engine on the driving front wheels surely felt quite heavy in all these corners he had to negotiate. Fortunately, the car and its immediate predecessor, the 11BL, were the first mass-produced front-wheel drive automobiles, which would do much better than competition if there was any snow, which rear-wheel drive cars would surely dislike.

Their main challenge, so much less difficult than earlier ones, was the need to stay awake. The mountain pass route did not really offer much scope for rest in a hotel, or to buy gasoline anywhere: the roads were indeed almost totally deserted, with the occasional farm on the right or the left. Jules had been warned of the potential problem and had bought extra gas that he placed in a five-gallon container inside the trunk, which thankfully was quite large, though it was by then so full that a few packages had to be placed on the rear left seat next to Edith.

They were surprised that crossing the border at Morgins was as uneventful as it turned out to be, having in fact anticipated all sorts of complications none of which came to pass. They assumed that the early hour in the morning explained the relative ease of their entry into Switzerland.

The gentleman had been correct. They found a decent hotel in Ollon where they were able both to have a decent lunch, rest during the day, and spend the night. They could find all the gas they needed the next morning. They drove north until they reached the north shore of Lake Leman at Montreux, which they followed westward driving through Vevey, Lausanne and Nyon. Eventually, they reached Versoix and the house which her mother and father had purchased and furnished with money from the silkworks and maintained until Edith and Jean had taken it over.

The one thing which Annabelle and I could not miss in the letter which Edith said she had written was that as soon as she, Jules, and Marie got to the house in Versoix it displayed the totally mixed emotions Edith was feeling at the time. She was elated to be safe in a place she knew and loved. A paragraph illustrated that feeling in spades:

"We are now at the house in Versoix. So far, the area has not been invaded and I even heard someone say that though the Germans had drawn an invasion plan for Switzerland, called Operation Tannenbaum, I believe, they decided against executing it. They were seemingly worried that every Swiss citizen was armed and ready to fight."

At the same time, she was heartbroken as she had not heard anything from her husband or her son, conjuring up the awful realization that they had probably been taken away to concentration camps in Germany or Poland. A simple quote tells it all:

"I'm home. I so wish Jean and Albert were with me!"

The place was a nice, but not outwardly fancy home near Geneva, on the shores of Lake Leman. Yet, one should concede that the whole area was considerably more desirable than many other parts of the Canton of Geneva, particularly since the home was on the lake's shoreline. Unbeknownst to Edith, or even her father, though homes on the shoreline of the lake and close to Geneva would always be in high demand, the proximity of Geneva airport and, more importantly, the orientation of its sole runway would eventually lead Versoix and its immediate surroundings to be less desirable than other locations. Versoix would be on the flight path of departing and arriving flights, and noise pollution would become an issue, except at night when the airport curfew would kick in. The runway indeed runs north-northeast to south-southwest: arriving flights would start their final approach pretty much right overhead the house. Obviously, air traffic was minimal at that time, though the airport was indeed opened on October 11, 1919.

The home with its garden was located on the north side of the lake, within the township of Versoix, a half a mile south of Port Choiseul de Versoix. It stood less than a mile from the border between Geneva and Vaud cantons, and a couple hundred yards at most from the Church of Saint Loup, a Catholic Church built in 1841. The house was smaller than many of the surrounding homes, many of which additionally boasted very large gardens, a couple of them designed to look like grand French gardens. Yet, the house was on the shore of the lake, and thus had direct access to it with a dock that could handle up to medium-size cabin cruisers or sailing boats. A ramp leading from the lake to a barn on the west side of the property allowed dry storage of a boat during the winter months, as the lake at that location was still relatively shallow and would normally freeze over. At the same time, a curved seawall starting a couple of houses north of it offered useful protection against the waves which could be triggered by strong winds.

Edith's letter also explained to Stephane that she had had to contact the gentleman who looked after the home in her absence. She reminded him that the gentleman worked full-time for one of their neighbors, who kindly allowed him to help manage the house when the Schneiders were not there, which was most of the time. She did not need to remind her brother that a quarterly payment was sent to him by his "mother's local friend." Although the house was in tip-top shape when it came to cleanliness, Edith would need help to have all utilities reconnected, which usually would have been done. Normally, she would have called ahead of their arrival, giving time for the caretaker to deal with all practical details, and even to fill up the refrigerator with milk and eggs. But the reason for their departure from Paris and the general circumstances explained why she had not called ahead. She promised that she would call Stephane as soon as telephone service was restored.

The next letter Annabelle picked up had a passage that drew her attention:

> *Can't tell you how surprised I am to read your telegram that I should avoid communicating with Rose at all costs. She has been so faithful to me for so long. Yet, your point that she cannot be excluded from the list of suspects that could have pointed us out to the authorities in Paris is sadly reasonable. She does not know of the house here, though I am sure I must have talked to her about my love of the Jura area. But, after all, the Jura region is quite wide as it covers a part of both France and Switzerland. If you feel that I should not even call her from a post office, can you find a way to call her and tell her I am OK. Tell her also that I will reach out to her when this wretched war is over.*

Annabelle assumed, correctly as it turns out, that Stephane, looking for people who might have denounced Edith and her family, had concluded that Rose could not be excluded. In fact, had Edith spoken to Stephane about it, he would have told her that she was the primary suspect, although he also had doubts about the friends with whom she was doing her daily shopping. Edith ostensibly understood her brother's feelings, though, in her diary, was a note to the effect that she could not believe that Rose could have had anything to do with the police's sudden incursion into the Paris apartment.

Edith's letter continued:

> *By the way, I did talk to the person Mom called "her local friend," and everything is in order. He confirms that Mother's financial inheritance, mostly the money from her shares in the silk business, is safely in a joint account in both yours and my name. He said he bought gold with the funds, as he saw that at the time as the safest investment. I don't know how you feel, but it seems reasonable to me. On a different note, I also talked to our family attorney here. He tells me that I should move both what he already has custody of and any art or artifacts I do not need or want to keep in the house here to the Geneva Free Port (you know, the art warehouse within the Free Port that was opened in the late 1800s). He feels that everything would be considerably safer than where things are currently. Could you call him on the telephone number I know you have and let him know what you think please? He'll take instructions from you.*
>
> *Talk to you soon. Still no news from Jean or Albert. I fear the worst. My heart is broken.*

Her next letter said:

> *One last thing. Thank you for having contacted Rose. You say she is OK but seemed harried if not*

worried. I wonder why. I know she always seems to have money problems and sometimes I wonder why this happens. I cannot believe that it is just bad luck that things keep breaking up in her apartment.

Edith's fears were ultimately proven real. Word did come out through the local Paris Jewish grapevine that Jean and Albert had been taken into Germany. Apparently, Rose heard about it from one of Edith's neighbors and she sent a telegram to Stephane since she could not contact Edith directly. By then, word had come out that being sent to Germany meant that someone was very unlikely to come back. Edith tried as hard as she could to remain hopeful, but she could not hide the fact that she was inconsolable for several weeks. Yet, with the war still in full swing, she could not do what she wanted most: travel to the U.S. to see and be with her brother. Fortunately, they were able to correspond by telephone when necessary and by letter the rest of the time. We are thankful for all these letters as they are the only source of information that we have to get to know about Jack's family. The close bond which always united them became even closer, as he effectively coached her through the hard times she was experiencing. With the fate of her husband in limbo, she was not prepared to make any change to her affairs, though she could within reason enjoy the freedom of life in Switzerland. She had made absolutely sure that no external sign was anywhere on the house or elsewhere within the property that she was Jewish, and Jules and Marie were just as careful to hide their ancestry as well. There was no *mezuzah* anywhere in sight!

Annabelle and I decided that we had to work harder at "cracking the code" of the secretary desk. We discussed the fact that our initial foraging into the Louis XVI desk and the armoire had not revealed anything of value, other than the letters and clippings which had allowed us to get a clearer sense of who Jack was, and, more importantly, who his parents and even his French relatives were. Thus, at that time and in our minds, the only place where we still had a defensible reason to search had to be the drop-leaf secretary.

We both agreed that the key had to be for us to find a way to open the hidden vertical drawers in the lower part of the piece which we were still convinced were part of the architecture of the secretary desk. Annabelle remarked:

"I know it has not worked so far, honey, but I really liked your idea that the bronze elements in the upper structure might well hold the key to the opening of these two drawers . . ."

She paused for a second and added:

"If they actually open and a secret compartment does really exist."

Her smile made it clear to me that she was not doubting me as much as wondering whether we were both barking up the wrong tree. I immediately wondered whether the candlestick on the middle column, which looked unnecessary, particularly as we had already managed to open that specific drawer, might be a decoy to take our attention away from the other two at either end of the gallery. Could these be the real McCoys? I directed my attention to the one on the left side of the gallery and tried to move it up, down or sideways. Still no result. I was beginning to lose both patience and hope as I was about to turn my attention to the right candlestick. Coincidentally, Annabelle had come closer to me as I was attempting the same maneuvers again. She startled me:

"I'm sure I heard something. I can't tell you what, but I heard a muffled sound as you were moving the candlestick forward and down."

"Are you kidding? Not nice to try and fool me!"

She persisted in her excitement. Though still unconvinced but given the lack of alternatives I replied:

"Let me give it another try. Here we go . . ."

This time I closed my eyes as I was slowly maneuvering the candlestick concentrating on any sound I might hear. Though I honestly did not hear anything, Annabelle exclaimed:

"The handrail. The wall-side handrail . . . It is moving. It's moving. Look!"

Though not fully convinced yet, curiosity was getting the best of me. I repeated the exercise, this time focusing my eyes on the wall-side handrail. And sure enough, it was extending outward in response to my moving the candlestick. In fact, looking at it more closely, I noticed something which I should have observed earlier. It might well have given us a clue: the rail was not continuous from the bottom of the stairs to the top. It had been made in two parts. There was this small line after the first four steps, separating the rail into two pieces. Therefore, the two parts of the banister could move independently. In fact, I noticed that a similar line could be found on the other side of the stairs, the side opposite the wall. On a hunch, I tried to pull the wall-side handrail further out, still gently as I did not want to break anything. I exclaimed:

"That's it. There's a "click." I think it's coming from the staircase."

Annabelle was equally delighted. Though in her usual cautious style she added:

"I still have not seen anything move; I mean anything other than the handrail."

I was about to agree and lose my calm when I realized that the reason neither of us could see anything moving was because we were not looking carefully enough. The "click" we had heard had started a small rotation in the bottom four steps of the staircase: the part that faced right toward the other staircase across the surface of the desk. That rotation was around a vertical axis located at the tip of the left side of the fourth step. Carefully, as we were still quite concerned that we might break something, we rotated these four stairsteps a bit more. Sure enough, there was a small cavity behind the bottom of the staircase. After having blown into the cavity to chase out the small accumulation of dust, Annabelle started exploring the cavity with her fingers, principally its floor and its back side. Suddenly, she almost yelled:

"There's a button. There's a button."

Without waiting for me to say or do anything, she pressed it and the column on that side of the cabinet, the left, below popped out a third of an inch. We were both excited like two young children when we gently pulled the drawer. It came out completely. We placed it on the floor and looking inside, we found a thick, yellowish envelope. We did not even bother looking at the other column right then. We grabbed the envelope and gently opened it. In it, a single folder and on the cover, it said, in French, the equivalent of: "S.S. Collection." We seized the first document within the folder. It fully documented the purchase by David Schneider of an oil painting by Claude Monet, providing both the date of the transaction (December 11, 1898), the price paid, and it mentioned: "purchased from the artist." I was jumping up and down like a child as I said:

"Bingo. The painting was purchased by David Schneider. He must be Jack's grandfather. Good thing we kept looking!"

Though Annabelle was not sure whether my statement was truly neutral or meant as a barb against her, she elected not to respond. She did not want another spat any more than I. So, together, we immediately repeated the same exercise on the other side of the cabinet, the right side, with the candlestick that hung on the right side of the desk. We were sorely disappointed when we had to accept that we were not getting the same results, though I was not too surprised as I had fiddled with it earlier and obtained no satisfaction. Annabelle asked:

"Do you think there is only one secret drawer below?"

I was shaking my head. I could not believe that the woodworker would have wasted space and only created one hidden compartment. Made no sense to me. So, I replied:

"Could surely well be. But I'm still surprised. I remember that there were always at least two sets of hidden drawers in the secretary desks we had at home when I lived with Mom and Dad."

Annabelle was not going to let me get away with that affirmation. She said,

"Hold it, Mike. This does not hold water."

I was surprised at the aggressiveness, but for once kept my mouth shut, thought a bit and then replied:

"What do you mean?"

She replied:

"We've already found several secret compartments in the upper section. Could it be that there is only one in the lower part."

"Again, it's possible. But remember, our thesis was that it made no sense for the space behind the columns to be wasted. It has been proven correct on the left-hand side. To me, it sounds even more compelling to think that there's got to be something on the right side as well."

I paused for a few seconds and started to think out loud. *If we assume that the maker wanted to have both drawers really secret, we have to accept that he would not likely have used the same mechanism. Having the same mechanism doubled the chances that the secret would be found as there would be two places in which to look, and once you had found one you almost automatically had the other. So, we must think of something different. Here, we have two options. First, the craftsman could have located the second mechanism in the same corresponding location as the other, with enough of a variation that one would lose patience if repeating the same steps did not work. Second, he could have placed it in a totally different position.* I hoped we were looking at the first alternative, because the number of possible variations would be almost limitless if the woodworker had decided to cover his tracks and make the second mechanism as different as he could from the first.

Chapter Nine

2001
NAPLES, FLORIDA

Annabelle and I continued to work on the drop-down desk. We were delighted to have found a way to confirm that there was at least one hidden drawer, the one located on the left side of the secretary and be able to open it. Yet, I could not abandon my conviction that there had to be some symmetrical set-up on the opposite side of the piece, on the right. The key was to find how we could make it open.

We started looking for variations on the theme we used for the left side, accepting that the woodworker had wanted to use different mechanisms so as not to give away the second whenever the first was uncovered. We kept fiddling with the candlestick, but this time, rather than bringing it gently forward and down, we tried forward and up. Didn't work. We looked at all the various parts of the banister along the "gallery" since I had already attempted to work with the center candlestick. Still no success. Annabelle asked:

"What if the craftsman had bypassed the step of the candlestick? What if we touched the wall-side handrail? After all, it popped out on the other side, maybe it does not need to pop out to trigger the mechanism."

"Makes a lot of sense. Let's try . . ."

Still no success unless we needed to pull much harder than either of us was comfortable doing. At the same time, I noticed that the banister running against the wall of the staircase was also in two pieces as it had been on the other side. I added:

"There's got to be a way to trigger the same rotation as on the other side. The two banisters match."

Annabelle asked again:

"Unless it's the other one. How about the other handrail, the one away from the wall."

I tried manipulating it both up and down, toward the inside of the stairs and away from them but still was not achieving anything. I could only say:

"Well, no success. So, since the banister is also in two pieces, I bet that the staircase is made of two pieces. Just like the other one. There's got to be a trigger somewhere."

I ran to my office to get a magnifying glass I had received at some function as a memento and used it to look as closely as I could at the staircase. Quickly, I exclaimed:

"No question. It's made in two pieces. The bottom part comprises the first four steps plus the portion of both banisters that go with it, and the other, upper part, which has the remaining stairs and their two banisters."

Pointing to a spot on one of the steps, I added:

"Look, here must be the top of the vertical rotation axis. I can see a minute piece of wood that looks like it was glued onto the step. It must be there to cover where the axis likely is. You could not see it without this magnifying glass; it must have been glued there after the craftsman drilled the hole for the axis."

Looking at the other side of the cabinet where we had seen the lower half of the stairs pop out, I argued:

"We've got exactly the same setup here. I can see the same small wood dot where the axis would come out. I can't believe that this is not the other secret compartment, or at least as we had on the other side the place where the trigger to a secret compartment is located."

I paused and concluded:

"Makes no sense unless the craftsman was so devious that he made this side in two pieces like the other side just to confuse people like you and me. Somehow, I can't believe it. I'm sure they were trying to hide their triggers, but the idea of launching people on wild goose chases seems a bit farfetched. At this point, unfortunately, it seems we've just run out of options, don't you agree?"

She conceded the point but was surely not willing to give up or at least not yet. She started thinking out loud in her turn.

"OK, I see your point, but somehow, I'm like you. I can't believe that narrative. There's got to be a hidden drawer. If that's the case, the trigger, the button I mean, must be close to the column. I bet the action is a direct one."

"Action?"

"Yes, I mean the mechanism that opens the drawer. Somewhere, there has to be something which slightly moves a piece of wood allowing some spring-loaded mechanism to take over and push the drawer just that much out."

"So?"

"Well, I bet that the link between the button and that trigger must be direct. They had no electronic stuff in those days . . . The indentation in the mechanism releasing the opening of the column must be physically activated by the button being depressed."

She added:

"Obviously, the mechanism might use mechanical relays, wooden or metallic. Yet, though possible, I don't believe it is reasonable for there to be more than one of these relays if any: there would be too many ways for the trigger to risk failing."

She paused, smiled, and added:

"And then, when it failed, how would you fix it without having to disassemble the whole cabinet? And if the relays were visible so that they could be fixed in case of a problem, then they would not be hidden, would they?"

She paused again and corrected herself:

"And if the relays were hidden and the woodworker was no longer alive when the mechanism failed, how would anyone know what to do. No. It does not make practical sense for the mechanism not to rely on a single, direct interaction between a button or something equivalent and the trigger."

I hated to interrupt her train of thought, but conceded she had a solid point. I asked:

"If you're right, then the trigger must be more or less in the same place. In a cavity in the general vicinity of the stairs. Right?"

"Agreed."

"Now, how do we get the stairs to pop out?"

"Well, if you accept my theory on the need for a direct linkage, then the trigger must be very close to the front right side of the cabinet."

We both immediately looked or rather felt our way along the full height of the inside front right of the upper cabinet and sadly concluded that there could not be anything there. Every piece of wood was either polished or sculptured, and whatever was sculptured did not seem to want to budge. Annabelle was getting closer to abandoning the search. She walked away from the piece and started glaring at it; a bit like *"I'll look at you until you deliver your secret!"* Suddenly, she exclaimed:

"Mike, the drawer above the folding desktop. Have we really looked at it closely enough?"

"Well, we both felt our way around the cavity and found nothing."

"I know. I know. But I don't think we had any conviction then. Let's try again, focusing on the side right next to the right-side panel of the piece."

I did as she had suggested and suddenly exclaimed:

"Got one."

I felt a small patch, something that protruded from the wood surrounding it, but only so slightly. I could easily have missed it if not going very slowly and methodically along the wood. I immediately realized that this was exactly what happened the first time around. This time, I pressed on it but could not get it to produce any result. Annabelle tried again but thought of pulling the asperity up with her thumbnail rather than pushing it down. Sure enough, that did the trick. The first four steps of the stairs on the right-side popped open; we helped them complete their outward rotation, revealing the pendant to the cavity we had found on the other side. And, in that cavity, we found the same button as on the other side; depressing it gently, we saw the other column pop forward. We pulled it out completely and set it on the floor next to us. It revealed another thick brownish envelope. We grabbed the envelope and gently opened it. In it, a folder and on the cover, it said, in French, the equivalent of: "E.S. Collection." Annabelle exclaimed:

"Must mean Edith Schneider. Let's look at the first document in it. It was a bill for an oil painting purchased directly from Pierre-Edouard Renouard on January 15th, 1902. It also documents the price paid and mentions: 'purchased from the artist.'"

I was jumping up as I said:

"There are two collections, not just one."

Annabelle could only reply:

"Now, the question is whether the second collection is part of what we have bought or still somewhere else."

One thing Annabelle noted in the correspondence between Edith and Stephane (although she could only see one side of it, Edith's letters) was that there was less and less discussion of what one might call important matters and more and more conversation providing "local color" and classical sibling chit chat. That led her to assume that the most crucial stuff could then be handled by phone, though direct links at that time were quite difficult: no automatic dialing, every call needed to go through at least one or two operators; there could be substantial delays ranging up to more than twenty-four hours between the time one initiated the process and when the call was actually put through, and the costs were prohibitive.

Edith did not really talk of the impact of the war on her life. In truth, with the house having been in the family for quite a while and the car which by then had been registered in Geneva, most people might surely consider Edith as a local resident. Yet, there were neighbors who might have been suspicious and asked questions. Whether they did or did not, Edith does not discuss the matter. In fact, one gets the decided impression that she really kept very much to herself. She discussed "putzing" in the garden and spending plenty of time in the library reading. She was clearly quite distraught that she had no news whatsoever of the whereabouts of Jean or Albert but demonstrated quite a bit of inner strength in her letters. She repeatedly made the point that unless they had been freed, there was no way that anyone could call her with any news. Nobody in France knew where she was. Annabelle commented that, had she been Stephane, she would have wondered whether Edith repeated the same rationale more as a means to keep herself convinced rather than in order to convince him.

Edith commented also on the fact that life in the house was quite different than when she and Stephane visited with their parents, or when she and Jean came there to spend a few weeks on holiday. She said that she had chosen to use her own "old" bedroom rather than that of her parents, which she had started to use when she came with her husband. With an upstairs bedroom, she needed to climb the stairs somewhat regularly. The house indeed had been built in such a way that the "owner" or, in their case, "the parents" could live on the ground floor without needing to go upstairs. In addition to the common rooms such as the living room, a small sitting room doubling up as a sunroom to the southeast of the house, the library, and the dining room, the first floor indeed had the master bedroom and its bathroom, though the concept of "*en-suite*" bathroom did not quite exist yet, and the European tradition of not mixing bathrooms and toilets was clearly respected. The second floor had three bedrooms and a playroom. The garage was detached and provided living quarters for Jules and Marie, who had a kitchen and living/dining room on the ground floor, effectively adjacent to the garage, while the second floor, more of an attic in fact, had two bedrooms with dormers for windows and a bathroom, the toilet being downstairs.

There was no central heating in the house, which got its heat when needed through the various fireplaces in all the main rooms, with a wood-burning stove in the kitchen. The shed where the wood was stored and, when needed, cut up, was between the main house and the garage, though somewhat recessed so that the two outbuildings represented the other two corners of a triangle formed by the three of them. Right next to the service entrance was the external entry to the cellar to which there was no direct access from within the house. This is where one would have stored things that were unneeded and kept wine and possibly fresh fruit or vegetables, as the temperature was more constant because of the thickness of the walls and the space being below ground. The driveway ran along the east side of the property, passed in front of the main house, and continued with a slight switchback toward the north to reach the garage. Doing so, it would allow direct access to the kitchen and pantry area, and then the servants quarters before reaching the garage. A large tree in front and slightly to the east of the garage made sure that guests coming to visit would not have their eyes attracted by the servants' area. To complete the picture, one could see the boat shed due west of the house, with a ramp leading to the dock on the lake.

In fact, at one point in a letter, Edith was reminiscing of fishing off the dock with the nanny who used to travel with her and her parents. The comment was prompted by her observation that food was not always as readily available as desired because of the war. Thus, Jules would occasionally take a fishing pole and try to catch those small "perch fish" whose fried filets were a delicacy around the lake. Little did she know that pollution would eventually force the Swiss to import these perch filets from Eastern Europe, particularly Estonia, as those fished in the lake were no longer considered appropriate for human consumption. By contrast with the relative difficulty to find meat and fish on a regular basis, Edith noted that dairy products, as well as fruits in season, were quite plentiful, which should not surprise anyone who knew the Swiss reputation for milk products, particularly cream and cheeses, and fruit liquors or jams.

Chapter Ten

1880 – 1932, 2001
VILNIUS, LITHUANIA, LYON AND PARIS, FRANCE

A picture was emerging in our minds. Though we had hoped most recently to learn more about Jack, the person whom we were beginning to get to know was David Schneider, Jack's grandfather. We had indeed found a very interesting document in the second yellowish envelope. Obviously, we had first focused on the folder entitled "E.S. Collection," as it contained a bunch of bills of purchases. Yet, there also was a diary which was apparently written by David. That was going to give us better insights into the prior generation.

Reading it was not as easy as perusing Edith's diary. We quickly determined that the language had to be a variant on German, which we assumed was Yiddish. Yiddish shares a lot of its vocabulary with German, but still has borrowed many Hebrew, and to a lesser extent, Aramaic words. Later, when most European Jews moved eastward, Yiddish borrowed words from Slavic languages. Annabelle's knowledge of German, in which she was truly fluent, as well as of Danish and Swedish, which was considerably rustier, allowed us to make some progress. Though it would be a while before we fully understood everything.

David Schneider was apparently born in Vilnius, Lithuania, in 1865, to a reformed Jewish family. It seemed that his family was quite assiduous in its synagogue service attendance on the Sabbath, but certain comments he made about food led us to conclude that he was not abiding by all the dietary rules which Kosher Jews follow. For instance, while he seemed to avoid pork and pork products, he did not seem to worry about eating meat and dairy products at the same time. It seems that he emigrated from Lithuania soon after finishing medical school in 1890. He settled in Lyon, France, where he pursued his medical specialization in ophthalmology. While a student in ophthalmology, he simultaneously worked in a hospital as a general practitioner as he needed to earn a living. There was no indication as to why David settled in Lyon, though it was one of the few places where Jews had assembled following their emancipation in 1831. One might, however, have thought that David would have more naturally chosen Paris where a much larger Jewish population lived. At any rate, David became acquainted with the professor who headed up the ophthalmology department, a jovial Gilbert Grune, who was Jewish as well and had in fact added an "e" to his last name, *Grun*, which meant "green" in German.

Dr. Grune one day invited three of his residents to a dinner at his house, somewhat of an unusual practice in the day. Though we certainly do not know for sure why the invitation was extended, and David's diary does not discuss that, we concluded that a couple of factors may have played an important role. First, looking at the date, Monday April 30th, 1894, it looked as if it might have coincided with the celebration of Passover, which that year, 5654 in the Hebrew calendar, saw *Pesach* run from Friday April 20th to

Saturday April 28th. We doubt it was a was an actual *seder* meal, as tradition has the meal celebrated on the first or second day of the seven-day Passover period and never after it had ended. That meal is served on a special plate containing symbolic foods to show all the elements that comprised the ideas of the people of Israel. Yet, it could be viewed as a meal in the Passover season. Second, we take it as an important clue that David emphasized that all three guests were of Jewish ancestry and that undercurrents of antisemitism were beginning to be felt.

The famous *"Affaire Dreyfus"* was less than 10 years away, a case where a Jewish military officer, Alfred Dreyfus, was accused of treason. More precisely, he was accused of selling French military secrets to the Germans, who had been at war with France less than 25 years earlier. Though the slip of paper discovered in a German military trashcan—which served as the main piece of evidence—could not definitely be linked to Captain Dreyfus, he was still condemned. Many have assumed that the fact that he was rich, and Jewish, played a significant role in his conviction, more so as he came from Alsace, the region which was taken from France by Germany after the Franco-Prussian war of 1870-1871, returning to France in 1919 after the end of the First World War. The press invented at that time the famous "international Jewish conspiracy" which would serve as the backbone for antisemitism.

David was immediately surprised by the opulence of Dr. Grune's house, which was surrounded by other homes, each one seemingly as beautiful as the others, at least from the outside. First, there were the four rounded stone steps with sculpted marble banisters on both sides, narrowing as they came close to the ornate front door. The front door was solid, sculpted, unpainted, dark wood. It was framed by small windows on either side, with wrought iron bars protecting them. Once he had rung the bell on the right-hand side of the door, a butler in an old-fashioned uniform greeted him and took his umbrella and hat, while he was admiring the beautiful hallway, with beige limestone tiles, enhanced by small, dark green marble tiles wherever four of the large tiles came together. He also noticed the green fabric-covered walls, the ceiling height, the heavy drapes on either side of the front door and, towards the back, the majestic staircase with bronze banisters ostensibly leading to at least two other floors. There was also a magnificent crystal chandelier hanging from the ceiling of the third floor.

He was ushered in what looked like the main reception room, probably a living room, with the same kind of heavy drapes with matching valences as in the entry hall, two beautiful silk-covered sofas, family portraits, and other elegant paintings on the walls, each with its own lamp to provide it with optimal lighting. He could also admire a couple of display cabinets with miniatures in them, as well as a couple of bronze sculptures on a sideboard, probably dating back to Louis XV. Dr. Grune was there to welcome him with a bright smile. David thought that his two associates had not arrived yet, or at least that he did not see them. Dr. Grune suggested they move to the next room, a beautiful library filled with a wide variety of neatly bound books. As he commented on the books, Dr. Grune simply said with a wide smile:

"Oh, can't say I've read them all, but they make for a wonderful décor."

As they were still alone together, a waiter, with what looked very much like a white tuxedo jacket, approached, and took a drink order. David was surprised that there would be more than one choice when he simply ordered a scotch whisky. Moving toward the side of the room, walking past a desk which he assumed had to be Dr. Grune's own desk, his host introduced him to a couple of people, one of whom was one of David's associates. The other gentleman looked a bit like Dr. Grune, which was confirmed when he was introduced as his brother. Moving on to a third reception room, a more intimate sitting room, he was introduced to Dr. Grune's wife and the women with whom she was chatting: Dr. Grune's sister-in-law, her daughter, and Dr. Grune's own daughter, Martha.

The one thing which David later remembered is that he had not seen a single, silver vessel which would traditionally be found in Jewish homes. It immediately reminded him that, though less unpopular than in Lithuania, being Jewish was not something one advertised in France at that time.

He would eventually find out that Dr. Grune was a pure product of the Lyon Jewish silk aristocracy, though he had chosen to become a physician rather than running the family company. David knew enough of the history of the town to have heard of the two revolts of silk workers, the "*canuts*," in 1831 and 1834, with silk being one of the main industries in Lyon at the time. Later, he would learn that the Grune family company simply was the most recognized one in the silk business in Lyon; he admired that Dr. Grune was discreet enough to not let any of that slip out at the hospital. In some ways, Dr. Grune was drawing income from two different sources: his professional practice which included work at the hospital and in a private clinic and the dividends he received from the family business run by his younger brother. The opulence was explained.

He could not help noticing the exquisite furniture as well as decorative items in every one of the four rooms which he got to see that evening rivaling one another in terms of beauty and cachet. He was also impressed by the quality and discretion of the service provided both before, during and after the dinner in a dining room which probably had space enough for eighteen people, if not more. Yet, the one element of the experience which stood up most in his mind was the beauty and charm of Dr. Grune's daughter. He took pains devising a stratagem to try to meet her again, the sooner the better in his mind.

Seated at the dinner table that evening with David and his two colleagues were Dr. Grune, his wife and their two children, including Martha, as well as Dr. Grune' brother, his wife and their two children. Conversation was very animated within the confines of proper etiquette. David, who had coincidentally been seated between Dr. Grune's daughter and her cousin, thoroughly enjoyed learning more about Martha and had to make an effort to pay attention to his other table companions. As he was leaving Dr. Grune's house, David intentionally "forgot" both his hat and his umbrella, focused as he was on saying his goodbyes to Martha.

Having "forgotten" his hat and umbrella, he would therefore have to be back at the house the next day to collect them, and, he hoped, have a chance to chat a bit more with Martha. The ploy must eventually have worked as the diary talks of a wedding less than a year later. As they were later reminiscing on the occasion, David and Martha could not help but joke that it seemed that Dr. Grune's intentions were ostensibly to introduce his three assistants to his daughter and her cousin. This was a time when marriages were still arranged, and they both felt that Dr. Grune had to have been so impressed with his associate, David, that the dinner was his way of "arranging" a marriage.

The wedding, in 1895, helped David a great deal, though it was a wedding based on love and not societal convenience. It put him simultaneously on a sound financial footing, as an in-law heir to the family fortune, and eventually professionally as a likely "preferred second-in-command" to Dr. Grune. The diary is quite discreet on the early years of the marriage, other than the birth of Stephane in 1897 and Edith in 1900, but it does suggest that the couple was quite happy. It does not expand much either on the eventual move to Paris, though a short comment suggests that Dr. Grune recommended his protégé to his opposite number in Paris. Whether David and Martha wanted to be in Paris or the opportunity to extend his influence over ophthalmology in France led Dr. Grune to dispatch his son-in-law and his daughter to Paris, we could not find any reason to lean one way or the other. The one thing which became quite clear, very quickly, is that David must have been introduced into the artistic circles in Paris, with a particular emphasis on impressionist painters.

Indeed, soon after they relocated to Paris, he started purchasing paintings, initially from seemingly secondary artists, as the trace provided by the various bills clearly suggested. Soon thereafter, the paintings that were acquired were the work of the famous members of the French impressionist group, and they were at least in part seemingly exchanged for ophthalmologic services. Fancy furniture was notably purchased at the time of the relocation, a proof if we needed one, that the two sources of income which David now had, just as his father-in-law, were giving him opportunities to "live it up." That also explained why he was able to acquire an apartment in one of the nicest areas of Paris, which would otherwise have seemed out of the reach of a young, and promising doctor though we did not know whether the apartment was in his name or his wife's name; a note in his diary talks of Dr. Grune having lent them the money needed to buy the apartment. Yet, in somewhat of a tradition within the people of his ancestry at the time, his "living it up" involved acquiring property or art rather than participating in what many called forms of debauchery, when aspiring, young, creative people flocked to the

City of the Lights to revel in its renewal which was marked by the 1900 Universal Exposition where the "Eiffel Tower" was "unveiled and thus discovered by millions of visitors from around the world." Yet, it goes without saying that David and Martha's life must have included attending numerous receptions, particularly those which involved art.

Though he does not discuss in any detail the early and even teenage years of his two children, David dedicates several pages of his diary to the conclusion of the Affaire Dreyfus in 1906, though his focus was, interestingly maybe, more on the famous letter written by Emile Zola entitled "I accuse" in 1898, about four years after Dreyfus was accused of treason. The letter supported the author's assertion that the army was covering an error that saw Dreyfus sentenced and sent to a penal colony, Devil's Island, off the coast of Guyana. Some other officer, Major Ferdinand Walsin-Esterhazy, whose handwriting seemed a better match to the note found in the German trashcan, appeared a more likely suspect. Yet, George Picquart, the man who pointed the finger away from Dreyfus and was head of counterespionage at the time, was demoted and accused of being a spy himself, while Ferdinand Esterhazy was acquitted, and Dreyfus reconvicted. Picquart was eventually rehabilitated and promoted to the rank of Brigadier General,

Yet, Annabelle noticed that the tone and content of the diary kept evolving. David indeed appeared to be spending less and less time focusing on current affairs or even his own life in general and seemingly more and more time discussing his budding art collection. For instance, one might have been surprised not to find any reference to what the French called the *Années folles* which characterized the 1920s, where, just as happened in the U.S. with the *Roaring Twenties* or in Germany with the *Golden Twenties*, people felt freer to create and enjoy life as they emerged into the post-World War I economic boom. They could finally forget or at least leave behind the blood, sweat and tears of the war which wiped out a good part of the male population of a generation.

If David was no longer offering much of a commentary on his life and on current affairs, the diary became replete with reflections about the art world. The first thing that we noted was a discussion, where he went into several arcane details, of the fact that impressionist painters were not making use of the expensive mineral-based pigments favored by their predecessors, but rather of cheaper alternatives that were often of organic origin. While he did not criticize the colors that were used or their effects, he was bemoaning the fact that future generations would enjoy different paintings than those he was himself seeing. He was arguing that organic pigments would tend to degenerate over time, while mineral pigments would have been considerably more stable. Interestingly, it led him to a couple of conclusions, one of which ended up being quite right and the other quite wrong. He believed that the cheaper pigments allowed painters to work more quickly and thus predicted that their work would be plentiful and thus capture the imagination of a generation. That proved absolutely correct, though even that took some time. By contrast, he argued that impressionist paintings might lose some of their appeal over the next century as the colors which the artists had chosen gradually became paler, thus detracting from the canvases' beauty or appeal. That was proven quite wrong and still is wrong today.

His diaries had comments on several artists, which, because of the nature of a diary, were mostly chronological. Interestingly, one of his final paragraphs amounted to a recapitulation of the era, noting that those he thought were the greatest names in the group of artists he considered were all born between 1830, with

Camille Pissarro born in St Thomas in the West Indies, and 1853 when Vincent Van Gogh was himself born in a small village near Antwerp. In between these two eminent representatives of the generation, one could find Edouard Manet, Edgar Degas, Paul Cezanne, Alfred Sisley, Claude Monet, Berthe Morisot, Pierre-Auguste Renoir, Armand Guillaumin, Jean-Frederic Bazile, Paul Gaugin, and Gustave Caillebotte to name but those whom David included in his chronology. His comment that impressionism was a generational phenomenon had been proved quite insightful.

Actually, David delighted in tracing the real onset of the movement when Monet, Renoir, Sisley, and Bazile met in the early 1860s, studying together under Charles Gleyre. The one element which seemed quite important in the development of the school was that certain artists were quite poor while others, for instance Manet, Degas or Caillebotte were wealthy in their own right; the wealthier among them were thus able to promote the work of the whole group.

A fascinating side note in David's diary focused on the reasons why impressionism did not experience immediate success, and it returns partially to his comment on the paint pigments which the artists used though it is much more general in scope. Impressionist painters all had to work very hard for very little rewards, all the while being roundly rejected by the cannons of the day, embodied in the "Salon," the crucial annual exhibit held by the Académie des Beaux Arts. The rejection was on the grounds that their works did not meet the norms which the Académie set, not a surprising observation with any new styles which conflict with prior habits. That added to the general distaste of the public for the relative "common nature" of their subjects, following in a way the Japanese who also responded to the onset of photography by turning to everyday scenes in their pictural art. Furthermore, critics concluded that the impressionists could not draw (as their subjects were at time not very well delineated), their colors based on organic pigments were vulgar and their compositions strange.

Eventually, the group of artists got together, led by Claude Monet and a couple of others, and elected in 1874 to create their first collective exhibit. Seven exhibits later, by 1882, the new school was well-established and the prices for their paintings started to climb and make a few of them less poor if not rich during their lifetimes. David seemed to relish the fact that he had acquired several paintings, sketches and drawings before prices rose dramatically, in effect following the same route as Caillebotte, from whom he did in fact buy paintings, both his own and those that Caillebotte bought from fellow impressionists. The chronology, however, led Annabelle and me to note that David was not among the very first buyers, but rather found himself in the second wave as prices had started to rise but were still modest, at least when compared to the heights they have now reached.

In 1920, about twelve years before he died in 1932, David even seemed to have founded some art company, maybe a gallery, with its own letterhead. His art-related activities increased substantially in volume, with transactions including purchases as before, but also an increasing number of sales. In 1926, if not a year or two before, he even appeared to have brought Stephane into the business, though the latter was simultaneously pursuing his medical studies; he had earned his medical degree but was completing work on his radiology specialty.

David's love for his father-in-law seemed to have been quite genuine as he devoted a full chapter of his diary to the last days and the eventual death of Dr. Grune. He described how distressed Martha was when it happened and noted that it took her quite a while to recover from it. The global economic crisis of 1929 might also be blamed for it, as it inflicted serious challenges on the silk business. Yet, David was quick to mention that the company had to curtail certain expenditures but was never in any way under the threat of having to cease operations. Interestingly, the records which we have of his art trading activities do not suggest that there was any need to slow down, even during these difficult times. In fact, at the margin, it would appear that David added to his collection and incited his two children to start on their own. A handful of purchases indeed around the time bear special mention that the paintings were bought by either Stephane or Edith. He does mention that the death of Dr. Grune led to the sale of the mansion he had in Lyon, while David's mother went to live with her other son, who remained in Lyon, and probably had similar accommodations as did his parents.

That entry makes specific mention of a Louis XVI secretary desk which he described in glowing terms, specifically as being one of the most original and best constructed pieces of furniture which he had ever seen. Reading between the lines, David seems to be wishing good luck to anyone that stumbles on it and does not know how to access what he calls "its treasures" which he claims he, Dr. Grune, only revealed to his son-in-law, David, and that not very long before his health started failing; this suggested to us that he wanted to make sure that its secrets were not lost after he died and bequeathed it to David. In some way, it surely made Annabelle and me feel quite good that we were able to discover these treasures on our own, though I certainly believe that by "treasures" he meant the secret compartments, while we tend to think of their contents . . .

But more to the point, we felt pretty sure that we had by then a rough outline of Jack's family history correct. Jack's grandfather was a wealthy art collector, and he incited both Jack's father and his aunt to follow in his footsteps. It's reasonable to assume that they both benefited from the extra financial resources that were available to them through the in-laws of Jack's grandfather's family. At that point, we stopped asking ourselves questions as to whether the goods we had purchased for a song were valuable or mere reproductions. We knew then that they had to be quite valuable. We thought that the next step in our investigations had to involve matching the items we saw with the various bills which we found in the two folders pried out of the Louis XVI secretary. On the surface, it quickly became quite clear that we were missing more than a few, but we wanted a precise accounting and that, we knew, was going to be tedious.

Chapter Eleven

2001, 1941 – 1946
NAPLES, FLORIDA AND VERSOIX, SWITZERLAND

Our discovery of the two folders led Annabelle and me to decide to take a short inventory of what we knew and did not know. Our work so far has added quite a significant amount to our knowledge of the art collection that David Schneider, and later on his two children, had accumulated. We knew that David had evolved from the medical world to the art world, taking advantage of the unusual combination of having been introduced into the art world as a solid ophthalmologist, while simultaneously drawing some significant additional income from the fortune of his wife.

At the end of the day, we became convinced that his passion was the main driver for the collection, which the wealth of his wife's family certainly enabled him to build. We also came to believe that David had played a role not too dissimilar to several emerging art merchants, who had chosen to invest heavily in the new school of painting which the impressionists represented. It did not take too much imagination to realize that the combination of wealth and interest in the school would allow one to build a fortune, in David's case a second fortune, since his in-law's business had created the first. The collection which the two folders described was quite impressive. Together, the two siblings seemed to have purchased or inherited at least a couple paintings of every one of the best-known artists, plus a few who might have been known then but somehow did not continue to enjoy the same fame later, not to mention the sketches, drawings or watercolors which they had managed to purchase as well and would enhance the value of the oil paintings to which they related when they did.

Yet, something was telling us that there was a lot we did not know, and, moreover, we had no idea whether that would or would not interfere with what we were starting to feel we should do with respect to the "Schneider Collection" as we had begun to call it. We had a few loose ends which, as we both had learned through life, can have a way of becoming a major element without giving you any advance notice.

Annabelle and I sat down and using the laptop in my office started to draw up an inventory of what the two siblings had bought and kept as per the documents in the two folders. Intentionally, we kept focusing solely on paintings, though we knew that we would have to include furniture and other works of art in due course. We dutifully recorded the name of the artist, the title given to the painting, its dimensions, the date of purchase, the name of the seller and the price which was paid. In the end, only six paintings had been received by David in exchange for his services. We smiled when we found a couple of letters from Theo Van Gogh, the artist's brother, and sometime agent, duly confirming that he was the one who sold the Vincent Van Gogh paintings to David.

We were delighted but also a bit miffed when we discovered an interesting piece of paper as we were coming to the end of the stack of receipts in Stephane's folder. Ostensibly, it had been drawn up by David's notary, the French lawyers who handle estates. It listed the paintings which Stephane received from David, with an estimated value at the time of David's passing. Had we found it earlier, it would have made our own inventory easier to compile. The fact that a good part of David's collection came directly to Stephane and Edith when he passed appeared a bit unusual to us, to the extent that we knew from other papers that David's wife, Martha, had survived him. Why did David transfer things to his children and not first to his surviving wife?

Looking through the papers in the folders, we did not have to remain surprised a lot longer. A second list gave us what Stephane had inherited from his mother when she died. We could not miss a note scribbled at the bottom of the page which, translated into English, said:

"Remained in France when we left for Boston."

That simple mention showed us that the question for us now was to determine both what Stephane and Simone had first brought to the U.S. and whether anything which was labelled as "remained in France" was later brought to the U.S. or left there. Could there be stuff still in France belonging to Jack? And what would that mean for us?

A quick look at the list of the goods that remained in France allowed us to answer the second part of the question: none of the works that were supposed to have remained in France were among those we bought at the consignment shop. Thus, we had to conclude that these other paintings listed as having remained in France were either still in storage there, in storage in the U.S.—but where?—or had been sold at some point. We realized we needed to look for other documents to answer that question.

Edith's folder interestingly contained a couple of comparable lists, though the one which followed her mother's death did not have any special mention at the bottom of the page: it did not need to as she had herself remained in Europe. As we had noted that all the paintings we had "bought" at the consignment shop came from Stephane's first list, it raised a crucial next question: what had happened to the paintings Stephane inherited from his mother and to those which passed onto Edith?

Again, we asked ourselves whether we should continue our current path or revert back to Jack's collection as it came to him from his father. We concluded that we should focus first on Jack's collection because this was our initial project. Yet, the inkling which was getting bigger by the day that we had uncovered a story that was bigger than Jack and that ought to be told led us to agree not to avoid the larger picture. In fact, that bigger picture might deserve, if not need, to be a part of the Schneider Collection, as we were calling it.

Annabelle and I concluded that our next step had to be to try and classify all the drawings, etchings, sketches, and the like which we found in the large artist folder we had bought at the same time as the rest at the consignment shop. There were no more than twenty pieces, with three actual oil paintings which we noted did not have a signature readily visible. It took us seconds to find that the signatures had been hidden as had been the case for the paintings which we had bought framed. Annabelle could not help exclaiming:

"Stephane was surely thorough. He even hid the signatures of paintings that were neither framed not on display anywhere."

The other seventeen pieces were all unsigned, although we found it relatively easy to identify the artists in about a dozen of them: six were obvious studies or sketches for one of the paintings we had bought; three were studies for different subjects, but the style of the drawings looked quite like the others we could identify, so we simply assumed they were the same authors; three others were etchings which we similarly attributed to artists based on style and subject similarities. Five would require the help of our friends at Sotheby's. We dutifully added these works to our Excel compilation, though the amount of detail we could record was obviously considerably less.

Comparing our list to those we had found in the two folders, it was crystal clear that the number of works that were listed, particularly on Stephane's inheritance from his father, was higher than what we had in our possession. Annabelle and I went back and forth as to what that might mean, conceding that it was entirely possible that works were sold over time, even possibly since Stephane had moved to the U.S. Yet, I could not convince myself that we had the whole thing:

"Honey, imagine that you are Stephane. You have ostensibly kept a number of secondary works, the unsigned drawings, for instance. Does it make sense for you to sell works that seem valuable given those on the list which are missing?"

"Really don't know, Mike. It's quite difficult, not to say impossible, for me to put myself in David's or Stephane's position. Why are you asking?"

"Well, assume that you wanted to bring a few more paintings, but, for instance, had them in your possession in France but had not been framed."

"OK, so?"

"What would you do?"

"Mike let's stop this game. I know you well enough. I know you have an idea. Let's come out with it and spare me the Q&A part."

"OK. You do know me. And you are correct: I have an idea, but I am not sure."

I explained to Annabelle that I suspected that paintings might have been smuggled along with the furniture. I could think of only two possibilities: they might have been hidden in the seats of the chairs, or they were in one of the other pieces of furniture. If the latter, I could exclude the drop-leaf secretary which I thought we had thoroughly explored. The only two places that remained were the armoire or the Louis XVI writing desk. Annabelle agreed with my logic and added:

"The seat of the armchairs, or even of the desk chair seem possible, but I would not call this discreet, unless you assume that Stephane or his wife were able to reupholster furniture themselves before they left France. If not, would the upholsterer required to reupholster the chairs not have raised questions?"

"Totally agree, although we know, clearly with the benefit of hindsight, that artworks owned by Jews were stolen by the Germans. Thus, it would not be crazy for Stephane to try to protect against that, potentially using means that appear extreme and maybe a Jewish craftsman who he assumed would not talk."

"Cannot disagree. But what about the risk that rather than looking for the art hidden in the seats, the thieves would simply have stolen the chairs, since we know they were made by Jacob, a very well-known maker?"

"Grant you that. Let me briefly go palpate the seating surfaces and backs of the armchairs and see if I can detect anything underneath."

I returned with a grimace on my face saying:

"I'm not saying there's nothing there. But one thing is clear: if there's something it's well- hidden; I can't feel anything with the palm of my hand."

"Did you check both the seat and the back?"

"Yes."

"The part we see as well as the other, the bottom of the seats or the back?"

"Yes, again."

Shifting the topic, I added:

"Let's focus on the armoire, as I can't imagine how you could smuggle enough in a desk."

Annabelle had the last laugh:

"Unless you found a way of drilling cylindric cavities in the legs . . ."

We both went back to the garage to inspect the armoire, which, in fairness, we had not really considered until then, though we had no difficulty thinking of a home for it in one of the children's bedrooms. I could not help noticing again that there was no marquetry work anywhere, while the wood was exquisitely sculptured, on almost every surface except the back. I immediately looked for a possible signature of the woodworker and found the same two as for the secretary: one on the very bottom of the armoire, and the other on the top, right behind the crown on the left side. It was also a piece of work by Gosselin. I noted that I was not aware of the fact that he had done work that did not include wood inlays, but Annabelle immediately chided me:

"Let's be honest, Mike, how much did either of us really know about him before we started on this project?"

"Touché," was all I could say. The armoire had two magnificent doors that opened revealing a beautiful inside, though there were no carvings in there, if one excludes the handles to the drawers. There was a set of three horizontal drawers about four feet above the floor of the armoire; they occupied the whole width of the piece. I explained to Annabelle that in my parents' apartment, in my own bedroom in fact, there was a Regence piece that looked like this armoire, though not nearly as beautifully sculpted. These drawers were where one would place small, folded items such as underwear, socks, or handkerchiefs; I added:

"In those days, I'm talking of my youth, in the post-WWII period, there were no built-in closets, at least in older buildings. In my bedroom, for instance, there was my bed with a wraparound piece of furniture—a cozy—at the head and along its right side, the armoire, a convertible sofa which would allow one of my brothers to sleep in my room, giving his to a visiting grandmother, an armchair, a writing desk, and a chair. That's it."

Back to the armoire, the space above the drawers was totally empty, allowing the owner to place folded shirts or sweaters. The bottom part of the piece was where one would hang suits, dresses, and other outerwear, from a wooden rod that ran the whole width of the armoire, just under the drawers.

Annabelle immediately offered:

"Unless we missed the paintings in the drawers, or there is a false bottom to the whole piece or a false top above the three drawers, I don't see where you could hide anything."

"Agreed, but only up to a point."

As I was making this affirmation, I literally walked into the space reserved for hanging clothes. I had to fold myself almost in half as my six-foot frame had to be made to fit in a space that was a bit less than four feet high, as the wooden rod from which the pieces of clothing would hang used up another three or four inches. I looked as carefully as I could at the sides and then underneath the drawers above my head and had to concede that I could not see anything odd. I was looking more carefully at the right-hand side of the armoire from the inside, focusing more specifically on the place where the hanging rod was fixed. I don't know why, but something caught my attention. I came closer, my neck twisted to the point where I almost felt some pain. I could see something right behind the spot where the hardware was attached. I invited Annabelle to replace me, as she was a good six inches shorter. It would be easier for her to inspect the spot. Within seconds, she was saying:

"That small piece of wood you saw . . . It rotates up and down around a horizontal axis."

I had to ask:

"Anything move?"

"You mean other than the small piece of wood I assume. Not really. Wait, let me try this."

She toggled the small piece of wood and was simultaneously applying her other hand against the very back of the armoire. She exclaimed:

"Mike, it's moving; not by much but it's definitely moving. I bet you it's not a false bottom, but a false back. There's got to be a space between the outside back and the inside back if I'm making any sense."

"Great. Smart, very smart. Who would have thought? Now there's got to be something like the small piece of wood quite near the bottom."

Annabelle went on all four and it took her but seconds to find another toggle a centimeter from the floor, attached to the frame of the armoire.

"This is it!"

"Two done, two to go. Is there something similar on the other side?"

She did not bother getting up. While still on all fours, she turned around and checked the left-hand side of the armoire, and another toggle was there. She got up, found the last toggle in the same spot I had near the other end of the hanging rod. Immediately, the whole of the back of the armoire started to lean forward; though about a half inch less wide than the actual back on either side, to allow space for the toggles. I pushed back against it while Annabelle climbed out of the armoire. Then, with both of us gently assisting the false back down to the horizontal without letting it tumble too fast, we discovered several canvases, all lying down, flat one against the others and now resting on the wooden plank, flat at our feet. With some real excitement in my voice, I said:

"We have just found another group of paintings. Let's count them."

A few seconds later, I added:

"We now have another group of fifteen paintings."

I looked at one of them and could not hold back:

"And naturally, the signature is hidden. Bet you it's the same for the others. But, darling, unless I am completely off, you're looking at another fifteen impressionist paintings!"

We brought them carefully into the house and Annabelle repeated her gauze trick to find the signatures which had been hidden. Three hours later, comparing the now appropriately signed canvases to the lists which we had for Stephane, Annabelle exclaimed:

"Well, now we know. We have everything on the list."

"We do. For one thing, it means we won't have to go check the legs of the desk!"

"Very funny, Mike!"

"However, honey, we still don't have those which his note said were initially, at least, left in France . . ."

"Are you becoming greedy?"

Chapter Twelve

2001, 1941 – 1946
Naples, Florida, Versoix, Switzerland and Skokie, Illinois

Meanwhile, Annabelle was still using Edith's letters and her diary to try and reconstruct as much of Edith's life post the police raid on her apartment as she could. So far, we knew that she had arrived safe and sound at the house in Versoix, but not without a couple of real frights with Jules and Marie.

Life in eastern Switzerland at that time during the Second World War was clearly less harsh than in France, occupied or not, but it was still hard. The Swiss's armed neutrality based on the topography of their country and the policy to have well-armed and trained citizens provided them with significant protection. Yet, it would be a mistake to think that they felt totally secure. The risk of a German, or Italian invasion was always present. It could be the reason why though willing to help up to a point, armed neutrality also meant that they could not allow themselves to be a safe haven.

In fact, after the border had been closed, many cantons simply failed to respond to a question as to how many refugees they would be willing to accept. History shows that "Appenzell-Ausserrhoden said it would take 25 refugees—if necessary. Ticino refused to take any; St. Gallen agreed only on condition that the emigrants be distributed evenly among the cantons—which amounted to a refusal. Geneva, on the other hand, agreed to provide places for 400 people in the canton—a figure that would triple in just a few months."

Given the situation, Edith recalled in a letter that one of the first things she asked Jules to do was to help get Swiss registration plates for the car. She could honestly say that she was not "just a common refugee" since they had owned the house for many years. Their "local friend" provided help, although the story of how the family came to use him is intriguing.

The Swiss bank which had historically catered to clients of Jewish extraction had been Dreyfus, which was based in Basel and, even to this day, has no branch outside of that city. Though David had been introduced to Dreyfus by Martha's family, he wanted to have both his bank and his residence in the Geneva area. He wanted to put as much distance between him and the Germans as he could. He found a way to get introduced, by a Dreyfus banker, to Pictet, another private bank which was founded in 1805, based in Geneva. Though arguably a very well-placed member of the Protestant community in Geneva, the bank agreed to assist David; ostensibly someone owed a favor to the banker from Dreyfus.

Going back to changing the car's registration, the family's Pictet banker expedited all the various formalities as a part of their "classical concierge service." Edith had been very careful that only she had the contact with her banker. Though she was sure that both Jules and Marie had to be aware that she had money in

Switzerland, or, if it was not hers, that she had access to money in Switzerland, they could not be allowed to know more. In this case, she only told Jules to go collect the license plates, which, she said, had been dropped by a dear friend where she asked him to go. Annabelle and I have been told since those events that the service provided by Swiss private banks has been and is still so discreet that it was totally reasonable to assume that Jules had no way of linking Edith to Pictet as well as any other private bank.

In fact, whenever she had to meet with her Pictet banker, Edith recorded that the meeting was apparently held at an address which no one knew had any connection with the bank. It was a simple, though very nice and exquisitely decorated apartment in a nice residential building which the bank maintained precisely so that clients were never seen at the bank. More importantly, the apartment had an underground garage which allowed visitors and bankers alike to drive into the building without being seen, though someone with suspicions could always observe and write down the license plate numbers going in and out. Yet, there could be quite a few residents in the building, which would have made tallying entries and exits quite tedious and possibly not terribly fruitful. She added that she knew of at least two of these apartments, and assumed that there might well be a few others, most likely not in the same building.

A note in Stephane's papers mentioned that he had immediately registered his brother-in-law and his nephew as missing persons as soon as he had heard of them having been arrested and eventually sent to Buchenwald. He had registered them with his local synagogue in Skokie, Temple Beth Israel which had been founded in 1917 in the Albany Park neighborhood.

While initially, there was little that anyone could do other than praying for the captives, Jewish organizations both in the U.S. and even more in Europe started trying to determine the fate of those captured, knowing that the camps were in fact extermination camps and that they were thus searching for lists of victims rather than for survivors.

With the war over by then, Stephane must have told Edith at that point that he was starting to look for Jean and Albert as a letter from her in Stephane's file displayed a lot of emotion and asked him to help her start the same process in Europe. He must have told her to stay in Switzerland and to remain in hiding, as her next letter agreed to the recommendation, though she asked when he would be able to travel to Europe. We were not able to find anything more that described either the nature and results of Stephane's efforts in the U.S. or anything he might have done on Edith's behalf in Europe, although we do know that he did travel, possibly more than once.

However, we eventually found a document dated in late June 1946 which officially informed Stephane that both relatives were among those that had been killed at some point before the Liberation, the end of the war, on May 8th, 1945. Up until then, the sense was growing in both Edith and Stephane's minds that things did not look good for Jean and Albert. Camps had indeed been freed by Allied or Russian troops, with Buchenwald liberated by U.S. troops on April 11, 1945. The camp held thousands of prisoners, mostly slave laborers. There were no gas chambers at Buchenwald, but hundreds, sometimes thousands of prisoners still died every month from disease, malnutrition, beatings, and executions. Further, Nazi "medical personnel" performed medical experiments on inmates, testing the effects of viral infections and vaccines. History seems to recall that Buchenwald was second only to Auschwitz in terms of number of Jews killed. However, at Buchenwald just as at Auschwitz, certain prisoners managed to survive. Coincidentally, one of the most famous prisoners freed from Buchenwald was Elie Wiesel who would go on to receive the Nobel Peace Prize in 1986. Jean and Albert might well have met him at one point in the camp.

By the middle of 1946, enough prisoner records were compiled that the fate of most prisoners and victims was known, if not with absolute certainty, at least with a high degree of confidence. Fortunately, the correspondence shows that Stephane was with Edith when she found out that her worst fears were justified. We assume that Stephane decided to travel to Switzerland with the news, as he knew full well that she would need his support at that delicate time. Additionally, with no one aware of her whereabouts, there was no way she could have been contacted directly. The news did bring closure to Edith, but she initially was inconsolable. So much so in fact that Stephane invited her to join him and Simone in the U.S. for a while. It would seem that she flew back with him and Simone when they returned to Skokie. Unfortunately, but understandably, we have had no correspondence between the siblings while they were together.

The correspondence resumes in December, after *Hanukkah*, still in 1946. We assume that this is when Edith returned from her long visit to the U.S. In the first letter, Edith talks of the beauty of the landscape, kidding that the temperature and the presence of snow is not the real difference she noticed between Geneva and Chicago, but the presence of majestic peaks covered in snow. From the house in Versoix, she would be looking due south and on a nice day she would be seeing Mont Blanc, the highest peak in Europe, covered as it was with perennial snow and ice, and forming what certain locals claim is the outline of a sleeping maiden. Edith alluded in these letters to missing her husband and her son, but reading between the lines, Annabelle and I concluded that she seemed increasingly at peace, and thus ready to embark on this, the next chapter in her life.

Among the topics which she mentioned was an interesting note that covered her friend, Rose. She knew from Stephane that Rose was alive and would love to see her again, and her letter was thanking her brother for having agreed that the risk of Rose doing harm to her, if she was the one that denounced the family in 1941, had greatly diminished if not totally vanished. She was telling him that she was expecting Rose to visit soon and was truly looking forward to it. She rehearsed the points she had agreed with Stephane could be discussed and those that should be sidestepped. In particular, she clearly said that she agreed she should not mention her suspicions as to who denounced the family. Annabelle, reading between the lines again, noted that Edith still seemed to want to ask her if she knew anything about what happened prior to her forced exile. At the same time, Annabelle seemed for some reason to believe that Edith would likely, somehow, sometime wish to join her brother in the U.S. rather than return to Paris. This perception came more from a comment she made about the future for Jules and Marie than any other point.

Annabelle called my attention to a passage in Edith's letter which she thought was troublingly nice. It said:

My dear brother,

It still pains me when I think of Jean or Albert and have to accept that I shall never see them again.

Yet, I must move on, as you and Simone so kindly and repeatedly advised me when I was with you for probably much too long a time in the U.S. You will not believe it, but there is one topic which I recently realized was very important to me and which, somehow, we did not discuss face to face. We both agreed that it made sense for me eventually to consider moving to the U.S. I am not sure I should settle right next to the two of you; you have enough to do with your own affairs and those of Caroline and Jacques. But there are plenty of spaces where I could build a second life in the Chicago area.

Yet, I suddenly realized that such a move to the U.S. would likely close the whole European chapter of our lives, both mine and yours. This brought up two important issues in my mind. What about the artwork, yours, and mine, which now share the same storage facility after you moved the part of your collection which you did not take along and what Mother had left for you after her death? We now have collectibles which belong to the two of us there. Should we not consider what ought to be done with it? Does it make sense to keep everything in the Geneva Free Port rather than having it moved to a similarly safe place in the U.S.? The second issue relates to our financial assets. As you know, there are two accounts. One which we share and arose from the settlement of Mother's ownership in the family business; and the other which represents my financial assets. In contrast with you, I do not have any income independent of these assets, though I do not know whether there will be any compensation accruing to me from the death of my dear son and husband. I will need financial assets in the U.S. to live on.

One final point which we did not discuss and really should have: the house in Versoix. At this point, unless you violently disagree with me, I would like to leave the house to Jules and Marie with the requirement that they cannot sell it or anything in it unless you and I have died. Let me explain. I feel that Jules and Marie went above and beyond their duty to help all three of us escape from France. They shared my fate, and I can only sing their praises. Jules, in particular, as the only one with a driver's license, must have felt the whole brunt of the stress. After all, he was the one going out in the open to scout possible routes, who spent some time in prison because of it and who yet never left my side. I know they needed to escape just as much as I did, but that does not change the fact that they could have easily let me down at some point. Think of the moment we were in Archamps. The gentleman was telling us that it would be easy for two people to get into Geneva if on foot, but that our having a car and the car being registered in France at the time meant that we had to make what did amount to a couple of hundred-mile detours. They could have left me there and taken their chances.

Plus, without me employing them if I was in the U.S., I am not sure how they could live unless they are prepared to return to France, which I for sure am not. They do not have work permits here and thus could not work for any Swiss employer. I would like them to have a home and a modest annuity which I could easily take from my financial assets to allow them to live and maintain the house. What do you think? Is it too much? Plus, since they do not have any descendant that I know of, should I simply let them use the house, rather than own it, until the last surviving of the two of them dies? Since they are younger than you or me, what provisions should we make for the sale of the house after the last surviving one of the two of them dies since neither you nor I may not be around then? And of its contents? Is this something you think the person I have come to call "my local friend" could handle as well?

Chapter Thirteen

2001
NAPLES, FLORIDA

Given the situation, Annabelle and I decided that we had two important pieces of work ahead of us. We needed to find out more about Edith's decision as to whether to stay in Switzerland or join her brother in the U.S. if we could, and that meant going through all the letters which we had only skimmed. We had not yet given up figuring out what happened to her own art collection, as we were pretty sure that she was no longer alive. Did she stay in Switzerland and remarry, thus changing her will and taking her collection out of the "family sphere?" Did she move to the U.S. and, if yes, did she take the collection with her immediately or later on? If that, where was the collection now, assuming that it should still be a part of the family wealth accruing to Jack, unless she came to the U.S., got married and gifted the collection to her second husband? Whatever she did, what if she changed her will and gifted her collection to a charity or a museum?

The second task, more important in our eyes given our priority relative to the art we had "purchased from Jack" so to speak, was to locate any additional information we could. It was clear to us that the drop-leaf desk had more likely than not disclosed all its secrets. I briefly debated the idea of having the piece of furniture x-rayed, but it quickly became obvious that this would likely be both expensive and probably futile. After all, if there was anything more that we had missed, the only part of the secret mechanisms which might be revealed would be the small springs which they contained, unless those were also made of wood. All the rest would have been made of wood and thus would not appear on any x-ray. We also had found the folder with the paintings hidden inside the armoire.

Yet, at that point we were stuck. We had what it should take to provide provenances for all the works we had purchased; we could therefore stop right there, after having verified with Jack's banker that we had satisfied all requirements. However, we knew very well that we could not create a "museum" for Jack's collection with just what we had purchased, though we could surely fill at least a couple of rooms in some already existing institution; after all, we had twenty-seven paintings, plus the drawings. Yet, that would mean that we would be giving everything we had bought and would thus be left with nothing to show for our efforts, other than the satisfaction of showing that Jack was not simply a great pianist, but in fact the scion of an art-loving family. At the same time, we felt we had uncovered enough to have a chance both to create a real foundation in Jack's honor and selfishly to retain a few of the goods we had in the end purchased in all honesty. Any other document we might uncover could be the key that we were missing. Indeed, the one thing we knew was that we did not have is any contact in Switzerland. Thus, we could not investigate any further whatever we knew likely existed but did not know where it was stored.

We therefore decided to "attack" the last piece of furniture that we had not yet fully "inspected" though we still had looked at it in at least a cursory manner: the Louis XVI writing desk. Before we even started, Annabelle said:

"The last time we looked for secret compartments, we ended up fighting. Let's make sure that we're not going to go crazy this time. I will try to be more patient, and you have to be less stubborn. Deal?"

I wasn't sure what the stubborn thing was about, but I liked the proposition and simply acquiesced.

We surely had already inspected the three drawers that opened to the front of the desk. After all, that is where we found the initial documents which launched our more detailed investigation. Yet, I had a nagging feeling that we were missing something, anything which would allow us to broaden our search beyond the goods we had purchased. We went back to the garage where the desk was still "stored." We removed all three of the drawers, placing them on the floor, next to the desk. Annabelle beat me to the punch:

"Hey, the middle one is shorter than the other two . . . quite a bit shorter in fact."

She was absolutely right. In fact, placing them in proper alignment next to one another in the way they would be inside the desk, it became obvious that the middle drawer was at least eight inches less deep than the other two. I immediately slid under the desk to look for something to help me understand what was happening. Not surprisingly, I could not see anything. The drawers were sliding into or out of shelves which were attached to the writing surface; however, since the shelves would be better described as "boxes" there was no external access possible. The sliding slots were not accessible from below. While the writing surface had nice marquetry work following its outside contour, as did the sides of the desk, the bottom part of these boxes, I will call them the floors below the drawers, were in plain "unfinished" and unvarnished wood.

The second thing which was immediately obvious from under the desk was that there was extra space allowing whoever was seated at the desk to place their knees. In fact, it made me consider that the desk might be from the Transition period rather than Louis XVI. I made a mental note to myself that we should have that element checked. Indeed, desks in the Louis XVI period often did away with what we might call the footwell, with all drawers on the front of the desk aligned both top and bottom. But on this desk, there definitely was a footwell: the bottoms of the two side drawers were deeper than the one of the middle drawer. The contour of the drawers created an inverted wave, initially rising then, starting in the middle of the left drawer, gradually falling to create the footwell, and repeating the pattern in a symmetrical fashion on the other side. The slots for the drawers generally followed the contours of the front of the desk (the same at its back); More importantly, there were small ledges that framed each of shelves in which the drawers fit. At the same time, there was no outward sign that the top drawer should be shorter than the other two. I asked Annabelle:

"Honey, can you please look into the slots where the drawers fit?"

Almost casually, I added:

"I wonder whether the space for the middle drawer is shorter than for the side drawers . . ."

Within seconds, she replied:

"Good call. There is something at the back of the middle drawer. The middle drawer could not be any longer than it is."

Finally, one of my guesses had been proven right. I replied:

"Bet you this is another secret compartment. Never heard of anything like that, but then again what do I know? Couldn't possibly find out about it unless you knew where to look, removed all three drawers and inspected the cavities where they fit. Not impossible, but surely not obvious!"

Careful not to get any splinters, I proceeded to follow with my fingers each of the ledges, starting with the two on either side of the middle drawer. Just as we had when trying to break the secrets of the drop-leaf desk, I was looking for any kind of button or cavity hidden somewhere in a ledge, assuming that this would deliver the key we were seeking. Unfortunately, that effort proved futile. Annabelle suggested that the next logical place for a trigger of a secret mechanism would have to be within the cavity into which the middle drawer would slide. It made a lot of sense and we both investigated the cavity with a great deal of care, looking with both our fingers and when that failed with our eyes helped by a flashlight. Yet, the result of our investigation was still unchanged—nothing!

Looking at the back of the desk, I noticed that there were marquetry motifs which mirrored the design on the front of the desk. More than that, I noticed that the motifs were on what seemed like false drawer fronts. And these were very similar if not exactly the same as those we could see when seated at the desk. The woodworker had taken the trouble to create what I can only call false drawer fronts on the back of the desk, so that someone sitting across from the desk would imagine that he or she could open the drawers. They seemed stuck to the back frame of the desk, probably glued to it.

I immediately turned to the false front for the middle drawer, in part because that was the drawer on which we were then focusing and because I had noted that it seemed to be less precisely adjusted to its frame than those on either side. That told me that it was probably "movable" once we had located the trigger to open it. It pushed on it as gently as I could and was initially delighted when I felt that it was indeed moving just so much that I could feel a small "spring effect." I jiggled it up, down, sideways hoping that this would be enough to pry it free, but I was again defeated by the ingenuity of the woodworker. Annabelle, just as she had been the more focused and hard-headed of the two of us when we worked on the secretary desk, simply said:

"Honey, we know more about this desk than we did when we hit the wall with the secretary desk. I'm surely not about to give up. Let's go back to the kitchen, serve ourselves a good cup of coffee and search with our brains rather than our fingers or our eyes."

I could not debate the idea as a cup of coffee felt quite welcome. Once seated at the kitchen table, I asked the obvious question:

"There must be something with the back of this middle drawer. More to the point, I'm ready to bet that there is a trigger that has the false front of the middle drawer at the back of the desk pop out . . ."

Annabelle replied:

"I'm generally on board with that, except for one thing: I can't believe that the woodworker would take the risk of having the nice piece of inlaid wood fall on the ground as it is popped. I bet it is somehow tethered to the desk. But, no matter, it does not change your conclusion."

"Can agree with that, but so what?"

"Well, going back to the mechanism for the second drawer in the lower cabinet of the secretary desk, I think we learned one of two things. Either the trigger mechanism is very close to the wooden cover so that you simultaneously trigger the move and catch the piece of wood before it hits the ground, or it is somehow attached to the desk by a chain or a ribbon."

"Can see that, but would argue that we've been there, done that, and should have received the T-shirt . . ."

"Agreed. So, the second option is that the trigger mechanism may not be as near to the drawer as we think, but in that case, I bet you that there is something which prevents the piece of wood from falling. Maybe it rotates . . ."

"Great idea, Sherlock. So, what's next?"

Annabelle smiled and started thinking out loud:

"Let's assume it is away from the middle drawer. Let's also assume that it is sufficiently hidden so that one could not happen on it just by accident."

She continued:

"Mike, where would you put a trigger if you had those two thoughts in mind?"

"Great question. Let me think. Let me first think of where I would not put it. It would not be anywhere on an outside part of the desk . . ."

Annabelle interrupted:

"Outside part?"

"Yeah! I mean anything that is immediately visible when you are seated at the desk or standing around it."

"I see. So, you would not exclude it being below the top surface?"

"Absolutely. In fact, come to think of it, where else would you put it? Can't be inside any of the drawers, as you would pick it up. Correct?"

"I'll grant you that, but I have a thought."

"Pray tell."

"You said that you would not exclude any place below the top surface. Yet, to me, this is not discrete enough. You could happen upon it by accident. Agreed?"

"Agreed, but I can't see where it leads us."

"Let me see."

She went back to the three drawers and started focusing on their inside, looking for any possible trigger. Her reasoning was that there would be papers and all sorts of things inside which would allow the trigger to be less concealed and yet still difficult to find. We went through all three drawers and unfortunately came back empty-handed. Suddenly, I could see my dear wife initially frown and then light up almost like a Christmas tree:

"Mike, how about the outside of these drawers?"

"Wait, you've lost me again. How would that connect to a mechanism that has to be inside the desk."

With her irresistible smile, she proclaimed:

"Let me show you . . ."

She first picked up the middle drawer, and finding nothing, she followed suit with the left drawer, with the same results. Undeterred, she picked up the right drawer. Within a few seconds, she exclaimed:

"Hello!"

She was pointing to a small cavity on the inside left ledge near the bottom of the right drawer. It was right near the vertical side of the drawer, about six inches from the front. She pressed on a button she felt in it and a section of the outside right ledge of the drawer, near the back of the drawer extended out a centimeter or so. As I could hardly believe my eyes, she matter-of-factly explained:

"When the drawer is partially opened, you press on the button. The side of the ledge extends. The drawer has to be drawn open just the right amount so that the piece that jots out presses against the side of the slot in which the drawer is located. I bet you there's something there, inside the slot for the right drawer, which can be squeezed ever so slightly and that this opens the back of the middle drawer."

"Can't believe it. Still, let's see. If you're right, there is a spot on the inside left wall of the drawer slot. We must have missed it."

"Failed to find it is a better word. I was not looking for what might be a piece of wood that moved. I was looking for a button. Let me see."

She used the flashlight to look into the slot where the right drawer would slide. She noticed that the inside wall of that slot was made of a series of one-inch-long pieces of darker wood, each piece seemingly slightly detached from those before and after it. Sure enough, she moved from one to the next until she felt one that seemed like it could move. Yet, it did not. I could see her disappointed face, looking as if she was missing something big. Suddenly, it was my turn to have an epiphany. I asked:

"Look at the bottom of the slot for the drawer. Near the side where you were looking. See anything?"

"See nothing, but . . ."

And her voice went up probably ten decibels:

"There is a small ramp that protrudes. Let me depress it and try again pressing on the one piece of wood that seemed willing to move a bit."

For some reason, I can only blame on intuition or excessive drama I said,

"Don't. What if the woodworker not only created a hidden cavity but also added something to protect it?"

"What do you mean?"

"Well, what if there was a blade ready to pop out if you maneuvered in the wrong way?"

"A blade?"

"Yep, a blade which would probably spring out of the back of the desk and hit you in the hand, or worse."

Annabelle clearly had not anticipated this development, which, quite frankly, I had not considered either in any of our earlier searches. So, we both agreed that unless the woodworker was truly cynical or even evil, the blade or whatever contraption he had built into the mechanism would protrude in a way perpendicular to the back of the desk. So, we both decided to proceed with caution, both of us standing where we could not be hit. I was ready to press the button when Annabelle jumped up:

"And what if there is something which is designed to hit whoever is sitting at the desk?"

We decided to move to a position where we felt the risk of being hit was negligible. I pressed on the ramp. Before either of us could say anything, I heard the mild "pop" we had been waiting for. We were still not done with our surprises. The pop was not caused by the back of the middle drawer opening, but by the back cover of the right drawer. It had moved just a smidge, but enough for Annabelle to slide a nail into the opening, noting that she could use a nail file or a small screwdriver to achieve the same result. Standing to the side of the desk, to avoid any possible internal defense mechanism, she pulled the piece of wood without any effort noticing, as she had expected, that it rotated around an axis located to its far right and did not separate from the desk. Behind it, she found a small cavity in which a button was visible. She pressed on it while holding on to the back piece of the middle drawer which, as predicted, popped out and was tethered to the desk by a short leather ribbon. Behind the opening, there was a metallic box, which we removed from its resting place. We opened it and we both were able to see that a few folders were inside. I joked:

"Have we found the holy grail?"

Annabelle laughed and simply said:

"The woodworker was quite smart. To find the secret compartment, you had to go through a series of steps which were very logical and in fact simple for the owner of the desk who presumably knew what he or she had to do. But it was quite difficult as we saw to detect if you did not know even if you were looking for it."

She paused for a second to take her breath and continued:

"The trick was on the right side of the chair on which the owner would be. You had to pull the right drawer just ten inches. Then you looked for a small cavity on the outside bottom of the drawer, about six inches from the front. Now, if the drawer is pulled too little or too much the small, wooded ramp inside the slot would remain up and the mechanism could not operate. You would have to be in the right spot for the ramp to be down and your finger pressing on the right spot. Our inspection originally did not work: first, because we were looking in the wrong place, second, we were doing it with the drawer outside of its slot and then, even with the drawer in its slot, it had to be placed in exactly the right spot."

And I had to add:

"And no defense mechanism! Hats off to the craftsman!"

Chapter Fourteen

2001, 1948
NAPLES, FLORIDA. VERSOIX, SWITZERLAND

Though we only perused them, we could not help noticing that the two folders we extracted from their hiding place at the back of the middle drawer of the desk were intensely personal. Stephane must have decided that the desk was where he would hide everything that was most important, though Annabelle cynically asked a perfectly valid rhetorical question:

"Who knew how to get to them since they were in a hidden drawer?"

While I surely did not know for sure, I punted:

"I bet you the people who were supposed to be in the know must have received some copy of it."

"Unfortunately, it seems that Jack didn't know or at least didn't remember . . ."

It contained official documents such as his latest will, specific dispositions that applied to Jack because the documents clearly demonstrated that the father knew very well at least a few of the issues which his son was facing. I added:

"I bet you that his lawyer and banker have a copy of most of these."

"You're probably right."

In fairness, even as recently as the mid -'60s, autism was not frequently diagnosed. Hard answers were very hard to come by, and the notion, which is mainstream today, that there may be five different forms of autism would have flabbergasted everyone. Having generally found it impossible to determine with any sort of confidence what might cause autism led the medical community to shift its stance toward blaming anyone or anything that could be connected to it. Often, it was described as a form of childhood schizophrenia and the result of "cold parenting" the latter of which many observers today would agree was very much the "normal approach then." This is best illustrated by noting that among the many names which clinicians used in the 1950s and '60s one can find "dementia infantilis (or childhood dementia)." That said it all: it was not a disease; it was a condition. Had Stephane lived only five to ten years more, he would have found studies which first suggested that autism was rooted in brain development, the conclusion which was further specified in the 1980s when autism was described as a "pervasive developmental disorder" separate and distinct from schizophrenia.

If Stephane had been looking at the issue today, he might in fact have concluded that his son suffered from a form of Asperger disease, which is often described as comprising up to ten traits, which surely seemed to fit with Jack's behavior, particularly after the accident that took the lives of his parents and his sister: *underdeveloped social skills, difficulties with non-verbal behavior, trouble with expressing emotions, lack of coordination, fixation on rituals and routines, limited range of interests, erratic behavior, self-absorption, unusual communication styles and extraordinary cognitive and creative ability.* Of the list, only one, lack of coordination, ostensibly did not affect someone who became an exceptional piano virtuoso. At the same time, as Annabelle and I were reading the documents and reflecting on them, we kept thinking that a few of the traits listed above could really apply to someone who very early discerned a vocation, here a musician, which may or may not have been accepted by his family. Add to this the trauma which the accident caused, and it may very well be that Jack was considerably closer to "normal" than many imagined. I could not resist adding:

"You know, honey, we've seen many people like him: super creative artists or even the proverbial absent-minded genius."

Annabelle nodded and simply replied:

"The provisions which Stephane put in place effectively removed from Jack the need to be concerned with any of the everyday stuff; that could very well have played right into it."

"You said it."

The second folder reserved a major surprise for us. It started with a telegram which Stephane had received on July 12th, 1948: it was from Jules and told him that Edith had been found dead in her bed that morning. Though it might surprise several younger readers, older contemporaries might not be surprised by the fact that the news was shared through a telegram; I surely remembered telegrams received from France for our wedding among others. That was the main, cheapest, and simplest means of long-distance communication at the time. Jules would probably not have had Stephane's phone number or might not have dared call if he had it. By contrast, telegrams were the simple solution, and by far the least expensive.

For obvious reasons, we both decided to dive into this folder immediately and to return to the personal documents afterwards. We found a couple of copies of a short obituary in French, one published in *Le Journal de Geneve* and the other in *Le Figaro,* the French newspaper with the most popular section announcing births, engagements, marriages, deaths, and similar notable events. The announcement said that the funeral was private, as it was published after the funeral had been conducted. We assumed that this simply reflected the fact that despite Jewish customs that dictate that a funeral should take place as soon as possible after death, Edith's funeral probably had to wait until Stephane and Simone could arrive and most likely organize it.

Coincidentally, Swissair had started to offer a transatlantic service to New York in 1947. It was a long flight, which did not originate in Zurich proper, but in an airport close by, in a Zurich suburb, Dübendorf. Swissair moved their formal base to Zurich from Dübendorf in June 1948. Stephane would still have to take a train from Zurich to Geneva.

A trip from Chicago to Zurich would take around twenty-four hours. Stephane chose Swissair because it was the only practical solution for him to land in Switzerland, as domestic U.S. airlines such as Pan Am privileged London for their initial transatlantic destinations early on, though it was not allowed to carry passengers between U.S. cities. Four domestic airlines, American, Eastern, TWA and United fought one another for that business. He would most likely have flown from Chicago to New York LaGuardia on a domestic airline and then jumped on a Swissair four-propeller Douglas DC-4. It would have needed at least two refueling stops, the first either in Stephenville on the west coast of Newfoundland or Gander on the east coast of the same Canadian province, and the second in Shannon, Ireland, all depending on winds and weather conditions. On the other hand, first class would have offered dinners served on porcelain plates and seats that reclined sufficiently to allow passengers to sleep, not to mention the today unthinkable gift of a pack of cigarettes!

Stephane's diary does not even mention the funeral, other than stating that it was quite private, that Simone was with him, and that Jules, Marie and Rose attended. The dates he mentions suggest that it took place about a week after Edith's death.

An entry which had both Annabelle and me jump up is the one where Stephane mentions that Edith did not die a natural death. Stephane says that he could not inspect the body himself as he arrived too late for that, but it says that the physician who was called by Jules when he said he found the body noted marks around her neck which did not seem normal. Though an autopsy was not ordered, the observation started a whole chain of events which transformed the recording of her death as being due to natural causes to something which triggered a murder investigation. The official cause of death was recorded as a combination of asphyxiation and strangulation. Stephane noted that other than Jules, Marie and Rose, there was no one else in the house at that time.

Stephane called the circumstance surrounding her death quite suspicious. He observed that Switzerland in general and the Geneva region were not crime prone. Occasionally, there might be a burglary here or there as there were many wealthy people living in the various neighborhoods. However, murders were exceedingly rare. And therefore, the likelihood of someone casually walking into the house and murdering Edith did not seem terribly probable. The front door to the house was always locked and all French doors on the first floor would have been locked as well, most with their shutters closed. There was no apparent break-in. There was always the possibility of someone entering through the service entrance. However, that door stood no more than twenty feet or so from the door to the cottage where Jules and Marie were living and was usually locked from the outside (though there was a way to unlock it from the inside in case of an emergency). Additionally, the ground in that area was covered with loose gravel, which was somewhat noisy when one walked on it. Finally, Edith had agreed to Jules's request to buy a dog which would be patrolling the property day and night; the fact that the doghouse was outside, in between the service cottage and the service entrance to the main house, in front of the woodshed, meant that any stranger that would have walked onto the property and attempted to enter into the main house would have been bound to wake the dog up and the dog would most likely have barked the deep loud bark of German shepherds.

Stephane seemingly could not shake a serious concern: it was hard to accept the theory of a random intrusion into the house. Then one had to accept that one of the three people who were on the property with Edith at the time of the murder had to be the prime suspects. He already had uncomfortable feelings with respect to Rose, whom he had suspected might have had something to do with the raid into the Paris apartment which took Jean and Albert away. He had accepted Edith's conclusion that with no proof she had no reason to keep her away now that the war was over. She liked Rose, considered her a friend, and had been so happy to be able to see her again after the end of the war. That was the reason that led her to invite her to visit for a week, just as she had done a couple of instances earlier since the end of the war. There was no proof with respect to the raid in the Paris apartment, and there was no more proof this time. Yet the suspicion remained; what was clearly missing was a motive. Stephane made a note to himself to have a private detective dig into Rose's past to see if there may have been any reason for her to want Edith dead.

As for Jules and Marie, the initial disbelief that they could have anything to do with the murder was even stronger. Edith could not stop saying good things about them. They had been in her employ for many years. And they had both played a crucial and supportive role in their flight from France to Switzerland. She had fallen over herself to sing their praises when she was in the U.S., and she had even shared with Stephane her intention either to give them the house once she left for the U.S. or at least to let them use it cost free for their lifetime, going as far as to provide them with an annuity to help them support themselves and maintain the house. Could she have gotten it that far wrong? Why would either one of them have done it? Yet, Stephane also made a note that he would ask whichever private detective he would hire to dig into their past as well. Did either of them have anything to hide? "Could anything in their past provide a motive?" This last entry into his diary included the mention that he would have to find a detective while he was in Geneva.

Neither Annabelle nor I could argue with a straight face that the resolution of this murder mystery was germane to our investigation into the assets of Jack and by implication as to what should eventually happen to whatever we thought we bought at the consignment shop. Yet, curiosity surely started to generate interest, and we wondered whether Stephane's notes would help us identify "who did it?"

The diary seems to indicate that Stephane could not stay in Geneva longer than a week, largely because of his professional obligations at home. However, the short week he was able to spend allowed him to get all the various processes started, including the work and coordination with the Swiss police and the estate settlement. Additionally, he had the time to begin answering a question which we had had for a while, the consolidation of his and his sister's assets in one place, though there would remain two dimensions, one focused on artworks and the other on financial assets.

As we were looking for more information on Edith's murder in that highly personal folder, we found a carbon copy of a police report, with a small magnetic tape reel, which we eventually found out was a more complete record of the questioning of witnesses. Annabelle could not help noting:

"Well, see, the reel-to-reel tape recorder that you refused to give away may finely be useful."

I could only nod with a wry smile.

The date on the police report suggested that Stephane obtained it and the tape before he returned to the U.S. with Simone, though a complement seemed to have been mailed to him subsequently, along with another, though smaller, magnetic tape reel.

The record put the time of Edith's death at around 3:00 a.m. though her body was not discovered until the early morning when

Marie went up to look for Edith who had not come down to have her breakfast at the usual 7:30 a.m. It said that Marie found her unresponsive though in her words "she looked like she was still asleep." Marie apparently called her from the partially opened door to her room and, receiving no answer, walked into the room. She said to Officer Rudi Marchand who questioned her that she did not fully approach the bed because, from where she was, all she could see was that Edith's eyes were closed. Everything else looked normal; the sheets were up to her neck, she was on her back and both arms seemed to be under the covers, though her left hand was visible outside the sheets on the side of the bed. There was no sign that anything was wrong. So, she assumed that Edith had had a difficult night and wanted to sleep some more. A note from the officer writing the report said that though it was unusual for Edith to sleep in, it was not so unheard of that Marie should not initially have suspected anything.

An hour later, she returned to the room and was surprised to see that Edith was still there, specifically adding "in what seemed to be the same exact position as an hour earlier." That is when, according to Marie, she approached the bed and noted that Edith looked quite pale. She came closer and touched the hand that was visible on the right side of the bed. That is when she said that she shrieked as she noted it was cold and rigid. She said that she ran downstairs to get her husband Jules. On the way, she met Rose in the morning room where breakfast was normally served and told her that Edith was sleeping and cold in her bed.

She then said that she saw Rose run upstairs but did not accompany her as her sole focus at the time was to get Jules. Jules had in fact only recently awakened as he had told her when she got up that he needed more sleep. He had been awake for at least a couple of hours during the night and did not have a pressing need to get up unless Edith asked him to go run a couple of errands. According to Marie, Jules seemed totally taken aback by the news and ran to Edith's bedroom, crossing the few yards between the door to their cottage and the servants' entrance which opened into the kitchen and the pantry room in only a few hops. He testified that he found Rose sobbing in an almost uncontrolled manner in Edith's room.

Stephane's diary seemed to express a measure of disappointment arguing that the three individuals who were in the house all seemed to have some solid alibi, though alibis that cover night periods are considerably less compelling: who can prove that anyone was not in bed as they claimed to be? No one in the case of Rose; and husband or wife in the case of Jules or Marie. More importantly, it seemed that there was no immediate reason why Edith might have been murdered. Yes, she was wealthy; however, who would believe that she did not have appropriate testamentary provisions? Jules and Marie, if it was either of them, would have had plenty of ways to get rid of Edith as they were fleeing Paris, and it would have been very hard for anyone to point to them, if only because they had intentionally not carried any identification papers, other than Jules who needed to be able to show a driver's license. As things were, they had a solid job and an employer who desperately needed them. The obvious next question was inescapable: could it be Rose rather than Jules or Marie? But then again, why? The whole thing made no sense. Plus, the police had not detected any sign of forced entry into the house. Could Jules or Marie have forgotten to lock the back door as they usually did? If not, who opened it and how if the murderer was not in the house? Stephane noted in pencil in the margin that the officer did not ask Marie the question of whether the back door was locked when she entered the main house the morning after the crime.

Chapter Fifteen

2001, 1948
Naples, Florida. Versoix, Switzerland

From our point of view, the only reasonable approach to satisfy our curiosity was to keep focusing on the police report and the magnetic tape reel. The report contained a further description of Edith's bedroom as Officer Marchand found it, with details as to what was not neatly placed in either the laundry basket or their proper place. Edith must have been a very meticulous woman, as the report noted that there was nothing on the floor, other than her slippers. It said that the left slipper was where it should have been had she removed it seated on the bed. On the other hand, the left slipper was a good one foot away, partially hidden under the bed. Officer Marchand remarked that it had to have been inadvertently kicked, first because it could not have been dropped where it was by someone sitting on the bed and second because it was on its side rather than flat on the floor as it should be. We looked at each other and postulated that the murderer must have been the one who pushed it and, maybe a useful piece of evidence, did not place it back where it should be. But then again, could it have happened casually as Rose or Marie in their panic were walking next to the bed? Or when Jules approached the bed to verify that Edith was dead?

The report also stated that each of the three witnesses had been separated as soon as the police officers had arrived at the murder scene. They had been told that they were witnesses and not suspects at that point, yet they needed to be kept in separate locations, each under the guard of a police officer who would stay with them and accompany them wherever they needed to go. We understood that they would be allowed to use the toilets but would be escorted there and back. Rose was allowed to choose first where she would be confined and selected the living room, where she could read or even lie down on a sofa if she felt too tired. Marie chose the morning room which was adjoining the kitchen/pantry area, where she could also benefit from seating accommodations. Jules was asked to remain in his home and thus not to enter the main house; Marie fixed a couple of sandwiches for him to take in case he was hungry.

The next section of the report turned to the interrogation of the three people who were in the house, both probably when the murder was committed and at the time Officer Marchand arrived.

The first witness the police interrogated was Rose Prestat, Edith's friend. The initial comment caught our attention, as Officer Marchand reported that she was visibly distraught. Even more, it said that she had to be given time to compose herself on more than a couple of occasions, as she found it difficult to keep up with the questioning without breaking down. Interestingly, her first comment as reported by Officer Marchand was that she was retrospectively scared. Indeed, she had mentioned that she could just as easily have been the victim if the murder was random. Her bedroom was indeed only two doors down from where Edith slept. Apparently, she broke down again then, bemoaning the fact that the war, the arrest of Jean and Albert, and Edith's ensuing flight had led to the two of them not being able to see each other for most of the war, and that, now that the war was over, and that she had been able to reconnect with her best friend, Edith was murdered.

Initially, according to the report, Rose said that she did not recall anything. She kept repeating that she was asleep, that she heard nothing and thus could not have seen anything. Officer Marchand told her he fully understood, but pushed a bit further, asking her, for instance, if she ever woke up during the night. She replied that she almost always did, if only to go to the toilet, but also after she had been having a bad dream. Officer Marchand naturally followed up asking whether she had gotten up during that night. She conceded that she had. Asked around what time she had gotten up, she said she did not notice, though she mentioned that she heard the church bell ring twice, meaning that it had to have been around the half hour, but she could not tell which hour because she was asleep when the bells rang again. Upon further gentle questioning, she added that it probably was earlier rather than later, as she usually woke up only a few hours after going to bed. Officer Marchand accepted her point and asked if she had awakened another time during the night. She was not sure, though Officer Marchand's gentle questioning seemed to be achieving its purpose: she was opening up. The story does not tell whether she was aware and in full control of what she was saying and not saying the whole time or had simply let something slip inadvertently.

Yet, the report noted that she said she was jolted out of her sleep when she heard a staircase creak a couple of times. Asked for a bit more precision, she simply said that it sounded like older wood often can when weight is applied to it. Officer Marchand asked whether the sound was likely to have come from a staircase or from the corridor. She replied that she felt the sound was distant, adding that it did not seem as if it came from right in front of her bedroom door. Officer Marchand noted that her room was closer to the service staircase, which led to an antechamber near the kitchen, than to the main staircase. Rose did not seem to object to the point, nor even to know why the comment was relevant.

Officer Marchand then asked her whether she remembered the material of which the steps of the main staircase were made. Her initial response did not help as the only thing she remembered clearly was that there was a rug running down the center of each step with a copper rod keeping it in place all the way to the foyer downstairs. Officer Marchand asked if she remembered the material that made up the floor covering of the foyer. There she immediately stated that downstairs was all tiled up, though a good portion was partially hidden owing to the few oriental rugs that were there. Officer Marchand mentioned that the tiles were in fact made of limestone. The report noted that at that moment she exclaimed:

"Then the stairs must be made of the same material."

Officer Marchand asked whether she had ever used the back stairs. She replied that she had and jokingly added that those stairs were all in wood, including the banister, if that was to be Officer Marchand's next question. He simply concluded:

"One more reason to assume that any creaking you might have heard came from the service staircase, not the main one."

The report said that she nodded and seemed comfortable with the conclusion offered to her. Officer Marchand then asked what the floor covering was in the corridor between the various bedrooms upstairs. Whether her memory had suddenly come back, or she simply assumed the answer given the exchange on the staircase that preceded the question, she immediately replied that upstairs there was only wood flooring, with a coarse tribal oriental runner neatly arranged in the middle. Officer Marchand calmly asked:

"Could the creaking have come from the corridor rather than the stairs?"

She replied that everything is possible, but she had gotten used to hearing the wood floor creak whenever anyone upstairs would use the sole restroom, which, as was the norm in Switzerland then, and still is today, was separate from the bathroom. She added that Edith and she were the only ones who would be walking there. She came back to her earlier affirmation saying that the creaking she heard seemed a bit more distant. Officer Marchand followed up on the last question by asking whether she had thought of doing anything, like getting up and looking for what might be causing the sound. The report noted that she smiled and said that everyone hears many things at night, particularly when half asleep. She then clarified her reply saying that she did not even consider doing anything after the first sound, though she did, briefly, after the second, Officer Marchand asked:

"How long between the two sounds?"

She looked confused. Officer Marchand helped her saying that she had mentioned that she had heard a couple of creaks. She said that she really did not know. She did not have an alarm clock and did not look at her watch, which would have required her to turn on the light. When pushed, she volunteered that there might have been ten to fifteen minutes but cautioned Officer Marchand that she was not even sure whether she had gone back to sleep between the two. He asked whether she had heard the church bell ring at that time. She replied that she did not. Officer Marchand suggested that it had to mean either that the two creaks were within fifteen minutes of each other or that she had fallen asleep in between the two. She initially did not seem to follow. Officer Marchand helped her again reminding her of her comment on the church bell which sounded every fifteen minutes and on the hour. She conceded the point and added that the two creaks had to be less than fifteen minutes from each other as she must have been asleep before the first and soon after the second. Officer Marchand did not disagree though he also added that the murderer would not have needed more than fifteen minutes to come, kill and leave, unless anything was stolen, and he had to look for it. The report states that she nodded but offered no comment on whether there had been a theft as well.

Officer Marchand's next line of questioning seemed to veer in a different direction: Rose's perceptions and actions vis-à-vis her relationship with Edith at the time of the murder. The report notes that Rose started to sob uncontrollably bemoaning the fact that she and Edith had only recently reconnected, and she was losing her again, a point which Officer Marchand noted she had already made earlier. Officer Marchand expanded his questioning in this direction. Rose said that she and Edith had been close friends ever since she and her husband had moved to the apartment on Avenue Paul Doumer in Paris, adding that she and her own husband lived quite close by. She confirmed that she and Edith had not known each other before yet noted that the two couples did not socialize as couples; it was just a relationship that existed between the wives. Asked why by Officer Marchand, she said she did not know, though she assumed that Edith's husband who was a well-to-do businessman may have preferred his own friends, as often happened in Paris then. She added that while Edith lived in an apartment from which she could see the park of the Trocadero, she, Rose, and her husband lived in a side street overlooking the Passy cemetery: she probably meant to convey the notion that they may not have felt they belonged to the same circles.

She did not seem to remember the exact circumstances of their meeting, though she self-suggested that she had a daughter that was about the same age as Albert. She said that she probably met Edith as she was walking to the local playground with her son while she was with her daughter. Officer Marchand asked:

"Are you married?"

"I was, but my husband died in the late thirties."

She paused and added:

"Edith was very kind to me when he died. Our two children were quite young, and she helped me cope emotionally, and a couple of times, early on even financially. It took forever to settle my late husband's affairs and in the interim I was worried about digging too deeply into our savings. In fact, you won't believe that, but I later found out that there was one savings account which I did not know existed. My husband used to give me a set amount of money each month to run the household and I would put in my savings account anything that I could squirrel away. That was nice, but not a huge amount."

Officer Marchand then asked whether she was interested in art. Rose replied that she was not as conversant as her friend Edith, though she did appreciate nice things. She said that Edith lived for the art which she received from her father. She asked:

"Do you know that she has an artist folder full of drawings and etchings? I had seen it in Paris and noticed when I came here the first time that she had invited me here, to the house in Versoix?"

Officer Marchand said that he certainly did not know. She added:

"She loved to put the big artist folder on the dining room table, untie the three black ribbons in the middle of each of the three sides that were not attached to each other via the folder's black spine and look at these drawings."

Casually, Officer Marchand asked:

"Why did she not have them framed and hung on the walls?"

Rose chuckled and simply replied:

"Do you see room for that here?"

Officer Marchand silently conceded the point and asked whether there was any reason she ever got mad at Edith. Rose seemed to pause for a short while and initially said that she could not recall any. Then she responded to further prodding that the one thing on which they frequently disagreed was their religious habits. She added:

"I am not Jewish, and I knew Edith was. But that was never an issue for me. What I did not understand was that one could profess a religion and not attend religious services. I surely would hardly ever miss Sunday Mass, while Edith only seemed to go to the synagogue on certain feast days."

"And you fought about that?"

"Fought. No, never. That's too big a word. We had arguments which always concluded with one or the other of us saying something like "to each her own" and that was it."

"How did you react to being sidelined by Edith?"

Rose conceded that it had made her quite sad and a bit disappointed. Her greatest sadness, she said, came from the realization that one of the reasons Edith did not want to talk to her or even see her during the war might be that she would suspect her of having denounced her. She said that she would never have done anything like that and started sobbing anew. She said she had never had a sister and viewed Edith almost like one. But she also said that she understood that the irruption of the police into their apartment must have shaken Edith. She added:

"I've never had to run for my life. I was sad and mad, but I gradually understood. In fact, I had forgiven her when I received the phone call from her brother telling me they were safe. I asked him where they were and, as best I can remember, he simply said that she would no longer be safe if anyone in France knew where she was."

She paused and added:

"I pushed a bit, but he was adamant. He added that she would surely call her after the war if she lived to see it end. I was hoping that we could put all that behind us when the war was over. And see, my prayers were answered."

Sobbing again, she concluded:

"And now, when will I see her again? Catholicism is not clear as to whether Jews can get into Paradise."

Annabelle noted that what Rose had just said according to the report was unfortunately true for most Catholics at the time. She could only add:

"How sad. I feel really bad for Rose. Having read this report, I cannot believe she did it."

"Neither can I, but criminals have a way of setting themselves in the best possible light, honey."

The taped interrogation record continued and veered in a direction which initially surprised Annabelle. Officer Marchand started to question Rose about her health. It said that she was taken aback and even asked, in her own words:

"What does this have to do with anything?"

The policeman assured her that he had reasons to ask and invited her to trust him. She volunteered that she considered herself to be in excellent health, at least for someone in her late forties and having been through menopause. He seemed to have asked if she ever had difficulties walking and she said she surely did not, though she noted that now and then she had a mild pain in her upper left thigh, stating that her doctor blamed it on a form of mild, early sciatica. The officer asked if she took any medication for the condition, and her reply was as simple as it was predictable:

"Not in normal circumstances, though my doctor told me to take two aspirin tablets when I needed to."

Though the report did not note this detail, historians of medicine have traced the birth of aspirin and argued that its history really goes back more than thirty-five centuries. Willow bark was then used as a painkiller and antipyretic. It thus did not all start with Bayer in 1863 in Germany!

Rose opened a bit further mentioning that she had some onset of arthritis in both of her hands. Although she said that it did not prevent her from playing the piano as she had for many years, she jokingly added that she would certainly no longer consider giving a concert. Officer Marchand asked whether she had given concerts in the past, and she answered that she had indeed; however, she mostly played as an accompanist for the church choir, using both a piano and a pipe organ. Officer Marchand continued along that line of questioning asking whether she needed medication to control the arthritic condition. Rose simply replied that her doctor's advice was to follow the same approach to the treatment of arthritis as for her sciatica: use aspirin, though she added that she had a prescription for a stronger concentration of aspirin with some other ingredient if the pain was to be too serious.

Annabelle was just as surprised as I was when reading the next section of the police report and listening to the corresponding part of the tape. Officer Marchand indeed asked Rose to grip his forearm with one and then both hands and squeeze. Rose did not see the point and initially refused. Officer Marchand explained that this was a simple exercise to test her strength. She asked why and he simply replied that he needed to see how serious her arthritis was impairing her normal functioning. She eventually agreed, offering that she still practiced the piano and could do her scales without effort. Officer Marchand concurred saying that probably owing to years of working her forearm muscles practicing the piano, she seemed still to have a great deal of strength. He stated that he did not say anything more though his report mentioned that Rose seemed to have sufficient strength to have strangled Edith.

Chapter Sixteen

2001, 1948
NAPLES, FLORIDA. VERSOIX, SWITZERLAND

Meanwhile, as the Swiss police were conducting their murder inquiry, Stephane, while in Versoix for the funeral, was also organizing meetings with his sister's estate attorney, whom she shared with him for all issues regarding Stephane's Swiss assets, and with their common banker at Pictet.

Stephane knew from what Edith had told him that given the death of her husband and only child, she was bequeathing everything she had to him. According to her attorney, there would be no Federal tax in Switzerland, and quite likely no canton tax either. Stephane also noted that the same attorney believed that estate taxes in the U.S. were charged to the estate and not to beneficiaries; thus, with the estate residing in Switzerland, he believed that Stephane would not have to worry about U.S. taxes either. Stephane's diary, however, noted that, even if he did not have to pay taxes, the fact that everything was left to him, lock, stock, and barrel, meant that the risk was serious that his heirs, children or grandchildren, would owe taxes when the time came.

Stephane's diary contained unusually long notes following his meeting with the Swiss attorney, Erik Sutter. He explained that there were two different pockets in Edith's estate. There were financial assets, as well as real assets, such as the house in Versoix, its furnishings and, more importantly, her art collection which, as he added:

"From what I understand it mostly came from her parents, your parents I mean. Though I have seen certain pieces added since your parents died, they were always purchased in her name, with her own funds. I do not believe that her husband ever purchased a significant piece of art, which is not surprising given the collection he knew existed."

When it came to the financial assets, there were those which were in her name, those which she should inherit from her husband, who as a successful businessman had accumulated significant savings, and the proceeds from the life insurance contracts that existed on both the life of her husband and that of her son. However, he immediately added:

"You should not expect any of this life insurance matter to be settled quickly. It may take years. There have been several lawsuits filed by several relatives of people killed in German death camps; your sister's family was not unique. Many families like hers had life insurance; predictably I guess, insurers are trying to seek government help, claiming that risks such as those we just saw occur were not covered. Just be aware that the insurance contracts were drawn up so that the beneficiary of the life insurance was not a named physical person, but a nominee company based in the Dutch Virgin Islands, Aruba to be more specific."

Stephane's notes mentioned that the company was owned by Edith, her husband, her son, and himself, with a provision that the shares of any one individual accrued equally to the others if that individual died. He wrote that he told Erik Sutter he understood the issue and was in no hurry to receive the funds. However, as a named beneficiary if Edith's whole family died, Stephane gave the attorney the power to manage the process within his own family if he, Stephane, should no longer be alive. The notes also said that the attorney went on to discuss the joint accounts which Stephane had with his sister, for the financial assets and artworks which they inherited from their mother, arguing that they were set up on a similar model, of an Aruba company with only Edith and him as shareholders.

Anabelle and I felt that Stephane's instructions on the resolution of the estate and the fate of the joint accounts were quite clear, though there was one element which he did not discuss. On the one hand, there were precise instructions for the attorney to consolidate all assets, financial or otherwise, under his name, with his wife and children as secondary beneficiaries, as and when they became available. On the other hand, contrasted with the relative clarity of the disposition of the assets once upon Stephane's death, the one element which remained totally unclear at that point was whether any of these assets were ever brought to the U.S.

Annabelle jumped on the issue:

"The will that we have here does say that whatever is left at the death of the last grandchild should be placed in a foundation, and if appropriate shared with the public."

"I saw that. The question in my mind is whether that provision of a U.S. will was shared with the Swiss attorney . . ."

"We'll have to find out. But I think that we won't get to that until we have had conversations with Jack's U.S. attorney and his banker. In the end, we can't forget that we are not police or IRS investigators."

Returning to Stephane's notes, we saw that the attorney added that, at that point in time, all the assets were physically in Switzerland, though the nominee companies through which they were held usually were in Aruba or Curaçao. It seemed indeed that the family had used nominee companies as a shield to add to traditional Swiss banking secrecy: bankers were not allowed to disclose the name of the owners of any asset, but, even if, somehow, the names of account holders leaked, they would be those of nominee companies, usually somewhere in the Caribbean, where banking secrecy also prevented beneficiaries to be disclosed.

In Stephane's notes, there follows a long description of the various assets, with the names of the companies which held them, which do not need to be discussed here. Suffice it to mention as an anecdote that all the company names were in one way or another related to the world of painting, as they were all based on a color associated with the name of a gemstone, Ruby Red, Emerald Green, Golden Topaz, Blue Sapphire, Amethyst Purple, and several others.

One thing Stephane was happy to note is that, in the end, Edith had followed his advice. She had decided to allow Jules and Marie to use the house in Versoix until they died or were otherwise obliged to leave it; however, it would eventually also pass onto Stephane or his heirs. She had simultaneously purchased a second-to-die annuity for the benefit of Jules and Marie, to provide them with the funds needed to maintain it and to live on; it was supposed to start paying them upon Edith's death. Interestingly, it was to be administered by her attorney, not her banker.

Given that we knew that everything which might have come to Stephane would have also gone to Jack upon the passing of Stephane, Simone, and Caroline, knowing what had happened to Swiss assets was crucial. That would have included all the assets we just saw listed, unless they had been sold in the interim, in which case the question would still be whether the proceeds from the sale were sent to the U.S. or kept in the current structure, that is in offshore accounts. Annabelle and I thus realized that there was a very important next conversation: we had to contact Stephane's U.S. attorney and his banker, who had taken on the responsibility of serving personally and through their successors the needs of Jack. This would not be difficult since we had a copy of his will, with the attorney's firm's name on it; though we had not yet found anything that told us who the banker was, we were pretty sure that the attorney, Richard McCormick, would know. The crucial question had to be: what happened to these assets between the time Stephane inherited them and the time he died? In fact, we were wondering whether Stephane had disclosed these foreign assets to anyone in the U.S.; he ought to have disclosed to the U.S. government any foreign income, as U.S. citizens and residents are taxed on their worldwide income. One could, however, argue that he may have managed to escape that provision of the tax code if the assets were owned in nominee names, i.e., by foreign companies, and if these foreign companies did not pay any dividend.

Secondarily, we needed to ascertain from Stephane's own estate attorney that the copy of the will we found in the secret compartment of the Transition desk (which we used to call Louis XVI) was truly the one that governed the execution of his estate.

Yet, in the back of my own mind, there was something which did not make sense: how could Richard McCormick have allowed the assisted living administration to consign and sell Jack's belongings, if they were known to be a part of a much bigger whole? The only thing I could think of was that, somehow, the European assets never came onshore in the U.S. and that Stephane's attorney was left in the dark with respect to the value of the art collection. When I broached the topic with Annabelle, we came up with a possible answer, which, we feared, would make our job considerably harder: what if Stephane had kept his U.S. attorney totally out of the foreign asset loop? In that case, the attorney might have started to work on creating the foundation which the will that we saw said should be put in place but thinking that the artworks in Jack's possession were not worth much and, as such, he would have had no issue selling them.

It was at that point that we started to ask ourselves whether we were correct in carrying out the investigation we were conducting. On the one hand, from an official standpoint, things had seemingly unfolded in a perfectly reasonable manner: the attorney should be working on a foundation with minimal funds other than the extant financial assets, Jack's piano had already been gifted in a "philanthropic manner" and worthless artworks had been sold to us as it turned out. On the other, even if the attorney had no knowledge of "the Swiss connection," didn't we have a moral obligation to reveal it? This would ostensibly not be for our own benefit, but it would fulfill Stephane's broader desire to have a U.S. foundation display the art accumulated by his family over time. Annabelle came up with the clincher:

"Why would Stephane have noted everything he noted about Switzerland if he never intended for it to be revealed?"

She added:

"I'm not here to judge whether the family followed the rules the way they should have. That will be for the family's attorney to judge and act upon."

With a wink, she continued:

"Given what we know, we must guess that one of the things we need to discuss with Stephane's attorney is what he wants to do about that. Are we talking of creating a Schneider Collection Museum?"

"I don't know if you're thinking what I'm thinking, but this looks a bit like the origins of the Dali Museum in St Peterburg, up the coast of the Gulf of Mexico. From what I remember, Mr. and Mrs. Morse collected over 2,400 works by Dali, with whom they had struck up a friendship. They used to display their collection in their home . . ."

"Not the whole thing, I assume."

"Probably not, but eventually, at least thirty or forty years before they died, they decided to donate their entire collection to the town, provided it would build at its expense a suitable home for it. So, the big difference with the Schneiders would be that their museum would be established after they had died. The Dali Museum opened in 1982 and has been a magnet for lovers of Dali's works ever since. I think people say it is the largest collection of works by Dali anywhere. I don't know whether they also did or did not give an endowment, as I know the museum has acquired additional works since it opened."

"I think it might be a wonderful idea. But it can't be our doing. In the end, the only thing we own, and even there I am having second thoughts, are the pieces we bought at the consignment shop."

I could not agree more with Annabelle, though somewhere deep down I still thought that we had bought what we did fair and square. So, from a pure legal standpoint, I did not see how anyone could argue that any of the stuff currently in our possession could not be ours. Yet, I could see how from a moral standpoint, having "gotten to know the family vicariously through letters, diaries, and the like," we could fail to sense our responsibility to them. Annabelle added:

"We really need to be careful. The more I hear us talk about the issue, the more I am concerned that we may be creating liabilities for ourselves. Wouldn't it be an ironic turn of events if our luck with the treasures we purchased was to come back and bite us in the tail? I don't want to be selfish, but at some point, we are going to find ourselves way over our heads."

"The funny bit is that I remember the early comments of Jeff Baker from Sotheby's. He saw the legal angle, principally because of the risk that we had bought stolen goods. The goods may not have been stolen, but there is a story behind them and it's bigger than us."

Chapter Seventeen

2001, 1948
NAPLES, FLORIDA. VERSOIX, SWITZERLAND

The next police record which Annabelle reviewed concerned Marie. The officer doing the questioning was apparently the same person, Officer Rudi Marchand that conducted the interview with Rose. Annabelle noted right off the bat that the way the questions were phrased as per the written report and even the tape was a bit harsher with Marie than they had been with Rose, or, at least, that the tone of voice on the tape appeared harsher. She asked me:

"Was that a case of class consciousness? Was he assuming that Rose was in the same social class as Edith while Marie was a part of the servant class?"

"Don't know. Who knows how things played out in those days?"

Then, rather than letting the matter drop and die the death it deserved, I asked a dumb question:

"Could it be a religious bit as well?"

Annabelle did not bat an eyelid:

"Well, dear, it's my turn to say that I don't really know. However, I remember reading a couple of examples which would suggest that there were probably at least as many anti-Semitic Swiss citizens in percentage of the population as in France. The first has to do with the refusal by the Swiss to accept refugees, often Jews, during WWII. The second is the case of Swiss banks initially refusing to pay back deposits placed by Jews, until they were forced to relent."

"Well, whatever the cause, we can see that Officer Marchand is tougher on Marie."

Returning to the important matter of the report, we could immediately see that Marie was initially not very helpful. At first, she had said was ready and willing to answer any question. However, almost whatever the question regarding the murder, she always seemed to answer the same thing: "I was asleep and did not hear anything." The report mentioned that Officer Marchand tried to ask several related questions and that he could not get Marie to deviate from her line of defense. Officer Marchand then asked whether she had had conversations about the murder with her husband. Marie apparently seemed to laugh a bit saying that it would be easier for her to answer that they had not discussed much of anything else. He asked what they discussed the most. She replied that they kept talking about Mrs. Edith, as they called her, remembering what a nice person she was, and reliving a few of the most uncomfortable episodes of their flight from Paris to Versoix. Officer Marchand asked:

"Did you talk of what you remembered from the night?"

"We sure did. But you know it really was not much; I was asleep before, during and after what we're told was the time of the murder. And I could only remember going upstairs twice, the first time to see if Mrs. Edith was OK and letting her sleep a bit more and the second time . . ."

She broke down sobbing. Officer Marchand gave her some time to recompose herself and she continued:

". . . The second time to find her dead."

"Did your husband remember anything that he might have told you?'

"No. He simply said that he had to give me a sleeping pill the prior evening because I seemed to have trouble falling asleep."

"Did he talk of him having heard anything?"

"Actually, he said he had slept very well and had not even been awakened by the dog once."

Officer Marchand then asked how come nobody seemed to have heard the dog, adding:

"If Mrs. Edith was murdered by someone from outside the house, the intruder would have had to come through the property. This should have awakened the dog, shouldn't it?"

Marie looked at a loss for a short while. Officer Marchand went further:

"Plus, since the front door and all the French doors were locked downstairs, the intruder would have had to come through the door that is almost right under your bedroom's window. The dog should have been barking right there. Don't you agree?"

Marie answered that she was by then completely confused. She returned to her earlier stock response, saying that she was asleep and had heard nothing. Though he did not state it as such, it appeared that Officer Marchand decided to shift his focus to try and pry information out of the witness, probably realizing that direct questioning about the murder would not elicit any useful insight.

He first asked whether she ever got up in the middle of the night. Her initial answer was a simple "no," though she then conceded that she would occasionally wake up and take the opportunity to go to the toilet. She also volunteered that her husband would occasionally get up as well, adding:

"In fact, he gets up virtually at least once each night."

But she said that she had gotten so used to him getting up that it hardly ever would wake her up, and if it did, she would fall straight back to sleep, often not remembering the following morning whether he had or had not gotten up. Officer Marchand seemed interested in the answer and asked her why her husband would get up. She replied that there could be many reasons, but the most relevant were that either he had been awakened by a dog barking or had drunk a bit too much beer the prior evening and needed to eliminate it. Officer Marchand asked:

"Did you hear a dog bark?"

She said she did not. She added that she hardly ever was awakened by dogs because she had gotten used to it. Officer Marchand asked how that could be. She replied that the property shared an access road with two others, with the road eventually leading to the main road, the Route de Suisse. There were plenty of opportunities to hear a dog in one of the other properties, in addition to their own dog. Officer Marchand led that answer slide by and then asked whether the neighborhood was generally noisy. She surprised him by saying that it really was not. She said that the house was sufficiently far from Route de Suisse that there was very little traffic noise. Annabelle noticing that I was right behind her noted that traffic in those days had to be minimal anyway, to which I replied that she was probably correct, though I assumed, without being able to prove it, that muffler technology was not as good as today and thus the noise emitted by each car may well have been more than today.

Marie seemed to have surprised Officer Marchand when, still on the topic of noise in the neighborhood, she had added that depending upon the direction of the wind, there were times when she could hear the bells in the church tower of Saint Loup as they rang every fifteen minutes. Thus, she said:

"If you are awake, you can tell what time it is. It rings once, twice or three times for the three quarters of an hour and then strikes the hour as well. I guess I mean you would have to hear what the hour is and then counting the number of rings for the intermediate fractions, you could tell the time. Or you are awakened by one of the quarter-hour rings and still are when the hour is rung."

Officer Marchand followed up:

"And you did not hear anything the night of the murder?"

"Didn't. I was sound asleep."

"Is that normal for you?"

"I usually sleep well, though now and then I wake up and have some trouble falling back asleep."

"What do you do then?"

"Not much. I would not turn a light on because that might wake my husband up. So, I count the church bell rings if I can hear them. Or I shift a bit in bed. Eventually I go back to sleep. I tend to feel these difficult nights the next morning, as I am not fully rested then."

Officer Marchand shifted his line of questioning, apologizing for having to ask personal questions. She said she did not mind though her facial expression did not convey the same message. She answered that she and Jules had been married for fifteen years, but never could have a child. She conceded that it had been a topic that had caused tensions between them for a while, particularly as she was the one that could not conceive. She added that it seemed that Jules had accepted the situation, even if it was a reluctant acceptance.

Officer Marchand followed up on the issue of marital trouble. She replied that they did not fight often, though they occasionally had what she called discussions on the topic of money. Officer Marchand asked why. She replied that Jules liked to bet on horse races and occasionally to play cards for money. Officer Marchand kept going on that line of questioning, asking if Jules was a heavy gambler. She seemed surprised by the question and simply replied that gambling was not something that consumed a large part of the couple's budget, though occasionally it might be more than usual. Officer Marchand was still not satisfied and asked how frequent these discussions, as she called them, had happened in the recent past. She replied that they were not frequent, though she noted that expenses related to drinking at the bar and gambling were related; shifting the topic somewhat, she volunteered that Jules had stopped betting with the onset of the war in Paris. She offered that she did not think he still played horses, adding that she thought the opportunities were limited in Switzerland. She conceded that it had also taken him some time to make enough friends since they arrived in Versoix, though she mentioned that he would more and more often go have a beer or two with friends in the center of town. Casually, she added that she would not be surprised if she found out they played a few card games while sharing drinks. Officer Marchand asked:

"Has he talked of missing the betting on horses?"

"Not really. He knows that I'm not very much in favor of it. So even if he did, I'm not sure he'd discuss it."

"Any other games?"

"The odd game of backgammon I think."

"Does he drive there?"

"By there, I assume you mean the café where he meets his friends. Anyway, the answer is: No!"

Marie replied that he uses a bicycle most of the time, if only because he would never use the family car for what he would consider personal errands. Asked what official errands might be, she told him that she would have him drive her virtually every morning so that she could buy what was needed to prepare the meals for the day. She added that she would at times get up earlier than usual and go to the bakery if there was too little bread left from the prior day for breakfast. She would need a ride there and back to be ready for Mrs. Edith's breakfast.

Officer Marchand then turned to how Marie reacted to Edith's friend, Rose. She thought for a few seconds and spoke first of the fact that she had only seen Mrs. Prestat a few times in Paris, in fact, only once inside the apartment at a dinner where she was with her husband. She then said that Mrs. Edith stopped seeing Mrs. Prestat as soon as they left for Versoix. She added:

"I never asked why, it's certainly not my place. Yet, I thought it was odd that someone with whom she would regularly visit or even talk on the phone in Paris suddenly left her life."

Officer Marchand asked when they reconnected. She replied that it was soon after the war was over. She had come to Versoix at least a couple of times before the current visit. She talked of Rose being quite interested in Edith's drawings and etchings. Officer Marchand asked:

"How many pieces were there in the artist folder, the one you call the green folder?"

"I would not know. By the way, I call it green because the outside in made of green cardboard, with black corner patches, a black spine where the two pieces of cardboard are attached to each other and black ribbons that allows the whole thing to be closed and to prevent anything slipping out from inside."

She paused to take a breath and continued:

"Now back to your question, "how many pieces?" Quite a few. I never looked at them by myself, but I saw Mrs. Edith looking at them once on the dining room table and there were many. Maybe two dozen? Maybe more?"

"Do you know anything else about these drawings?"

Marie initially replied that she could not think of anything and then caught herself, adding:

"Not really."

"Anything that you might have found odd?"

"Once I saw Mrs. Prestat look at them with Mrs. Edith and she stayed back and kept admiring them as Mrs. Edith needed to leave the room."

Officer Marchand seemed then to turn his attention to Marie's health which, she said, was excellent, except for, in her words:

"That darn infertility."

He asked whether she took any medication, and she replied she did not, though she seemed at that point to remember something:

"Wait a minute. From time to time, I have difficulty falling asleep. My doctor has prescribed something which he says is not very strong. I took some the night Mrs. Edith was murdered."

"Why?"

"Jules thought I was twisting and turning and offered to get me some. I agreed."

Officer Marchand asked to see the bottle from which the pill came from. She excused herself and went to look for it. Officer

Marchand looked at the bottle she had brought back and noted in the report that the main ingredient was listed as "barbiturates." He asked how many pills she would normally take, and she answered that she usually took one, or two if she felt particularly tense. Officer Marchand asked:

"Do you remember how many pills you took the night of the murder?"

She replied that she did not remember, though she said that she could not imagine why she would have needed two pills, adding:

"I can't think why I would have been that much on edge—a premonition?"

Officer Marchand asked how often she needed to have the prescription renewed by her doctor. She said that she had never needed the prescription to be renewed more than twice a year. Looking at the bottle, Officer Marchand noted that the date on the prescription was quite recent. He asked:

"Was this the first time you used the pills since you last went to the doctor?"

Marie looked surprised and replied:

"Actually, you know what? You're right. I didn't think of that. I had not needed any pill since I had gone to see the doctor."

Officer Marchand stated in his report that the bottle's original contents should have been 30 pills and that at present it contained 28. He asked Marie:

"It looks as if you took two pills . . ."

"Must have, but I can't understand why Jules gave me two pills. Could it be that he took one pill as well?"

Officer Marchand stated that this was an unexpected reply. He asked whether Jules ever took sleeping pills. Marie replied that it was very infrequent but had surely happened once or twice before. Officer Marchand took this opportunity to return to an earlier question: did Marie remember Jules getting up during the night? She replied that he certainly got up to fetch the sleeping pills for her. Officer Marchand asked:

"Only once then?"

She replied that it was the only one she recalled. Officer Marchand asked whether she remembered when she took the pills. She said that Jules had turned on a bedside lamp when he got up and she noted that it was around eleven fifteen. Officer Marchand asked at what time she retired to bed, and Marie simply answered that she usually was in bed before ten, because she needed to be up at 6:00 a.m. to get ready for Mrs. Edith who usually had breakfast at around 7:30 a.m. Officer Marchand further asked whether she had had any sleep before her husband got her sleeping pills. Marie replied that she had fallen asleep quite rapidly right after her head hit the pillow. However, apparently at least according to Jules, she had later been twisting and turning for a good thirty minutes before he offered to get her sleeping pills. Officer Marchand asked whether she had heard the church bells while she was twisting and turning and she said that she had not. She added with a genuineness which impressed Officer Marchand:

"No. Wonder why? The winds were blowing from the northwest, and I should have heard them. Must not have twisted long!"

Chapter Eighteen

2001, 1948
NAPLES, FLORIDA. VERSOIX, SWITZERLAND

We came last to the police documents on Jules and dove into it with bated breath. While neither of the other reports totally exculpated Rose and Marie in our eyes, it did appear to our uneducated eyes that they suggested that both women had solid alibis. So, we concluded that Jules had to be in the hot seat. We really wondered whether he would have as airtight an alibi as the other two witnesses, thus opening the way for the so far rejected hypothesis of an intruder.

Officer Marchand started by asking Jules if he had heard anything the night of the murder. He promptly replied that he had not. In fact, he explained that his wife had had some trouble sleeping earlier in the night. So, he had gotten up to get her a sleeping pill. He then went straight back to bed and said that he heard the church bells ring all the way till 1:30 a.m., at which point he got up again and took one of his wife's sleeping pills as well. He added:

"Since I take any of that kind of medicine extremely rarely, I fell asleep almost on the spot and did not wake up until when my wife called to say that Mrs. Edith was dead."

He added:

"That, alone, is unusual. I normally get up at the same time as Marie. I remember that morning that I asked her to let me sleep some more when her alarm clock rang."

Officer Marchand asked how his relationship with Edith was, and Jules could not stop singing her praises. He went as far as saying that she had surprised him a couple of weeks earlier telling him that she would let them both live in the house even if she left for the U.S., saying that at least they would both have a roof over their heads until they died. Officer Marchand was surprised as this was the first time this offer had come to light. Yet, the next question was obvious:

"How will you maintain it?"

"Mrs. Edith said that she would provide some money to be paid to us to maintain the house and supplement any income we can earn ourselves."

"Are you both Swiss citizens?"

"No, we are not even residents yet."

"How do you expect to get a job without a work permit?"

"At this point, we have not thought this through. But Mrs. Edith had strongly advised us to apply for whatever status we could get so that we could eventually become residents if not citizens. So, we started the process a few weeks ago."

"Why wait so long?"

"Initially, it was war, officer. Then, I don't know. Procrastination, I guess, and maybe simply the feeling that Mrs. Edith would remain in Versoix. Then, when she indicated she might move on, we realized that we had to do something. Quickly."

Officer Marchand shifted the questioning to Jules's duties in the house. He replied that he was still principally Mrs. Edith's driver. He, however, conceded that she had curtailed her travel and even her visits to friends since they had moved to Versoix. Thus, there was less need for a driver. On the other hand, there was more need for someone to help around the property. He added that he was doing some gardening and more importantly helping with the maintenance of the house, which had not been occupied permanently for many years before they arrived. Officer Marchand asked whether he had any qualification in the building trade, to which Jules could only reply that he did not have formal training. Yet, he immediately mentioned:

"As a professional driver, I have had to learn quite a bit with respect to basic mechanical work, as cars are still not terribly reliable."

"What does that have to do with the building trade?"

Jules explained that he was used to learning on the job so to speak as he was looking at what mechanics did and was able to do it himself after having watched them do it a few times. He added:

"That's the same with issues around the house. For instance, I used the extra time I had to observe and get some training from the electrician who originally came."

He paused seeing Officer Marchand's incredulity all over his face, and conceded:

"I know very well that there is quite a lot I still cannot do. That's when I know I must call a specialized tradesman. Yet, there are many minor tasks which I can safely handle. Things like woodworking, elementary masonry, basic electrical repair, and many of the trades that are needed. In fact, I can assure you that I do not have a lot of free time during the day."

Officer Marchand shifted the conversation to what Jules did when he had free time. Jules's demeanor appeared to change, marginally at least. He was becoming quite a bit less comfortable, but Officer Marchand kept pressing. He replied that he did spend some time at one or the other local bars having a few beers with people he had met in the seven years they had been living there. Officer Marchand asked why he seemed to be uncomfortable replying to the question. Jules seemed to hesitate and simply admitted that he and his friends would play a few games of *Jass*.

Jass is often considered Switzerland's national card game, just as *belote* is considered the national card game in France. In fact, both belong to the same general family of card games, though there are differences. Additionally, there are several variants of each which complicate the matter and allow one to score higher or faster. However, simply described, the ultimate goal of the game of *Jass* is to reach 2,500 points, or some other pre-agreed level, by winning tricks, where a trick is taken by the highest card of the suit that was led, or by the highest trump card played if anyone played one. Points are scored by counting the value of each of the four cards in a trick. The total value of all counters in a pack is 152, 62 in the trump suit and 30 each in the other three. As in the classical *belote* game, there is a bonus for the last trick, 5 points in *Jass* and 10 in *belote*; thus, excluding extras which do not need to be discussed here, there are 157 points at play for each time that cards are dealt in a Jass game. The game is played with a 36-card deck (from Ace to 6) by two teams of two players each, with the two players in a team trying to work together, but, like belote and contrary to bridge for instance, they do not know what their partner holds in their hand.

With Officer Marchand probably at least as familiar as Jules with the game, he came back with a tough question. He asked Jules if he ever played for money. Jules looked even more uncomfortable but had to concede that the game almost always involved some money. At times, it was simply because the losing team had to pay for the drinks consumed during a given game by both themselves and the winners. At other times, there might be some small bet, he said, such as a Swiss cent per winning point. Remembering his conversation with Marie, Officer Marchand pushed further:

"Never more than one cent? I've heard of games where the point is played for a Franc if not more."

"Very infrequently. Frankly, I don't have enough money to play at that level, Officer."

Staying with gambling, Officer Marchand then asked whether Jules was involved in any other form of gambling. He came straight out stating that he used to like to bet on horse races when in Paris, as it was both quite popular and accessible. He said that he knew there were horse races in Switzerland, but they were far fewer than around Paris. In fact, he noted in passing that in season the best horse races close enough to Versoix would likely be on the other side of the French border, in Divonne-les-bains. Officer Marchand fired straight back:

"It also has a casino, doesn't it?"

Jules' look became considerably more quizzical. Up until then, Officer Marchand's questions, though having narrowed onto a weak spot he knew he had, had seemed to flow quite freely and in a way that was thus not suspicious. The focus which he seemed to put on gambling made him wonder whether Marie had led Officer Marchand in that direction. A trained detective, Officer

Marchand sensed the witness's reluctance and chose to move to a different line of questioning, adding:

"By the way, I don't want you to feel that I am going in that direction for any specific reason. You gave me the entry into the topic when you talked of drinking in bars and the rest naturally followed. So, would you agree with the conclusion that you used to gamble, you still do in small amounts, but you have had to stop because of the unavailability of opportunities?"

"Fair. Totally fair. Plus, frankly a lack of longtime friends; we're still relatively new here."

"Wait, you've been here for more than six years . . . You haven't had the time to make friends?"

Jules realized that his statement that he was relatively new in Versoix was suspect. He corrected himself saying that there was little socializing during the war, and that the fact that neither he nor Marie were Swiss made it more difficult to make friends.

Officer Marchand did not seem truly convinced by Jules' logic, but still shifted the line of questioning to the issue of an intruder. He noted, as he had with Marie, that the most likely intrusion entry point had to be the service entrance which was quite close to the window of his bedroom. Jules agreed with him, and surprised Officer Marchand with his next point, which was totally unsolicited:

"The piece I don't understand is that the dog did not bark. I know him, he is a solid guard dog. He would have to have barked . . . Unless he has been tranquilized."

"How?"

"Your question! I have no answer for sure, but there are ways. You could for instance take something like the pills my wife takes, powder it one way or another and mix it with his evening meal."

"What does he eat?"

"Usually, cooked chunk or ground meat mixed with rice and a couple of vegetables."

"Would that one pill do the trick?"

"I don't know what the dosage should be for a dog like Marroik . . ."

"Marroik?"

"That's the name of our German Shepherd: Marroik de Riva Bella, in fact. He's a purebred."

"I see."

"As I was saying, he weighs about eighty pounds, which is about half my weight."

Officer Marchand kept playing the hypothetical game and added:

"What dose does your wife normally take?"

"Not sure where you're going with that . . ."

"You'll see in a second. How many tablets does she take?"

"Normally a full tablet, two if she is really stressed. And very rarely half, though I cannot remember when she took just a half."

Officer Marchand did not carry out the reasoning explicitly, but his report noted two important points. First, Marie had only mentioned that she normally took one tablet. He wondered what that meant if she really at times only needed a half a pill. Second, Marie would probably not weigh more than half as much again as the dog, say one hundred and twenty pounds. Assuming similar metabolism in her and the dog, a whole pill would surely knock the dog out for a while. Yet, at the same time, as a father himself, he knew that certain drugs tended to have the opposite of their intended effect; for instance, particular tranquilizers would excite rather than tranquilize certain babies, especially when administered in the wrong dosage, including too little rather than too much. Could it be the same with a dog? Was it not a high risk to drug him unless someone knew that the reaction would not be adverse? How would Jules or Marie know how the dog would react to taking one of Marie's pills? Suddenly officer Marchand asked:

"Have you ever had to tranquilize the dog?"

Jules seemed to be thinking and replied:

"Yes, in fact we had to do it once . . ."

"Why?"

"We needed to take him to the vet for some bowel problem. The vet gave us a pill for us to have him eat before we drove him to the vet's office."

Officer Marchand dropped that line of questioning and turned next to Jules's actions immediately after he learned that Mrs. Edith was dead. Jules seemed suddenly much more comfortable. He said that he went upstairs to check for himself that she was really dead and confirmed that she had no pulse in her left wrist and that rigor mortis had started to set in. He then rushed downstairs to call the doctor first and then the police. In the meantime, waiting for them, he dug up the address of Mrs. Edith's brother in the U.S. and dictated a telegram in French to the post office. In response to the question as to whether he touched anything in the room, he replied that he did not, other than placing her robe at the foot of the bed; he explained that at some point it had to have fallen off and he decided that the room had to look neat. Officer Marchand asked:

"Did Mrs. Edith usually place her robe on her bed?"

"She often did. You know, she disliked the cold and felt that the robe could serve as an extra blanket if needed. I assume that she must have moved at some point in the bed and the robe fell off."

"Do you remember whether the night of the murder was particularly cold?"

"Frankly, I don't."

"At that time of the year, in July, would she not more likely have been hot rather than cold? Also, could the robe be unintentionally displaced by the murderer? Could she had briefly fought with the murderer and thus kicked the robe off the bed?"

Jules conceded that the scenario was possible. Officer Marchand noted that there was a trace of embarrassment on his face. He asked how close Jules had come to the side of the bed. Jules seemed surprised, leading Officer Marchand to ask:

"Did you notice anything about her slippers?"

Jules thought for a while and replied:

"Come to think of it, I could only see one slipper."

"Did you look for the other?"

"No. Did not think it was important."

Officer Marchand noted that Jules had not seemed perturbed by the question. The final line of questioning focused on the use of the car. There was almost total overlap there between Jules's answers and those which Marie had given. In fact, Officer Marchand put a question mark in between parentheses after that remark, as if he wondered whether the two had rehearsed that point.

Chapter Nineteen

2001, 1948
NAPLES, FLORIDA, AND VERSOIX, SWITZERLAND

Though we certainly knew that we had not read everything we needed to read, we were interrupted in our efforts by a phone call. Richard McCormick, Stephane's attorney had long retired by the time we contacted his law firm, but, when we first called him, we were transferred to the voicemail of one of the current partners, James Henderson Jr. We left as detailed a message as we could and asked for a call back as soon as possible. Truth be known, the return phone call came late in the afternoon, a bit as if the lawyer had done everything he had to do before calling us back. Surely, we did not think as if he thought calling us back was a priority item.

I took the phone call, though I mentioned to Jim Henderson that my wife, Annabelle, would be listening in. He asked if it would be OK for him to tape the call as he did not have anyone to take notes at that time, and we immediately agreed. He asked for some background in addition to what the voice mail stated and sounded a bit startled when, before diving into the matter at hand, I asked:

"Do you want the elevator talk or the full version?"

He replied that the elevator talk might be insufficient, though the several hour sessions ought to take place later. We both briefly chuckled, and I launched into a quick introduction. We had information about a former client of the firm, as well as about his son, also a client, adding they were both deceased. Looking through furniture which we purchased from a consignment shop, we found a trove of documents which now raised a number of issues in our minds. I mentioned that one of these documents was a copy of the will of the oldest of the two clients, bearing the letterhead of the firm and the signature of Richard McCormick. Jim interrupted:

"Dick! What a great fellow. Yet, you know that he retired quite a while ago. I must also tell you that he died a few years back."

He paused and then continued:

"But since I inherited all his files, I believe I can help. The main question in my mind, excuse the legalistic lingo, is whether you have standing for me to discuss any of this with you."

I simply replied:

"Fully understand. Yet, I suspect that when you get to peruse what we have, it will become obvious that there is work for you to do, and we will likely have to do it together.

"Can you tell me a bit more?"

"Well, let's start with this. It's entirely possible, maybe even probable that your partner, Richard, was not aware of the whole of the client's estate."

"How come?"

"Well, what if a portion of it was abroad and undeclared in the U.S.?"

Jim's voice rose a few decibels expressing his surprise as he said:

"Wait. That would have been illegal . . ."

"Maybe, maybe not. But irrespective as to whether it was or was not an issue for the client whom Richard advised, his son most probably did not know the full extent of his estate and you, as his estate lawyer as I understand it, may thus have only done a partial settlement of his estate."

Jim's voice became considerably more serious as he interrupted me:

"Stop! That's enough. Do you have proof for any of this?"

I decided that I would stay as calm as possible and simply replied:

"We do. I must concede that my wife and I have not yet looked as deeply as we should at all the documentation we have, but there is nothing in what I just said that is pure speculation."

I paused for a short while, enough to let the point set in and then, almost casually, added:

"Would you agree that it would probably not be a bad idea for us to meet?"

Jim could only reply in an almost dejected tone of voice certainly thus lacking any form of enthusiasm:

"I guess so. When would you like to meet?"

I replied that the question was in fact a double one. One part was straight forward, we should have a meeting, and finding a time should not be too hard. The other was less clear, and it related to where we should meet. I did not leave Jim time to respond and simply added:

"We have a lot of papers and an equally large number of pieces of evidence which, quite frankly, I would hate to take out of the house. Would you be willing to come to our house so that we have full documentation available for you to consider?"

"Do you live in Naples?"

"Not Naples proper, but just north of Naples, in Bonita Bay."

"I know Bonita Bay; in fact, I have played golf there a few times. Great community. Great golf courses, five of them I think, correct?"

"Correct."

We had prepared a full "show and tell" for Jim when he arrived at our front door. We first casually took him to the second garage to show him those pieces of furniture which had not yet migrated into the house. We then walked into the house and let him admire the twelve framed impressionist paintings, which we had pulled from the closet under the stairs and casually lined up against the sofas and the armchairs in the living room. We also assured him that there was only minimal doubt that they were genuine. We then took him into our bedroom, which was next to the living room, to let him see the secretary desk and the two armchairs. We then showed the artist folder with the various drawings and etchings, which we had placed on the dining room table, as well as the fifteen unframed paintings which we had retrieved from the back of the armoire, and which were stacked up on a coffee table in my office. Triumphally, I added:

"And can you believe that we bought the whole thing for $5,000!"

"I know. I know. That's what they appeared to be worth in Jack's estate tax declaration. Any idea what they're worth?"

"Who knows? One of Monet's grain stack canvases went for $15 million this year. My guess is that the 27 paintings taken together must average at least \$1 million per unit, probably in fact quite a lot more. We have not taken the time to get a formal valuation of the whole lot."

Jim smiled and said:

"You had said you were in the investment business at some point, right?"

I could only agree. He then added:

"I bet this has got to be your best investment ever . . ."

"By a mile."

I smiled again but wanted to bring Jim back to the whole topic. I repeated that Stephane's will seemed to say that he would like anything that was left when his last descendant died to be placed in a foundation. I asked Jim point blank:

"Was there anything left when Jack died?"

"Well, Mike, I hesitate to answer because this should be a confidential attorney/client privileged matter. But given the work you have done and the fact that you are not doing it for yourself but for the Schneider family, I will tell you what I can. I'll draft a release which I will ask you to sign later if that is OK."

"No problem."

"There was some furniture in storage. In fact, the furniture is still there. I would have given it to the consignment shop, but I did not have the time to do a complete verification of the inventory. I was still planning eventually to sell it in the same manner. I estimated its worth as *de minimis* on the declaration, as we did not need to worry about estate taxes."

He paused for a second and explained that the current estate tax exemption at the U.S. Federal level was \$675,000. He conceded that there was some money left in the trust account, though he added that the total plus the de minimis value assigned to furniture and artworks still fell short of the taxation threshold.

Annabelle enquired as to the value of the apartment in the assisted living complex. Jim replied that Jack had agreed to take a reverse mortgage on his assisted living apartment, adding:

"The money in his own account included what he received. Yet, that and the remaining of the trust were not enough for his estate to have been subject to any tax."

"Unless the furniture in storage is worth more than the *de minimis* amount which was assumed."

"Correct, Mike."

He paused and then concluded:

"Plus, since whatever money is left is going to charity, this was a very simple estate. There was no need for probate."

Jim paused and I took the opportunity to interject. Rather than offering a long preamble with facts, I had decided that I would ask a challenging question, sort of out of the blue. I was hoping that the shock would lead Jim to come totally to our side. Without batting an eyelid, I asked:

"What would have to happen if it was discovered that Jack owned substantial assets abroad?"

"Wait. What are you saying? Which assets would those be?"

I smiled and explained that what I was going to tell him, however incomplete at that point, was the reason why I thought we should meet. I brought him up to speed regarding what we knew of the family, prefacing my point with a comment that we still did not know everything. I added:

"The main uncertainty is that we have reasonable information as to what was there when Jack's father died. Yet, I must add that what we absolutely do not know is what happened to any of these assets since then."

Jim looked quizzical and kept mumbling:

"What? What?"

I explained that we had a series of documents which we found in the hidden compartments in the furniture we bought at the consignment shop. One of them was a list which Stephane had prepared before he died. The list did not itemize anything he had in the U.S., presumably because his attorney would have known about that. Rather, it focused on assets that I said Annabelle and I suspected were still in Europe, unless we were to find out that he, Jim, or Richard knew about them and had brought them onshore. Jim immediately said:

"I can categorically say that no one from our law firm has brought anything onshore since the passing of Stephane Schneider. Better yet, we ignored that there was anything. I have never seen anything in the file that might as much as allude to foreign assets."

So, I replied:

"Fasten your seatbelt. The list mentioned what he had left in Europe when he moved to the U.S., what he owned jointly with his late sister and what he had inherited from his sister when she died, including the proceeds from her life insurance."

I added that there were also some further financial assets which should have come to his sister but came his way when the insurances on the lives of his brother-in-law and his nephew were finally settled. I paused for a minute and simply concluded:

"We still are not sure what all this is worth today, but Stephane's documents when he received the last payment from the two life insurances of Edith's husband and son, in 1960, placed the total on these lists at well over $10 million, then. I leave it up to your imagination to determine how much this might be today."

Annabelle and I had fun looking back to the performance of the S&P 500, the index which tracks the performance of the U.S. stock market; it was at 58 at the beginning of 1960 and at 1336 at the beginning of this year, that's up 23 times! I argued that we also knew that the price of impressionist paintings had followed more or less the same trend as global equities. So, I concluded:

"Take the $10 million listed by Stephane. I'd say it would not be crazy to say that they could be worth north of $200 million today, with about $60 million in financial assets and the balance in artworks!"

Jim sighed visibly and seemed pensive for at least a couple of minutes which felt to us like a lot longer. Initially, he could only manage a weak:

"Oh my God!"

I asked:

"That means that Jack's estate tax declaration needs a complete redo, correct?"

"I guess so. But how do we get the data we need? Stephane's 1960 estimates are a good start, but I cannot file an amended declaration without a lot more data. For a start, I must confirm that every piece on the list is still there; I mean that no piece has been sold at some point. I should have pictures of every piece of furniture or artwork. I must have expert confirmation that they're genuine, together with valuations and many other elements. We're looking at a detailed probate process. Where would I find the items at this point?"

Though Annabelle and I initially believed that we had completed our reading of the police records, we found out quickly that the document did not stop with the first interrogations of the three witnesses. When we had heard that they had isolated the witnesses preventing them talking to one another, we should have anticipated that we were only looking at round one. The follow-up reports, we could call them cross-examination reports, were equally instructive.

The second questioning of Rose related principally to what she had and had not heard. It seems that Officer Marchand walked her from the living room to her bedroom, on the first floor. They both sat in her bedroom, the door closed, while another officer, the one who had kept her company all along, was walking both up and down the back stairs and from the top of the back stairs to Edith's bedroom and back. Rose was surprised that there was more creaking from the floor in the corridor than from the back stairs. She initially argued that whatever intruder she had heard was more careful in the corridor than in the stairs. Officer Marchand dutifully asked his colleague to be more careful in the corridor than on the stairs. Rose smiled mildly when the creaking from the corridor was less audible, but definitely present. Yet, the interrogator still noted that however careful his colleague was, there was still almost as loud a sound in the corridor as in the back stairs. Rose was surprised when Officer Marchand, with both still in her room, asked her:

"Does the floor creak when you walk from your bedroom to the toilets?"

She replied that she had heard it creak loudly once, the first night, and had thus been terribly careful not to make any noise, adding:

"If you set your feet as close to the wall as possible, there is much less creaking."

Officer Marchand asked his colleague to check the assertion. Rose definitely had a point.

Officer Marchand returned to Rose's discussion of the whole event. He asked her again whether the crime could have been committed by an intruder. She replied that everything was possible, though she noted that Edith usually made sure that all doors on the main floor were locked, and, for several of them, that the shutters were closed and locked as well. She repeated that the only door that Edith usually did not check on the main floor was the back door, as Marie or Jules would have locked it themselves as they retired to their house. Officer Marchand was not done with that line of questioning and asked whether it was possible that an intruder could have come in through the back door. She conceded that this was possible, though she noted that the doghouse was between the house and the garage and thus that anyone trying to enter through the back door would have surely awakened the dog unless that person was known to the dog. With a mild smile on her face, she added:

"That's what guard dogs are supposed to do."

Officer Marchand noted the point and kept digging. He asked whether it was possible that an intruder might have drugged the dog. Rose displayed surprise but thinking about it for a few seconds said that it was indeed possible. Yet. she asked:

"How would an intruder have drugged the dog?"

Officer Marchand simply replied that he could have put some drug in his food. Rose chuckled and said that this did not make sense to her. Upon further questioning, she added:

"Marie or Jules feed the dog before they go to bed. So, the dog would have just eaten. How would one get the dog to eat any more?"

"What if they put the drug in its water?"

"Possible, but first how could someone do that and avoid the dog barking while the water is being spiked and second how much would the dog need to drink for the drug to have the desired effect?"

She paused and casually added:

"Anyway, there must be water left in his dish. Have you checked it?"

Officer Marchand replied that they did, but the water dish had been turned over and was empty. He added that there were not enough water traces for anything to be analyzed. Rose jumped up:

"To me, if your scenario is right, this says that the criminal was very careful and that the murder must have been premeditated. He even thought of turning the bowl over to make sure that no one would find any trace of the drug . . ."

As I was walking past her desk where she sat to read the document, Annabelle could not resist telling me:

"Rose seems to be saying everything to point to Marie or Jules and away from herself."

"How come?"

"You need to read this yourself."

Back to the second record of the police interrogation, Officer Marchand asked Rose:

"I never asked you how you felt about art, the kind of art which your friend collected . . ."

"Actually, I believe that we covered this the last time already. Anyway, I can answer the question again. I love to look at it. I would never have the money to buy any of these, so to me admiring them at Edith's house is a bit like going to a museum."

"How often did you look at them?"

"Come to think of it, I think we have looked at them at least once on any of my visits."

"This was your third visit I believe . . ."

"Correct. The third visit since she moved to Versoix. So, I must have looked at them three times."

"Are there many drawings in the artist folder?"

"Not sure, but I'd say a couple of dozens, plus or minus."

"Are you aware of their worth?"

"Not specifically. But I can read a signature as well as anyone. So, I must think that a sketch by Renoir must be worth quite a bit of money . . ."

Officer Marchand let go of this topic and asked:

"One question troubles me. Going back to an earlier comment, you mentioned that the murder might have been premeditated. So, you must be thinking that the murderer was familiar with the house. Is that correct?"

"I guess. I don't see where you are going though, officer."

"Give me a second. If the murderer knew the house, he would have known two things."

He paused and said in the report that Rose seemed to remain emotionless. He continued:

"He would have to have known that the back stairs and the floor of the corridor might creak . . ."

Rose interrupted:

"He or she would then have been careful, correct?"

"That could well be. But he also would have to have known both that the front steps would not creak and that the door to Edith's room was closer to the front staircase than to the back stairs. Why would he not have used the front staircase?"

"I had not thought of that. Maybe the fear of staying in the open downstairs for a while longer if he had, as we both seem to be assuming, entered through the service door."

"Who was going to disturb him in the middle of the night?"

With that, without allowing Rose to respond to his prior question, Officer Marchand asked:

"Do you ever take sleeping pills?"

"Me, hardly ever. I always have a couple I carry in my toiletry kit, but I can't remember when I last took one of these pills. I hate them anyway because I still feel woozy the next morning. They are quite powerful, at least as far as how I react to them."

"Can we look into your toiletry kit?"

Rose did not seem overly surprised by the question. She simply replied:

"It's in the bathroom. Let's go there."

"Do you mean that anyone has access to your toiletries?"

"Sure, mine and Edith's as well. There is only one bathroom upstairs in the main house, the other one is downstairs, for the room which Edith used to call her parents' bedroom."

"How many sleeping pills were there in your toiletries?"

"Two! I keep the prescription in Paris and never take more than two pills with me."

"Why?"

"I do get depressed at times. With only two pills with me, I know I cannot do anything stupid . . ."

"But what about when you are in Paris?"

"I have two pills in the bathroom, ready for me, and the rest is in my safe."

"Safe?"

"Yes, a small wall safe in the room my husband and I used as an office."

By then, they had gotten to the bathroom, opened the door and saw a mirror-fronted cabinet which Rose explained was where she and Edith would have their respective items. Officer Marchand abandoned his earlier line of questioning, as they investigated Rose's part of the cabinet, and she pulled out a small glass container where she kept her sleeping pills. He inclined the container so that an orange and red capsule rolled out.

Officer Marchand knew full well that capsules are made of a soft, gelatin-like, outer skin with the real medicine, powder, or liquid, inside the harmless outer skin. Once swallowed, the soft gelatin breaks down and the medicine is thus released and enters more quickly into the bloodstream than when using more traditional pills.

Suddenly, before Officer Marchand could say anything, she exclaimed:

"Hold it. There's only one capsule here. Who took the other?"

Chapter Twenty

2001, 1948
NAPLES, FLORIDA, AND VERSOIX, SWITZERLAND

While Annabelle kept going through the police data, I investigated a bit more of Stephane's diary and found myself at the spot when, still in Versoix right after the death of Edith, he had decided to hire a private detective. Interestingly, he seems to have requested help and recommendation from his Swiss attorney, Erik Sutter, who was unable to help him. He then went to see the family private banker at Pictet, Jean-Yves Lemieux. For some reason, the banker was able to rattle off a few names, though he noted that they were Swiss; I assumed that clients might more easily ask their bankers for help on such matters than their attorneys, though I was surely not ready to defend that assumption. Jean-Yves Lemieux said that any Swiss detective could find someone in Paris if that would help, but Stephane stopped him right there, arguing:

"I prefer someone who is used to being discreet. I am sure that any Swiss private detective would have contacts in the neighboring countries, such as France. I would rather establish a relationship with that person here, in Geneva, and let him marshal whatever resources he might need."

"Would you like me to make an introduction?"

"Unless you feel he will not talk to me without your help, I would rather contact him directly. I don't want anyone to know that you and I have a relationship unless I can't do otherwise."

"Very prudent, Mr. Schneider; very prudent. Let me give you the address and telephone number of someone we know and respect. His name is Felix Favre. You might be interested to know that Favre probably is the most common surname in the Geneva area."

"How convenient. Am I to believe that it might not be his real name?"

"I frankly don't know, but I must tell you that the thought had occurred to me."

Stephane appeared to have wanted to keep careful notes on his meeting with Felix Favre, as he dedicated a couple of pages to it in his diary. He first mentioned semi-jokingly that it took him some effort to secure a meeting with Felix because he would not disclose the name of the person who made the recommendation. He finally broke the ice asking a simple question:

"Mr. Favre, do you do much work with attorneys and private bankers in Geneva?"

"Certainly. In fact, they are my primary sources of clients."

"Assuming that I deal with one of them, do you think I would want you to know I have a relationship with a particular law firm or bank?"

"You said your name was Stephane Schneider, correct?"

"Yes."

"Well, Mr. Schneider, let me tell you that you must be one of the most careful people I have met in this business. I'll be happy to meet you. Do you have my address?"

"I do have an address. 7, rue des Alpes. Is that correct?"

"It is. You walk into the foyer that links the front of the building to the gardens at the back. The staircase and elevator are on the left. My office is on the last floor. It is not very big, but rents are quite expensive in this part of town."

Stephane arrived at the appointed time and met a gentleman who was in his early fifties. Shorter than usual, probably 5 feet 7 at most, athletic, with a round face whose most noticeable feature was two piercing blue eyes. His light brown hair had receded somewhat, which made his forehead seem larger than it was. He was dressed informally, with grey pants, a striped blue and white, open-necked shirt and a light blue sweater. Stephane could see a blue blazer hanging in the corner of the office to complete Felix's clothing in formal circumstances. He was impressed that Felix would not consider his meeting Stephane formal enough to dress up. Felix motioned Stephane into the room which served as his office, offered a cup of coffee, and sat down in a chair opposite the dark green sofa which he had pointed to Stephane.

"What can I do for you?"

Stephane started with a factual review of the murder of his sister, which Felix interrupted to say that he had read a couple of pieces in the local press. Stephane gave him details which he knew were known to everyone, adding that, so far, the list of suspects comprised three individuals who were in the house at the time, as well as anyone that might have come from outside. Felix asked Stephane for a description of the property, which he was delighted to provide, though, interestingly, Felix said that he would rather not be known to the three people that were in the house. Candidly, Stephane had asked:

"Do you want to come and visit under an assumed name? My wife is with me on this trip, and it would not be hard for me to introduce you as someone whom I met when I was much younger. I bet we are roughly the same vintage . . . I am 51."

"Well, you're right, I am 53. So, the story is plausible. Let me think about that. I assume that the police are on the matter."

"Absolutely, and it looks like they are doing a great job. In fact, if the murderer is an intruder, though I have reasons to question how he might have come in, I have total confidence the Swiss police will eventually find him."

"So?"

"I am more worried if the murderer is one of the three people that were in the house at the time of the murder. My sister came from France in 1941, fleeing after her husband and son had been taken away by the Germans."

Seeing that Felix was not following, he added a few words to the story of the intrusion into the Paris apartment, the possible role of Rose in the intrusion, the functions of the two domestic servants that were in the house and in fact fled with Edith. He then simply and quite calmly said:

"I would love to know if there is any skeleton in any of their closets, particularly in Paris."

Meanwhile, Annabelle was still busy with the second installment of the police documents. She was now ready to read and listen to what Officer Marchand had discussed during his second visit with Marie.

Officer Marchand seemingly wanted to learn more about how the dog was being cared for. He asked who usually prepared his food, to which Marie said that she did, adding with a chuckle:

"I'm not sure Jules would know how to cook rice."

"What do you normally give the dog?"

"I feed him twice a day. In the morning, I give him some rice as I always cook more than I need the prior evening and mix in a couple of root vegetables. I normally add a few pieces of raw meat."

"Raw?"

"Yes. The vet says that raw meat is what canines have always eaten in the wild and it is good to give him some, but not too much because it is harder to digest."

Seeing that Officer Marchand was satisfied with the answer, she continued:

"In the evening, I give him a bit more. Always still some rice, but I will give him at least a half pound of cooked ground meat, and still a few vegetables such as carrots, potatoes, turnip . . . Whatever is in season. I also add some broth in the bowl to wet the food a bit more."

"Do you carry the bowl to the dog?"

"Usually not, though I do it from time to time."

"Do you remember who carried it the night before the murder?"

"I do. It was Jules because I was a bit late fixing a special dinner Mrs. Edith had requested."

Seeing Officer Marchand open his eyes wider, she corrected herself:

"Oh! Nothing too special, but she wanted to celebrate her friend's visit. I think Mrs. Prestat was due to leave the next day . . ."

"The next day? But she did not, did she?"

"Mrs. Edith's death must have forced her to change her plans. In fact, I remember she called the train station as soon as she heard Mrs. Edith was dead. Very early that morning."

"How early?"

"Had to be around 9:00 a. m."

Officer Marchand did not follow up further on the dog's food or even the special dinner and turned to the behavior of the people in the house over the few days before the murder. Marie argued that things had looked quite normal to her. Mrs. Edith was cheerful. Officer Marchand noted that she stopped dead in her tracks and paused. He asked:

"Is "cheerful" the wrong word?"

"No. Not really. She was cheerful, but a couple of days before her death, she and Mrs. Prestat were having an animated conversation in the living room. I could not make out what they were saying, but their voices were raised a bit. It all eventually calmed down, but I could see something like a shadow across Mrs. Edith's face when she came to the kitchen to grab a glass of hot milk as she did every night before retiring to bed."

"A shadow?"

"I don't know how to describe it. But she is, I mean she was, usually so cheerful when she came to have her milk and say good night. That night she appeared concerned by something."

"Any trace of it the next morning?"

"No. Not on Mrs. Edith's face. She seemed to have gotten over whatever it was. But I thought that it was Mrs. Prestat who looked a bit concerned in her turn. Yet, they greeted each other as usual, and I surely did not note anything odd that day. In fact, I remember that they went to Geneva together that day. Jules drove them."

She paused and as an aside said:

"Jules gave me these details because Mrs. Edith rarely told me where she was going. At most she would ask if there was anything I needed for the kitchen."

Returning to the flow of her earlier statement, she added:

"But then, the next morning, Mrs. Edith was dead."

Officer Marchand was ready to conclude his report and, almost as an afterthought, asked another question about the dog:

"Would the dog let anyone approach him?"

"Anyone surely not. But either of the two of us, plus Mrs. Edith certainly. In fact, with Mrs. Prestat at the house for a week, he seemed to have adopted her as well."

"Thanks. Oh, a last question. Is it frequent for the dog to upturn his water bowl?"

"Why are you asking?"

"Well, one of my officers said that the bowl was upturned the morning of Mrs. Edith's death."

"Nobody told me. I'm sure it must have happened before, but I can't say it is frequent. If you look carefully at the doghouse and its very front, you'll see that there is a small depression as the cement slab on which the doghouse is placed stops and gives way to gravel first and grass afterwards. I've always thought that the grass prevents Marroik upending either his bowl or his dish, as we typically set them on the gravel. In fact, come to think of it, I remember Jules saying that he had dug a couple of shallow holes, depressions may be a better word, to place the bowl and the dish, precisely because Marroik would upend them too often earlier."

"Thank you very much, Marie."

<hr />

Officer Marchand then went back to Jules to complete his interviews. He had a good idea of the few areas where Jules could help him add the final touches to his understanding.

He first focused on the dog. It was clear in his mind that the dog and more importantly the fact that no one had heard him bark was a very important element in the current mystery. Indeed, either the murderer was known to the dog and known well enough that even if surprised in the middle of the night the dog would not bark or the dog would have had to have been tranquilized in one manner or another if the murderer came from the outside. Interestingly, Officer Marchand seemed to add an unexpected element: what if the murderer had come from the outside to commit a murder for which he might have been paid by someone inside the house?

"Jules, do you remember who fed the dog the evening of the murder?"

"Honestly, I don't. Marie always prepares it. I know that she takes the bowl to him most of the time. After all, we're talking a few steps from the service entrance, which is less than ten yards from the doghouse."

"Do you ever do it?"

"Sure. Sometimes she is busy, and I am not. I am happy to do it. The dog loves me."

"While I think of it, Jules, is the dog free to roam?

"Almost always. We would only close the door of its run if Mrs. Edith was expecting guests or any sort of delivery."

"I assume he did not like being locked up."

"Correct, he would bark for a while, then, eventually calm himself. But he might resume his barking at any moment."

"So, he could not have been locked up that night . . ."

"I'm sure he wasn't, except if he was locked up by someone whom he knew and been tranquilized first."

"Who else but Marie and you, other than Mrs. Edith?"

"Not sure, really. He had stopped barking at Mrs. Prestat, but I cannot imagine how she could have drugged him. And in addition, why would she have drugged him?"

"I'm not accusing anyone of anything, you understand?"

"I do."

"What if she was the one who had paid someone from the outside to come in and murder Mrs. Edith?"

"Why would she do that? I believe they were close friends?"

"How could you tell?"

"The way they talked to each other. Joyful and almost intimate at times."

"Any change in the recent past?"

Jules looked pensive for a few seconds. Then he blurted out:

"Well, you know, the day before the murder, I drove them both to Geneva, each of them had a different errand to run. Well, both on the way to and on the way back, they were more silent than usual."

"Thank you. Quite useful. By the way, back to my earlier question: what if Mrs. Prestat was the one who had paid an intruder to come in and murder Mrs. Edith?"

Jules thought for a short while and replied:

"Possible. However, anybody coming from the outside could be heard by people along the access road."

"Like, who?"

"Well, for a start, the old Bernard Reinhold."

"Who is he?"

Jules explained that Bernard Reinhold was the gentleman who had looked after the house when Mrs. Edith was away. He formerly was a police officer, and, when he retired, got an almost full-time job with one of the neighbors, serving as the caretaker of the property, which was at least twice as large as the Schneiders' and maybe even more. However, they had agreed to allow him a few hours a month to oversee the care of the Schneider house, as a favor to the Schneiders. Jules noted that Bernard's house was along the access road, against the wall that delineated the neighbor's property. Officer Marchand gave a pencil and a piece of paper to Jules asking him to draw a rough map. Jules first drew the gate to the Schneider property, then virtually alongside, though at a one hundred thirty-five-degree angle, drew the gate to the neighbor's property and right in between the two drew a vague rectangle which represented Bernard's house.

Annabelle saw in the report that Officer Marchand noted that he should pay a visit to Mr. Reinhold.

Officer Marchand, still interrogating Jules for the second time, noted that his next question was going to put Jules on the spot, but commented that he had to ask it that way:

"Now, put yourself in the shoes of an intruder."

"Not easy. Remember, I used to live in Paris, not in the countryside. I can imagine how someone would try to break into an apartment, not a separate house with a large garden."

"Understood, but still try. Imagine that you have a contract to murder Mrs. Edith. What would you have needed?"

Jules seemed to hesitate for a short while. Then saying that his reply was based on the murder mysteries he had read, he rattled of what he could think of at the time:

"I would need a car or a bicycle to get to the house, probably a car to get away as fast as possible, though it might be a bit noisier than a bicycle. I'm assuming that I would not normally live in Versoix. I would surely keep the car, or the bicycle parked outside the gate. I would have had to be given a map to the inside of the house."

Jules may have misinterpreted the officer's concentration on his reply for doubt, and added:

"How else would I know where to go?"

"Well, whoever asked you to commit the murder might be meeting you at the door . . ."

"Good thinking. That's possible. But that would mean that the murderer and whoever ordered the murder had met at least once. Would you want to leave witnesses around when you are a contract killer? Would it not be easier to provide the details to the killer and take a sleeping pill to make sure whoever ordered the killing was asleep."

"OK. I buy it. But you agree that my hypothesis is not unrealistic."

"Sure. In fact, my hypothesis may be more complicated. They would have to organize a dead drop somewhere for the murderer to be paid. Unless everything took place through intermediaries."

"Intermediaries?"

"Yes, someone who is known to both parties but who shields both parties from each other."

"I see. But then there would be one more person who would be aware of the crime."

"Agreed, let's abandon that route."

"Anything else?"

"Not really. However, note that we must assume that the dog is heavily sedated . . ."

"Or locked up in its run?"

"I know we discussed that already, officer, but the more I think of it the more I think it is too complicated and unnecessary. Why go to the trouble of sedating and locking him up? Plus, everybody knows he gets excited when he is locked up. So, you would need to give him a heavier dose to keep him quiet at least as the drug is starting to work. If that's your plan, just give him the dose and be done with it; he would sleep it off in front of the doghouse."

Officer Marchand noted in his report that, as he was walking away from the table at which he had sat with Jules, he turned around and asked another question:

"How often did you drive Mrs. Edith out of the house here."

"Well, it depends, officer. When she is by herself, she does not need to leave the house too often. I would drive her to Geneva probably once or twice a month, and another once a week for local errands here in Versoix, like a hairdresser appointment or something like that. She still has very few friends, other than the two neighbors, and she does not need a car to get there."

"How is it different when she has guests?"

"Then they usually go out at least once a day."

"Destinations?"

"Anywhere. The surrounding area, Geneva, Lausanne, sometimes they go as far as Montreux or Martigny, at the eastern tip of Lake Geneva."

"And with Mrs. Prestat?"

"They would go walk in Versoix almost every day unless they wanted to go on a trip a bit further. I took them to Gruyere once; there's a wonderful restaurant where they serve local Swiss dishes for lunch, you know, fondue, raclette and things like that."

"Did you ever drive Mrs. Prestat by herself?"

Jules seemed to hesitate and then replied:

"A couple of times, I think. Once, she wanted me to drive her to a florist so that she could buy flowers for Mrs. Edith. Another time, she needed to go to Geneva. Mrs. Edith was with us because she too had business there. I dropped Mrs. Edith near the Hotel Richemont, right in the center of town. She had simply said she had an errand to run. I often drop her off around there and pick her up at some later agreed time at the hotel. It's quite convenient, close to both banks of the lake and the hotel provides ample parking for chauffeured cars. Mrs. Prestat was not joining her and asked me to drive her to the Cornavin train station."

"When was that?"

"Actually, you know what? It was the day before we found Mrs. Edith murdered."

"Why was Mrs. Prestat going to the train station? To buy her return ticket?"

"That's what I thought; or maybe to confirm her reservations. She was due to leave the next day. But she was gone almost forty-five minutes. I can't believe there was that much of a wait at the ticket window."

"Could she have wanted to make a phone call?"

"There are a few public phones there indeed. But there is a phone at the house. And if she wanted discretion, she could call while Mrs. Edith was away . . ."

"Could she have met someone there?"

"Possible, but less likely."

"Why?"

"How could she give a precise time at which to meet? She was not in control of time, Mrs. Edith was with her errand, which I assume was an appointment with a banker or a lawyer."

"OK. Let's drop that one. What about the drive back to Versoix that day?"

"I drove Mrs. Prestat from the train station back to the hotel where Mrs. Edith was calmly waiting. Nothing special. You know, Mrs. Edith was a very patient person. She would not lose her calm on something like her friend or even me being fifteen minutes or so late. She was simply sipping a cup of coffee looking at the lake slightly to her left. She paid for her coffee, came in the car, let me close the door for her and we drove away."

"Any interesting conversation between the ladies on the way back to the house?"

"I do not listen to conversations. But I might notice if there was anything unusual."

"And?"

"Well, there was nothing unusual on that trip, other than the fact that they spent most of the time absorbed in their own thoughts."

He paused and corrected himself:

"Except maybe that they surely talked a lot less than usual. But remember, officer, this is quite a short drive . . ."

Officer Marchand was not finished. He asked Jules if there were interactions between him and Mrs. Edith and her guests. He replied that both he and Marie understood their positions and would not presume to mingle with guests. He added:

"We would only enter into any sort of interaction if invited to do so."

"Can you give me an example or two?"

"Sure. The day I drove Mrs. Prestat to Cornavin, I had to talk to her; she liked to talk, and I had to answer . . ."

He was going to stop and then offered another thought:

"Another time, it was not me but Marie, I know that Mrs. Prestat asked her help to look at Mrs. Edith's drawing collection."

"She asked without her friend being around?"

"Oh. I'm sure Mrs. Edith was in the house. But she asked while Mrs. Edith was probably upstairs. In fact, Mrs. Prestat called Marie very quickly afterwards to help close the artist folder, tie the three black ribbons, and place it back in its place."

Chapter Twenty-one

2001, 1948
NAPLES, FLORIDA, AND VERSOIX, SWITZERLAND

Though Stephane had to wait until he returned to the U.S. to hear from Felix Favre, the letter he received and kept in his documents was quite telling. It started with a simple statement to the effect that all three witnesses had a few issues that they probably would rather not discuss.

Apparently, Rose Prestat, though well-educated and with a solid reputation, was in some financial straits. She had had difficulties at the time of the death of her husband, but she was known ever since then to need to find solutions that bridged periods when money was running low. Nobody initially seemed to know what caused her expenses to appear to rise at certain times, but she found herself from time to time unable to pay her bills for weeks if not months at a time. From what Felix could uncover through a French *confrere*, she had to ask for the help of unregulated lenders to make ends meet in at least two or three instances.

Subsequently, Felix's *confrere* heard a rumor that her need for money might be related to gambling. Apparently, he found two bridge clubs, one near her apartment in Passy and the other near Park Monceau, closer to the center of Paris. He could verify that she had played there and had been requested to stop coming, because she evidently routinely failed to make good on the debts which she accumulated in the clubs. His report asked whether the client would like further digging, as gambling circles in Paris are still quite closed. He had added that one would find it hard to run up massive debts in bridge unless one was playing with very unusual people. However, it is not unusual for people to gamble across different games, and there surely were underground casinos where one could make or lose quite a bit of money.

Jules seemingly suffered from the same problem as Rose: he was known to be a gambler, though the bulk of his debts were incurred on horse races. He was known to be a heavy better and Felix was able to confirm that there were people in France that were still looking for him: they would like to have him pay back what he owed when he left in a hurry with Mrs. Edith and Marie. The word was that he suddenly disappeared in 1941. Certain people thought he fled to avoid having to pay his debts. Others postulated that he was Jewish and might have fled to escape arrest. Others simply thought he had been captured by the Germans and probably died in a death camp.

Marie's story was at the same time simpler and sadder. She was remembered as quite a good-looking woman who was both very nice and very discreet. Yet, at times she had had to resort to prostitution. She was not described as belonging to a particular group of underworld figures, or to have an assigned pimp. Rather she seemed to appear and disappear from time to time in fringe red-light areas. Cross-referencing this story with what he had learned about Jules, whom he knew was her husband, his most likely hypothesis was that she was a victim; she would agree to sell her sexual favors to help her husband cover his debts. Yet, she would have difficulties going back to Paris at present as a few professional pimps were still after her, as she had, in their view, stolen business from their women.

As she flipped the last page of Felix's first report, Annabelle could not miss a note which Stephane attached to the report. It said:

"Can see a motive for Rose and Jules: stealing something from Edith to pay debts. Keep looking for more on them. Marie looks like a victim. No need to dig further at this point on Marie unless something new and unexpected arises."

Back in our living room with Jim Henderson, the law partner who handled Jack's estate and had inherited the file of his father's estate from his law partner, we had just finished showing him that there could well be a lot more to the Jack's estate than anybody knew. I asked the next question:

"With Stephane having died more than thirty-three years ago, is there any reason you would worry about his estate tax filings and the fact that they did not disclose these foreign assets?"

"Thank God about that. No. The statute of limitation has run out. I won't bore you with all the gory details, but, in Mr. Schneider's circumstances, I believe that the Internal Revenue Service would have had to act less than six years after he died, and that includes the fact that omissions of foreign assets would typically double the normal period."

He paused and almost smiling added:

"But if you are correct with respect to Jack's estate, I will have to amend his filing. Your help will be needed if I am to complete this within the prescribed period."

He took a deep breath and conceded:

"Given what you have shown me, I am duty bound to report I have uncovered a possible problem and to investigate. You have given me reason to believe that the filing was incomplete. I must immediately inform the Tax Authorities."

Though I fully understood Jim's point, I still did not feel terribly comfortable in the position which Annabelle and I occupied. I wondered whether we were under any sort of cloud or might have financial liabilities. So, I asked what we needed to do next. Jim was quite clear that we had no liability, real or potential. He argued:

"I'll get back to your personal situation later, but there is nothing you must do. In fact, you did not even have to contact me. You might just as easily have kept those documents you needed and shredded what you did not need. You had no obligation to report since you knew neither of the two members of the Schneider family. On the other hand, now that you have contacted me and are placing on me the responsibility to act, I am allowed to ask for your full cooperation. In fact, you created your liability in contacting me, but it is not a financial issue."

He paused again and asked:

"So, where are we?"

The only reply I could give was:

"We have data, documents which we believe were created by Stephane Schneider. The issue is that everything which we believe was missed in the case of both Stephane's and Jack's estates is that they had undeclared assets abroad, and in the case of Jack's estate that the works of art that were sold to us were valuable. From our point of view, other than the documents, the only other thing we have is the name of two contacts outside of the U.S."

"You have a couple of names outside of the U.S.?"

"Yes. In fact, I believe that Stephane left coordinates for his lawyer and his banker, both in Geneva, in Switzerland. This was on a piece of paper, in the folder that was in what we believe was the most secret compartment in the furniture: the back end of the middle drawer of the Transition desk, which unless you can prove to me otherwise, I will believe was Stephane's own desk."

Jim was visibly starting to breathe more easily. He could see a way out of the mess in which he had been left by both his client and his client's father. Yet before he could ask further about the contacts, I asked another question, which I must admit, was pure curiosity on my part as knowing whether Jack's estate would or would not owe taxes was really none of my business:

"Does it make a difference that Stephane's letter of wishes and maybe his will if you have a copy of the final document give the specific instruction that any remaining asset at the death of his last descendant should go to a foundation?"

Jim nodded, saying first that it was an interesting question. He noted that the issue revolved around whether the receiving foundation existed when he would settle the estate, though in this case he corrected himself and argued he was not settling but in fact re-settling Jack's estate. Annabelle's and my face must have clearly indicated that we did not understand. Jim therefore undertook to explain his point in some detail. He stated that there was no estate tax if the whole of an estate was given to a qualified foundation. We nodded that we understood him, at least so far. He added that the first course of action that should be taken was to create a foundation qualified to receive the estate, adding with a wry smile:

"For as long as we cannot document the foreign assets, and I can argue that I cannot until I have a lot more than a list created in 1960, I can postulate that the foundation is created before the estate is fully known."

Annabelle could not resist:

"Sounds a bit fishy to me . . ."

"Maybe, but it's the law. Again, I won't take you through chapter and verse of the Tax Code, but this can be argued to be the equivalent of "earned" versus "received" in the Federal income tax code."

Annabelle was frowning, saying:

"It's even less clear now."

Jim explained that income taxes in the U.S. are due on income received, but not on income earned if that income has not been received. He added that income earned but not received would be called deferred income. He then said:

"I feel I can follow the same logic with respect to Jack's estate: you have told me, and therefore now I know, that there is more than I thought to the estate. However, in practice I still have no proof that anything really exists other than a list which you tell me is from Jack's father. Don't get me wrong, I trust that you are telling the truth as you believe it to be, but there is still a risk that I will not be able to put my hands on these assets. And what if what you believe to be true isn't?"

"How could that be?"

"Well, Annabelle, what if the attorney or banker whom you say were listed by Jack's father either do not exist, are deceased and we do not have a successor, or simply do not recognize my right to talk to them?"

Annabelle conceded that the question was fair. She asked:

"Would there be anything you could do?"

"I could go to court. But Swiss banking secrecy remains quite strong. I hope it won't come to that, because we might all leave it in the too hard basket."

"Wait, we know that Stephane wanted excess assets given to a foundation."

"You know that, and I know that. The key would be to be able to show the letter of wishes and the will to the Swiss attorney. That should be enough to convince him that we are all on the same side. Plus, my telling him that there is no known descendant and that there should be no tax because of the philanthropic disposition of the assets should be the icing on the cake."

Annabelle smiled and, as an aside, added that the situation would be like ours when we approached Jim's firm. The name we had at his law firm was his deceased partner, Richard McCormick. Jim nodded approvingly, though he added:

"But there has to be another scenario there as well . . ."

Annabelle and I must have looked totally incredulous, so Jim added:

"What if Stephane Schneider indeed had foreign assets and instructed his attorney or banker or both in that foreign country to sell all assets and give the proceeds to a foundation that he, the attorney, the banker, or even Stephane Schneider himself, might have created there as well? The foreign assets would have existed at one point but would no longer be available to any U.S. estate. They would no longer be his; they would belong to the foundation . . ."

I conceded that I had not considered that possibility. Shifting the topic, I asked Jim whether we needed to be involved in any way. His reply was crystal clear:

"Don't think so other than to the extent of helping me. Your nexus with the estate is your purchase at the consignment store. It was done with no prior knowledge on your part that the art was anything more than what it was described as—nearly worthless. The transaction is valid; the estate received your $5,000 minus the store's commission. You did make an incredible investment that day."

I could not resist sharing with Jim a bit more of the family story as it was developing. I prefaced my comment with the note that someone could be given access to all the documents we had in our possession and as I put it cynically:

"Proceed to reinvent the wheel."

At the same time, I added that we already had gone through quite a lot of the documents and would be able to help him save a lot of time if we remained in the background, unless Jim had in their office the linguistic capabilities which Annabelle and I have or want to spend the money needed to get them. I could not resist adding:

"And frankly, I really want to find out both who murdered Stephane's sister and why, and whether all the pieces listed on Stephane's 1960 list are still there or as you just suggested may already have been sold or given to a foundation."

Jim smiled and simply said:

"I welcome all the help I can get. Let me add something. I will have no problem having the two of you recognized among the people behind the creation of the Foundation here in Naples if we end up creating one. You surely deserve it."

He paused for an instant and then took his line of thought further. He argued that the knowledge that Annabelle and I had acquired going through the documents, together with the fact that we both spoke French and Annabelle was fluent in German might be of great help if we would agree to accompany him in his visits to Switzerland, adding:

"I'm sure I could describe what you have told me. However, you can describe, I'm sure in excruciating details, all the steps you went through to bring all these documents to light. This should facilitate communication and credibility."

I could not resist mentioning that we surely did not know if any of the furniture in storage at the Geneva Free Port might contain other secrets which would reveal other important elements. I could see Jim's face becoming quizzical. Rhetorically, I asked:

"What if Edith had maintained accounts that were not known to her brother? Why would she not have similar hidden drawers in some of her own furniture? While I doubt this would be in the house in Versoix—though who knows?—it could be in any of the pieces which she eventually brought back from Paris after the apartment there was sold."

Jim beat me to the punch:

"And since according to what you have told me Edith had designated her brother or any descendant as the beneficiary of her estate, there may still be stuff that should be added to Jack's estate tax declaration."

"Got it in one. So, Jim, what's the next step?"

"Are you willing to part with the documents, the time for me to have all of them copied and placed in our files? I assume you want the originals back . . ."

I looked at Annabelle and the message in her eyes was very clear. I replied on both our behalf:

"On your first question, the answer has to be an unequivocal yes; you can have the originals if only to create one or two sets of duplicates. With respect to your assumption that we want the originals back, we are less sure. Would you not want the Foundation to be their custodian? Whether they decide to put them on display or not is a decision that can be made later, but I do not see what claim we might have to any of them. They're the story of the Schneider family, not the De Barral family."

Chapter Twenty-two

2001, 1948
NAPLES, FLORIDA, AND VERSOIX, SWITZERLAND

The next page in the police report folder which Annabelle was reading dealt with Bernard Reinhold, the neighbor's caretaker. Bernard was indeed an older gentleman, probably in his late sixties. He had been around the area for many years. In fact, he was born in Collex-Bossy, the town to the immediate north of Versoix. He had served both as a custom officer and later a police officer. He had retired when he had reached his 60th birthday and had since been doing odd jobs in the area. He eventually accepted a position with the Reichenschmidts, the family who owned the large property right next to the Schneiders', in large measure because the housing conditions they would be providing to him and his wife; those seemed quite a bit better than what they had been able to afford on his official pension; a pensioned policeman did not expect to live along the lakeshore. Within a couple of years, he had lost his wife to complications from pneumonia. He wanted to be more occupied, as he found that staying by himself in the caretaker's house during the day was quite depressing; he was missing his wife of nearly fifty years. The Reichenschmidts were happy to allow him to do some work on the side provided it did not jeopardize his ability to serve them.

Officer Marchand asked Bernard about the genesis of the relationship with the Schneider family. Bernard was happy to explain his coincidental encounter with Mr. Dumas, whom he had to explain was the husband of Mrs. Edith Schneider. He sighed when he recalled how Mr. Jean Dumas was such a nice gentleman and how sad it was that he perished in the German death camps. He mentioned that the Dumas-Schneiders were seeking someone to look after the house in their absence. He was not expected to do work himself, but rather to coordinate the activities that should take place, such as the maintenance of the garden, monthly cleaning of the house and generally keeping watch over the property. The extra time he had to work was quite manageable, and yet it gave him some extra income which he was happy to share with his two children and three grandchildren.

Officer Marchand asked Bernard how much attention he was paying to the property. Bernard was quite straightforward answering that he paid a lot more attention when the property was not inhabited than when the Dumas-Schneiders were there. He even added that he had spent a lot less time since Mrs. Edith seemed to have moved permanently and bought the dog. Casually, Officer Marchand asked whether the dog barked a lot. Bernard smiled and simply said:

"Show me a German Shepherd that does not bark . . ."

Yet he added:

"He does bark but he is not annoying. Usually, he barks when there are people near the gate. Occasionally, he will bark when neighbors, such as us or those on the other side, come close to their side of the wall, but that was more so in the early days. I guess he has gotten used to our scents and only reacts when some new scent comes into the picture, or someone is trying to enter the property. But it's a deep bark, not an annoying yap!"

Officer Marchand asked whether Bernard heard anything on the night of the murder. Bernard was adamant that there was nothing unusual. He said he was awake around 3:00 a.m., though Officer Marchand noted that he had not been told that this was the time of Edith's death. He said that he could be definite about the time as he heard the church bells strike three times and some while later had heard the bell single strike once at 3:15 a.m.; then fell back asleep. Officer Marchand pushed a little bit harder, and Bernard simply could not offer any other insight other that saying that he had noted tire marks along the wall in between the two gates, adding it must have rained that night and the ground must have been softer and wetter than usual. Officer Marchand asked how he could be sure the marks were new, and Bernard simply replied:

"Honestly, I can't. You know officer, I remember from my days in the police or even in the customs and border patrol environment that you do not always observe things in an active manner. You notice something which seems unusual. My training tells me that the tire marks were unusual, but I sure cannot be sure they were not there the day before."

He paused and then right away corrected himself:

"You know what makes me think they were new? People do not normally park there. It makes no difference to the gate to the Reichenschmidt property as it opens in the opposite direction. But it could make it difficult for a car to leave the Schneider property; the right side of the gate might bump into the parked car when it is opened."

The next report in the folder piqued Annabelle's attention. Officer Marchand first noted that he had received the notes which Stephane's private investigator had provided. Just as Stephane had, he conceded that though all three witnesses did have circumstances in their past they might not want uncovered the two who seemed to be most relevant to the current investigation were Jules and Rose Prestat. The fact that both had gambling debts from time to time would suggest a need for money. Edith would clearly potentially be a source of money, though Officer Marchand remarked that the way to get the money most likely did not fit with murdering the person. At best, one might emit certain threats but killing the golden goose would forever deprive the criminal from access to the money; the victim's estate it would pass onto her heirs, and who knows whether the heirs would keep any of it. In passing, he added that the only rationale behind a murder would be that the person in need of money would have been caught by Mrs. Edith in the act of stealing something, ostensibly to resell it and use the proceeds to pay back their debt.

The report presented Officer Marchand's current evidence for or against a murder by an intruder. The first comment noted that all three witnesses would have had a way of murdering Mrs. Edith. All three had sufficient strength in their hands to strangle her and all three had access to her bedroom, with Rose Prestat having by far the easiest access. All three had what looked like solid alibis, though the alibis were virtually unverifiable: they claimed to be sleeping. How does one prove or disprove that unless Marie was prepared to denounce her husband or vice versa, which had not happened.

Officer Marchand further noted that two sleeping pills and a sleeping capsule appeared to have been consumed. He discussed the fact that there were at least four, maybe five different scenarios that would be consistent with the facts. The first would be that Jules did get one tablet for Maria and took one himself. This would leave open the question as to who used the missing pill from Rose's toiletry kit. The second would be that Jules got two tablets for Marie, suggesting that he wanted her to be sound asleep, hypothetically while he was dealing with Edith. An alternative was that Jules had used the second tablet to sedate the dog. Another alternative in the same vein was that Marie pretended to take a pill but did not consume it, and, having waited for Jules to fall asleep with the tablet he had absorbed, she would use the one she should have taken on the dog. In fact, a variant would be that she used the pill when she prepared the dog's food the prior evening, when Jules would then have only taken one pill from the bottle when he got it for Marie.

The problem with either of these two variants in Officer Marchand's mind was twofold. First, it did not make sense to imagine that either Jules or Marie had felt a need to sedate the dog. Unless the reason they did it was that they had conspired with a third party to have Edith murdered. In that case, clearly, they would not have wanted the dog to bark, and he would likely have since he would not have known the actual murderer when he came. The second inconsistency in Officer Marchand's mind was that it did not answer the question of what happened to the pill from Rose's toiletry kit.

A final scenario would have Jules and Marie both take the tablets Marie indicated that they had and have Rose using a capsule from her toiletry kit to find a way to sedate the dog. She would likely not have had the occasion to place the powder in the food, as the dog was probably eating it as soon as Marie brought it to him. However, she could have had the opportunity to spike the dog's water. This brought back the notion of an intruder and might even be consistent with instructions given to the intruder to upturn and empty the dog's water bowl before leaving.

The final sentence in this report was telling, but showed that Officer Marchand was still far from a conclusion:

"Nothing that we could charge anyone with at this point."

The next paragraph provided a list of the key questions which Officer Marchand needed to answer. Not surprisingly he felt he needed to resolve the question of the sleeping pills, and he noted that he should visit a veterinarian with the exact formula of each of the two types of medicine and ask what reaction he would expect consuming one of them would create in a dog of Marroik's size; secondarily, if the sleeping medicine had been dissolved in the dog's water would he have been likely to consume enough of it? He was still looking for motives both for the murder and, if possible, for its timing. His notes said that he needed to talk anew to the three witnesses to understand the more detailed timing of certain events. A final comment simply said:

"Mrs. Prestat wants to go back to Paris; I cannot prevent her from leaving, but I need her under discreet surveillance there."

The next sheet of paper in the folder brought everything to a head. Attached to it was a yellowed photocopy of an article in the Journal de Geneve, entitled: "Burglary at Murder Site." Bottom line, someone had broken into the main house at the Versoix property. Though no one had been killed, the intruder had used a gun, twice. First, he had shot at the German Shepherd; second, he had shot at Marie. The crime occurred around 2:00 a.m.

Officer Marchand was naturally asked to expand his investigation into the murder to include the burglary. He noted in his report that, the prior morning, he had allowed Mrs. Prestat to return to Paris, against a commitment on her part to make herself available if he called on her. He also mentioned that, as a precaution, he placed a notice in the Interpol system to have her under surveillance while in Paris. Yet, his notice and his comments in the report both bemoaned the fact that there was not enough conclusive evidence to place her in preventative detention, though there were several indices that pointed to her as a prime suspect. He however added that Jules could not be exculpated, as his suddenly leaving the Versoix residence at around 1:30 a.m. the morning of the burglary was decidedly suspect.

According to the police documents, Jules declared that he received an anonymous letter dropped in the family mailbox asking him to be in Lausanne at 2:00 a.m. the following morning, in front of the side door in the bell tower of Eglise Reformée St-François. He would then be given evidence that could clear him of any suspicion in the murder of Mrs. Edith and disclose the name of the culprit. When he asked her the question, Marie told Officer Marchand that there had been a lot of back and forth between the two of them on what Jules should do. Her position, she claimed, was that he should take the letter to the police and ask for help. His position, still according to Marie, was that he was tired of being under suspicion when he knew very well that he was sound asleep when the murder was committed. Marie conceded that she was sorry to see him go, but he had made her promise that she would not call the police unless he was not home by 5:00 a.m. the next morning. She was sobbing, according to the report, when she saw him leave and was worried that she would never see him alive again; she worried that the letter was a trap.

Marie's testimony then shifted to the next hour after Jules left the house, using the car that was still in the garage and which he felt freer to use since Mrs. Edith's death. She said that she had trouble going to sleep but refrained from taking any sleeping pill as she wanted to be fully awake when Jules returned. She still said that she set the alarm clock for 5:00 a.m. to be sure. She claimed that she had finally fallen asleep when she awoke suddenly at what she said was the sound of a gunshot. She said that she could not say where the gunshot was fired, other than being adamant that it had to have been fired within the property or if not just outside the gate. Officer Marchand asked whether she had heard anything before. Her reply was unclear, as she said she had not but was not sure. In fact, she added that she had been dreaming that the dog was barking. Hearing no additional sound, and not hearing the dog back led her to slip back into somnolence.

She claimed that she was then awakened by what she said was the sound of a door banging against its frame. She was sure it was not the door to their apartment on top of the garage, so it had to be the back door to the house. She said she got up, threw a robe over her shoulders, and ran down the stairs to see what was going on. She saw the house's service door ajar and heard steps as if someone was running in the garden. Looking toward the gate, she could see someone dressed in dark clothes and wearing a mask and a black beret nearly at the gate. He was carrying something, but she could not tell what; it did not look overly bulky. She yelled at him and in response the intruder fired one shot in her direction. It grazed her left ankle and she fell on the grass, probably more from the shock than the pain. She said that she then heard a car's engine being started and revved up as the thief fled. She managed to get back on her feet as the wound was superficial and ran to the gate where she found Marroik bleeding on the ground; she concluded that the shot had been fired from across the gate into the garden. She ran back to the house, called the vet first and the police second. Officer Marchand interrupted:

"At what time did you call us?"

"I'm not sure because I did not take the time to look at the clock, but it had to have been around 4:00 a.m."

Less than an hour later, as she was attending the vet who had arrived to treat the dog he had carried into the main house, she heard a car entering the property through the gate that had been left open. It was Jules who was driving back from Place St-François in Lausanne, where he said he waited I vain for an hour for someone to show up. He had in fact returned as he had suggested before 5:00 a.m.

Chapter Twenty-three

2001
NAPLES, FLORIDA, AND VERSOIX, SWITZERLAND

Jim Henderson had asked Annabelle and me to go with him to Geneva, at his firm's expense. He had booked us into the Hotel des Bergues, one of the top ten five-star hotels there and often argued to really be the best. Located on the right bank of the Rhone River right after it flows out of Lake Geneva, the hotel is perfectly sited being both quite close to the fancy places on the right bank and across the bridge from the Rue du Rhone, the main luxury commercial artery of the left bank in Geneva. Jim had arranged three different meetings and had obtained that we would be allowed to attend them with him: first with Edith's lawyer, Erik Sutter; second with her banker, Jean-Yves Lemieux and third, accompanied by Erik Sutter at the Geneva Free Port to inspect what was in storage.

Erik Sutter was initially somewhat surprised by the request for a meeting. He was indeed Stephane's local attorney, but he wondered what he should discuss with Stephane's U.S. attorney. Jim assured him that his goal was simply to find out whether he had himself forgotten something as he was settling Stephane's son's estate. He had just managed to clear that initial hurdle when the issue of having us in the meeting with him raised further questions and an additional discomfort in Erik Sutter's mind. Jim helped him over the objection by arguing that we were instrumental in bringing up some hitherto ignored information that was relevant to both Stephane's and his son Jack's estates. As rehearsed earlier, Jim explained to him that our goal was not to obtain anything for ourselves, but rather potentially to help achieve a goal which Stephane Schneider had left in both his will and in the letter of wishes. Jim had taken the precaution of having the two documents available so that Erik could consult them and see for himself. Erik Sutter still asked:

"Mr. and Mrs. De Barral, I must tell you that I do not understand your role, or rather your motivation. Yet, if it is to foster some wish that my client might have had, let's talk about it."

Before I could reply, Jim asked whether Erik had chosen to liquidate any of Stephane's estate at this death. He replied that he did not have instructions to do anything other than to keep everything as it was prior to his death. Having thus heard that the foreign assets whose existence we suspected were still around, I spoke up, directing myself principally to Erik:

"Please understand that I fully sympathize with your hesitation. I would react the same way if placed in the same situation."

As I continued and I started explaining what Annabelle and I had just been through, he seemed touched when I discussed the situation from the heart rather than from the head. I conceded that the purchase which we made at the consignment shop was a life changer for us. I humbly admitted that though we were relatively well off in our own right, both because of our work and because of our parents, our financial position was completely changed by the actual value of what we had purchased. I then said that this life change made us feel indebted to Stephane and David Schneider, more so than to Jack Schneider, as it was because of what they built and how they managed it that we had come into "our share" of their wealth. Rhetorically, I asked:

"Place yourself in our shoes, would you not feel that you owe the family something?"

He did not respond, though Annabelle swore that he had batted his eyelids. She took over:

"We have gone through most if not all the documents which they had carefully hidden away. In fact, for a while until informed by Jim Henderson that such was not a necessity, we even wondered whether we were the rightful owners of what we had bought."

She paused and took a sip of the cup of coffee with the dark Swiss chocolate tablet that had appeared in front of her on the table. Then she added:

"Assume with me that you just found out someone's wishes; not through hearsay, but because you have found a document which has these wishes in black and white. Now knowing that nobody would know of either the assets or the wishes if we did not reach out, would you not have tried to help the person's wishes be fulfilled, had you been in our place?"

Somehow her delivery and tone seemed to strike more of a chord with Erik Sutter who said that he understood. In fact, he briefly thanked both of us for what we were doing for his late client. Jim added to the narrative by saying both that we had agreed to help with the creation and initial management of the foundation which had been set up, and that we had indicated that we would surely donate some of what we had bought. Regaining his Swiss caution and cynicism, Erik interrupted:

"Are they getting paid?"

Jim beat us to the punch:

"Other than my firm covering their expenses, I give you my word of honor and would be happy to document it in writing that their work is free of charge to the estate."

Erik looked almost embarrassed and said:

"I am sorry if the question was offensive, but you will understand that I had to ask it."

Jim replied that he understood and that was why he was prepared to file an affidavit to that effect if necessary. Jim turned to the question of Edith's estate and asked Erik if the information which he had was correct, adding that he believed that her entire estate was bequeathed to her brother and if he was deceased to his descendants. Erik confirmed that this was correct and, prepared as he was for the meeting, he produced a copy of Edith's will. Jim looked it over, asking Annabelle to translate it into English for him, and compared it to the document which Edith had sent to her brother when she finalized her will. She had by then received the funds from the two life insurances for Jean and Albert and was getting everything in order, preparing as she was to consider moving to the U.S., permanently. Indeed, she wanted, as her brother had advised her to do, to maintain two sets of assets, those that everybody knew about and would bring with her to the U.S. and the others. Jim was gratified to conclude that the two documents were almost perfect overlaps, translation variation uncertainties aside.

These "formalities" behind us we were able to dig into the documents together with the various compilations which had been made first by Annabelle and me, and second by Jim's law clerk. Thankfully, as many of his compatriots, Erik Sutter's English was more than passable, allowing us to dispense with the inefficiency of having to translate back and forth. Our purpose was to ensure that we had everything covered and that the two sources to which we had access, Stephane's documents, and Edith's estate filings, would overlap perfectly. Any deviation from one or the other would be an indication that we had a problem which needed addressing. We were all delighted to see that there was an almost faultless overlap, except that Stephane was not aware of certain financial details. Edith had indeed at one point transferred all the accounts she had in Paris. Though the amounts were not terribly material in the greater scheme of things, she maintained a couple of savings accounts which were not listed. Erik noted that they had all been consolidated after her death, after he had conferred with her private banker.

Erik then directed everyone's attention to the other significant discrepancy. He reminded the group that the house in Versoix was not to be sold until Edith's domestic help no longer needed it. He therefore pointed to two additional items on his list: the proceeds from the house which had been paid into her bank account and the furnishings, furniture, and artwork, which had been added to everything that was in storage at Geneva Free Port. I remembered a letter from Edith to Stephane in which she discussed leaving some money for her domestic help and asked if that was in any way significant. Erik said that it really was not. That is when he told us that she had bought a second-to-die annuity which paid to her domestic help what they needed, adding:

"That annuity terminated when the last one of them died."

Out of the blue I asked whether anyone had investigated the furniture that was in storage to check whether any of the antiques might have secret or hidden compartments. Seeing the eyes of Erik Sutter open as wide as they could with surprise at the question, I explained that these were the places where we found all the documents we retrieved:

"They were in Stephane's furniture which his son Jack had inherited."

Erik looked again somewhat embarrassed to admit that he surely had not looked. He wondered what could be there. I simply replied:

"The real answer is we don't know. However, Annabelle and I learned a lot about secret compartments as we wrestled with the furniture we had bought. We might thus be able to help when the time comes. "

I noted that we had found old French Franc notes which had turned out to be near worthless. Erik could only say that we should discuss that when we were due to visit her banker.

To say that Officer Marchand, who had rushed to the house in Versoix after Marie had called, was not happy would be the understatement of the century. He was in particular very critical of Jules for not having brought him into the loop before going on what he called "his wild goose chase." More pointedly, he added:

"Don't you realize that this makes you a prime suspect in the second crime and could well point to your involvement in the first? Plus, even if what you're saying is true, you could easily have been killed if somebody had shown up!"

Jules was quite flustered, and the report said that he would not look his wife straight in the eyes as he replied to initial questions. Officer Marchand knew from Marie that she had tried to talk him out of going and had lost that battle. Turning back toward Jules, Officer Marchand said:

"I am going to have to detain you at the station and ask you a whole lot more questions."

Jules could only reply:

"How can you even suspect me? How can you imagine me shooting Marroik?"

He paused, wiping a tear from his eyes and added:

"Where was he shot?"

Marie was about to answer when Officer Marchand prevented her, saying:

"That is why I must detain you, Jules. There are things which you know and things which you should not know if you were not connected to the crime. That is why I cannot allow you to speak to your wife before you have answered all our questions."

With this, he ordered his sergeant to take Jules to the station. Marie was crying and Officer Marchand simply said:

"It's for his own good. We need to investigate the whole situation. The tire marks in front of the gate and on the pathway to your garage, do they belong to one car or two cars? What does Jules know and what does he not know? That's why I did not want you to tell him where the dog was when he was shot. That's also why I wanted him to be taken away before you said that you had been shot at. If he knows you've been shot at, then he must somehow be in the loop, maybe not the shooter, but a co-conspirator. If he does not know, it does not make him innocent, but it removes some suspicion. I could go on, but I hope you understand."

Marie nodded between sniffles. She added that she was afraid to spend the night alone at the house. Officer Marchand offered to find her safe accommodation at a hotel nearby. All of a sudden, she blurted:

"Wait a minute. Marroik was shot because he was barking at the gate. He surely would not have been barking at Jules if he had been the one trying to get in. He knows Jules. Most likely he would have tried to jump all over him and lick his face."

"This is a perfectly good point, Marie. Let me ask you another question: how does the dog behave when the *Citroën* comes back, say if Jules has taken it to run errands?"

"He runs toward it but has learned not to get too close to avoid being hit. A bit like shepherd dogs always do with cattle: scare the animals but avoid being hit by a hoof. Anyway, when the car comes back, he does not bark; at most he lets a few yaps go, but you could not confuse these semi-high pitches with his deep bark."

"Well, this is one more potential sign that him running to the gate and barking would more likely than not suggest that the car that was approaching was not the *Citroën and that whoever was driving it was not Jules."*

Marie was starting to relax and smile. She might have reacted differently if she had read the last paragraphs written by Officer Marchand in his report:

"Though it looks like Jules is unlikely to be the thief, he could have commanded the crime. He certainly could benefit from selling the contents of the artist folder, which according to Marie might include two dozen or more drawings and etchings. Jules not being there at the time of the theft was at the same time a blessing for him and for the thief. It certainly helped the thief who, had he not allowed the service door to slam and not even shut fully, might have escaped without being noticed other than by the dog. Not being there was also a good thing for Jules if he was a co-conspirator: had he been there indeed, he would have been expected to get up and chase the thief, which would have greatly complicated matters.

Though this does not directly play into the case of the murder of Mrs. Edith, it should be noted that the motive for killing her might simply be to allow someone to have freer access to some of the assets she kept in the house. Jules was in the house at the time of the murder, but allegedly sound asleep. He could claim to be asleep then because he did not have to interact with the intruder. First, one wonders what Jules would have to gain from Edith's murder, unless it was a means to an end . . . Remove the owner to steal enough from her house to pay back all debts and return to the life he knew and liked in France. What does that say about Marie? Is she a simple by-stander or a link in the chain?"

Chapter Twenty-four

2001
NAPLES, FLORIDA, AND GENEVA, SWITZERLAND

Our visit with Jim Henderson to Jean-Yves Lemieux was pretty much a carbon copy of the meeting with Erik Sutter. However, as we had taken the precaution of having Erik Sutter come with us, Jean-Yves's initial reluctance was overcome much more quickly and without the need for us to give a blow-by-blow account of our adventure. Jim was able to obtain a market value report of Edith's remaining financial assets and to give instructions, in his capacity as executor of Jack's estate, for the assets to be cautiously liquidated and the funds remitted to an account he had opened in the U.S. in the name of the newly created Schneider Foundation.

Our next visit proved to be quite interesting, particularly as it allowed Annabelle and me to discover something which is known by name but remains a real secret. The Geneva Free Port is said to host the world's largest art collection with an estimated value in the tens of billions of U.S. Dollars. Again, though there is no official tabulation offered, the Free Port is said to hold a collection containing 1.2 million pieces; as a matter of comparison, the

Louvre in Paris is said to own 380,000 pieces of which no more than 35,000 are typically on display at any one moment in time; and the New York Museum of Modern Art owns "only" 200,000 artworks. Furthermore, it has been estimated that works by the greatest and most sought-after artists such as Da Vinci, Monet, Renoir, and Van Gogh to name but a few with which Annabelle or I are quite familiar make up a large part of the total. In fact, many people consider the Free Port as the world's largest museum, albeit one which nobody can visit.

Though the Free Port was originally located in La Praille, an industrial area only a few kilometers away from the French border, it has grown over the years and come to consist of several warehouses scattered across the Canton of Geneva. The need for space has indeed increased manifold, with the Free Port called to host wine collections—it is considered the world's largest cellar—or even classic car collections as it would be the world's largest garage were it not for the free-standing parking structures which have popped around the world or car dealers' lots in the U.S.

The minibus organized by Erik Sutter dropped us in front of a large, windowless concrete block surrounded by barbed-wire fences. We were told that it stood above extensive basements, representing the tip of an "iceberg" designed to resist natural catastrophes, such as earthquakes and fires. Erik who had made the appointment managed to get all of us into what Annabelle whimsically called the "dungeon." We entered a non-descript hall with a bank of three elevators on the far side of the room. Additionally, there were doors leading to what we assumed were galleries at the back and on the sides of the room. Once having again produced our credentials and gotten them approved, we were led by two men, both of whom were in military-like uniforms and ostensibly armed, to an elevator which took us to the fourth floor, where our "room" awaited us.

Getting there from the elevator required us to walk along a maze of corridors with nameless armored doors every ten to twenty meters (thirty to sixty yards) on both sides. Judging by the door of our room after it was opened, each of these doors had one panel that had to be at least six inches thick if not more, and, right behind it, there was an additional steel door with vertical bars. They gave access to a large hygrometry-measured and temperature-controlled room. The entry to each room frankly looked to me more like what one finds in the vaults of many a bank than somewhere where I would expect to find works of art. These doors, which are supposed to hold out against explosives, were each equipped with biometric readers to limit access to those who were allowed in. In this instance, Erik Sutter was the prime permit holder, though he assured us that his firm had two other individuals either of whom would succeed him should he no longer be available. There was no risk of ever being locked out of access to the room in perpetuity.

Erik told us an interesting anecdote. He said he had heard that quite a few masterpieces had been bought and sold several times, without ever leaving the Free Port. Indeed, the port serves as a secret and quiet locale where trading in art can take place without attracting taxes or being known by the custom administration. Thus, both buyer and seller would typically house their own collections in the Free Port; any transaction simply involved the object being transferred from one vault to another. I could not resist noting:

"This is an invitation to trade in stolen goods. How does one control for that?"

Erik looked mildly embarrassed and simply replied that he knew the topic had come up several times and added:

"There is a lot of resistance as you can imagine. Lots of very powerful interests. Just like bank secrecy. But I don't doubt that things will eventually perhaps change before I retire and most likely before any child of mine retires."

The door we had just opened had only one marking, which consisted of four digits: 4.21.2. We entered the space which I found surprisingly large. I noticed that one of the men who had accompanied us took a position outside of the armored door, ostensibly to shut the door with the vertical bars and maybe even the main door if there was any menace to us. The other walked in with us and took a position just inside of the frame of the armored door, right next to the small panel which would read the biometric inputs as and when we desired to leave. I was told that the original room was smaller, in fact that there were two rooms, one for Mr. Schneider and one for Mrs. Dumas-Schneider. However, everything had been consolidated into this single room after Mrs. Dumas-Schneider had died. The room therefore contained works that had belonged to Edith as well as to Stephane.

My biggest surprise was that the goods were not all packed up as if ready to be moved; a few pieces were hung from the walls. As a whole, however, the goods were not ready for display either, as they were simply placed on nice "storage" shelves. I noted an interesting vertical contraption which held several paintings vertically in display frames that rotated around a vertical axis. I was told that this would allow an owner to come and admire several pieces of his collection; he would sit on the nearby sofa and use a remote-control unit to call the painting he wanted to see; once done with that painting, he could call another one. We were told that this setup was in fact not the latest available version, as there were even more complex systems. Erik pointed to the opposite corner of the room and said:

"See the sofa and a couple of armchairs, together with a coffee table in the far-right corner. That's the way it used to be. Owners would come and have a couple of people with them who would use the half walls around that area to present some or all of the collection."

He paused and added:

"When an owner does not simply want to admire something but is in fact considering selling it, he would come with a couple of people again, but would have them remove the one or two pieces he may be selling, and they would take them to one of the spaces reserved for trading. The center has a private gallery or a space that could be used by anyone, only one at a time obviously."

It was clear that Erik had finished his introduction, which, speaking for myself, was surely an eye opener: I had never seen anything like this and was pretty sure I would never again visit the place. Jim and Erik turned to Annabelle and me as Erik asked:

"How do you want to proceed? Do you want to check each piece against this detailed inventory? I know you have yours, but I believe we have agreed that they are both quite similar, except for the furniture which we added after the house in Versoix was sold. Or do you want to check only a few pieces?"

I replied that my main concern, and Jim's as I suspected, related to the antique furniture. We were not looking to discover pieces whose existence we ignored. I wanted to check if any of the pieces might hide any secret. Erik noted that this should not take too long as he could only see a limited number of items, though he added:

"As I just said, the furniture and artworks from Versoix were moved here, as I did not know what should or should not be kept.

However, it is segregated in this corner, and I even had the staff place these half walls so that we could easily delineate them from the rest."

I could not resist asking:

"I can see a few other half walls. What are they for?"

"Oh. Simple. I should have told you earlier. They divide the non-Versoix stuff into three unequal areas. Here you have Mrs. Dumas-Schneider goods, there you have the goods which jointly belong to Mrs. Dumas-Schneider and Mr. Schneider, which they inherited from their mother, and over there are the goods that belong to Mr. Schneider, which I believe all came to him from his father."

I smiled and jokingly added:

"And in the right corner you have what I'll call the special viewing area . . . Frankly, I am not sure it is terribly necessary as all descendants are by now deceased . . . Who would ask to view the canvases?"

Erik smiled. Annabelle beat me to the punch saying that, to her uneducated eyes at least, there were certain pieces of furniture which looked exceptional and others that looked more common. I agreed and, looking around, elected to focus on a half a dozen pieces, all dating from a period starting with the Regence (which covered the time between the death of Louis XIV – 1715—and the time when Louis XV was old enough to reign—1723) and ending with the death of Louis XVI in 1793. I noted that there was no desk, though there were several chests of drawers, at least four secretaries, two of which looked like the one we bought and the other two much smaller, with a sloping folding top, three dressing tables and two large armoires. I elected to ignore the chairs, dining room table, sideboards, armchairs and even a nice Louis XV sofa. It was not a case of any of these not being nice—I would quite easily have had any of them in our house. It was simply that I discounted the odds of anything being hidden within them. Yet I added:

"Erik, we will need complete inspections of any piece of furniture before it is sold. We do not want to presume there is nothing and miss out on something important. But right now, if you agree, let's focus on those pieces most likely to hold anything interesting."

Erik nodded.

Annabelle and I decided to divide and conquer. She chose the two secretaries which looked like the one we had bought, on the grounds that she knew what we had done and could repeat our maneuvers, though she quickly discovered that the inside of each piece was different and neither looked exactly like the one we had. She let me deal with the smaller secretaries, which were often called sloping desks as the desk could be used when the folding top had been brought down from its resting inclined position to the horizontal. Though there were two small drawers on the front and below the horizontal axis around which the top revolved, there was nothing further down. Both pieces, which tended often to be used by women, were stunningly beautiful, with marquetry involving the wood of several fruit trees, as well as bronze ornaments at the top of each of the two front legs. They ostensibly dated back to Louis XV. I quickly located the woodworker signature, the same for both, Pierre Roussel.

Inside both, the number of possible hidden compartments was limited, if only by the relatively small volume of the space under the folding top. I quickly dispensed with the compartment that was just at the back of the articulation of the folding top. It was empty and did not seem to include any trigger mechanism. On the first piece I inspected, I found two small compartments which opened in an odd fashion: instead of popping forward, they popped up. There was one on either side in the body of the desk, at the back. I almost dejectedly noted that there were only a few gold ingots in each. I was smiling interiorly noting that I would be jumping up and down if I had found anything like that in a piece of furniture I had bought before the consignment shop adventure. The other sloping top desk proved a variant on the same scheme; ostensibly, Pierre Roussel had not been asked to be very original in his triggering mechanisms. Again, a few loose gemstones were found, one of which, a nice emerald-cut emerald was in a pouch with the mention that it should be given to the first male grandchild to use as the engagement ring he would give to his fiancée.

Annabelle was not more successful than I was from the point of view of finding interesting documents or something pointing to another batch of family heirloom. Yet, she did find a few letters, apparently addressed to Martha, David Schneider's wife, from Stephane and Edith. The letters, somewhat of an important tradition at that time in France, were sent by each child on the first day of the year and offered their best wishes to their parents for the coming year and thanked them for whatever "special favor" they felt they had received during the prior one. The letters were written in French and Annabelle simultaneously felt touched by how nice a custom they were and embarrassed that she was reading such private correspondence. I simply said that they would make wonderful exhibits in the museum the foundation was going to build.

We also found a few drawings done by Stephane or Edith when they were children in the middle drawers of one of the armoires, together with a collection of mementos which had to have been assembled when the children were very young. There was also a nice collection of family pictures, though, unfortunately, there was no legend to tell who was who. I winked at Annabelle as I turned to Jim to say that several of these would be wonderful when displayed in the foundation museum, I was now convinced we were about to build, though I wondered how we could figure out the identity of the main characters. Always the logical lawyer, Jim simply replied that there were enough that they might be able to do so through multiple comparisons.

Annabelle and I had the definite feeling that we were through with our discoveries. That some stuff might possibly still be left out did not seem probable but was always possible. Though Edith had indeed received the two life insurances that had been bought on the lives of her husband and her son, there was no trace anywhere that she might have inherited anything from her late husband's family. That gave us an idea. We both went straight for the corner of the room where furniture from Versoix had been placed. We identified what we believe had to have been Edith's personal desk. We could not take much credit as it was the only very nice piece of furniture in the Versoix lot. It was a Louis XVI cylinder desk, with three drawers set horizontally above the cylinder and three drawers below; it was covered with fine marquetry and had simple yet very elegant bronze decorations at the base of the legs and at their feet.

We rolled the cylinder back and were delighted to see the usual central well at the back of the writing surface which we had found in several other pieces. We slid the two wooden panels which were above it and found a couple of folders which seemingly nobody had even looked at. Jim asked Erik:

"Did anybody look into any of these pieces of furniture after Edith died?"

"Not really. I am told that Marie had gone through her personal effects and discarded or given away what she deemed not needed, but I do not believe anyone investigated any of the drawers."

I interjected:

"Hold it there. From what we know, the house had been left to her domestic help. Doesn't that mean that they would have used that furniture for themselves?"

Erik replied:

"Excellent question. Unfortunately, as we all know, they are now deceased, and we cannot ask them any question."

I felt I needed to ask that someone take a close look at everything that came from Versoix, if only because one would probably not want to sell pieces of furniture with personal documents in them. Jim seconded my point and offered to provide help to go through that task. That episode led to an interesting though short debate with Erik asking:

"Jim, do you want anything you do not want to keep sold here and the money sent to the U.S., or should we send all the goods to the U.S. and let you take care of selling what you do not need?"

Jim seemed to hesitate for a short while. This allowed me to offer a thought, though I was increasingly wondering why I felt so personally implicated in these decisions. I suggested that antique, period furniture prices have not been doing well in Europe, in part because younger buyers were more interested in practicality than historical worth or artistic significance. I mentioned that we had noted this fact when we visited a few auction houses in the South of France and had been flabbergasted at how cheap certain surely valuable pieces were selling. From that, I concluded that good quality French furniture, particularly if they could be said to be period furniture and not only furniture in the style of a period, would most likely get a better price in the U.S. Jim did not seem to disagree when Annabelle offered the cherry on top of the cake:

"We must bring some of the high-quality stuff anyway. So, while we need a container, we might as well be sure it is as full as possible."

Chapter Twenty-five

2001 AND 1948
NAPLES, FLORIDA, AND VERSOIX, SWITZERLAND

Meanwhile the official police investigations continued. One could almost say that it was accelerating as the original focus on a murder had just been augmented to include a theft involving breaking and entering as well as the use of a firearm twice.

With respect to the murder, the investigation had not made significant further progress. Officer Marchand's report clearly noted that he was still far from having any hard proof or even a motive. The points he was making in the report were indeed all conjectural, but they did seem to point in the direction of a criminal conspiracy. Indices had been identified to suggest a murder committed by some outside intruder: tire traces right outside of the gate and the fact that the dog did not bark, among others. Officer Marchand still noted that he had contacted Interpol asking for legal and discreet surveillance of Mrs. Prestat's whereabouts, particularly as it related to two items: gambling and the sale of works of art.

The convenient absence of Jules at the time of the break-in and the theft, and a desire to prevent any direct conversation between him and his wife in the early stage of the theft investigation had led Officer Marchand to place him in custody, at least for as long as he needed to complete his questioning. The continuation of Officer Marchand's report noted that Jules appeared contrite, maybe because he had not even met anyone. He suddenly realized that he was more a suspect than a witness and, to make matters worse, he did not have anyone to defend his alibi. He was able to produce the anonymous letter that gave him the appointment, though Officer Marchand noted he told him that anyone, himself included, could have prepared it. Officer Marchand continued the questioning asking for facts that Jules should not know if he was not guilty:

"Do you know when the crime was committed?"

"The only response I can give you is that I left the house just around 1:00 a.m. and returned just before 5:00 a.m. So, the crime had to be committed in that time window."

"What did you do as you waited for your rendezvous in Lausanne?"

"Initially, I stepped out of the car and paced the pavement along the north side of the church. Then I decided to walk around the church to avoid looking like I was on patrol. You know, Officer, an hour is a long time, particularly when you're waiting."

"You stayed out of the car the whole time?"

"No. It was parked right on the plaza by the north side of the church. Eventually, I got tired of walking and went back and sat in it. Before that, I turned the car around so that I would be facing the church and see whomever I was supposed to meet, if he or she was coming from that direction. By the way, a couple of times, I was a bit scared when I realized that I would not see anybody coming from behind. So, I positioned my rearview mirrors such that I could see anyone who would be approaching from the left rear of the car."

"Back to the scene of the crime. How many shots were fired?"

"Again, officer, I don't know. In fact, how would I know since one thing is clear: I was not there."

"I see. How many shots do you believe were fired?"

"Again, how would I know? I do know that whoever the intruder was, he shot at Marroik. How many shots, I would not know. By the way, how is the dog?"

Officer Marchand replied that no vital organ or bone had been hit and that the wound was thus only muscular, near the top of the right shoulder. He added that the dog's life was not in danger and turning to Jules he cautioned:

"That's not necessarily good news for you from our point of view. We knew you loved the dog and if you were involved you could well have asked that any shot fired not kill the dog."

Jules broke down. Sobbing he pleaded:

"I'm done. How can I prove anything? See what you just did. To you, the fact that I would not hurt the dog does not mean that I would not have fired at him. Rather, combined with the fact I was not there means that I had asked for the dog's life to be spared. Not fair."

He paused and then regaining his posture he turned the tables around and asked:

"By the way, from the time parameters I gave you, the shot was fired between 1:00 a.m. and 5:00 a.m. I would guess it was earlier than 5:00 a.m. because you and the vet were already there when I arrived. Agreed?"

"Agreed. Where are you going with that?"

"Simple, Officer Marchand, have you ever tried to shoot at a moving, barking dog which is partially black, in the dark, and honestly expect that you can control where he would be hit?"

"Interesting question, Jules. Interesting question. Now do you know what was stolen?"

"Sure don't. If there was only one person, it couldn't be furniture as that would be too heavy and bulky. I know that Mrs. Edith had a safe in her bedroom. Could the thief know that and have tried to break into it? I don't know what was in it, but you'd have to think it's valuable."

"I'll grant you that, but wouldn't that suggest more a casual thief rather than someone mandated to steal?"

"Maybe, maybe not. Do you know what was or is in the safe?"

"No, I don't."

"Well, imagine that the thief was looking for valuables, wouldn't a safe be the first place he'd look?"

"Grant you that. So, you don't know what was stolen?"

Jules was adamant:

"No, I don't. What else could have been stolen? First, I'll assume right away the silverware as it is quite bulky, though she had a few large silver vessels. Could these have been stolen? There are nice paintings about the house, though I could not tell you which is worth a lot, and which is simply worth a more modest sum."

He paused and with an air of renewed desperation on his face said:

"Officer, I am back to my earlier point: how can I prove not only that I did not do it, but that I did not conspire with someone else to have it done? I'd hate to keep going with a list of things to steal. Eventually, I might stumble on whatever was stolen. Will that prove that I was in on it?"

Officer Marchand noted in his report that he told Jules that he understood his predicament. Yet, Jules should know that the only way to get to the truth short of a confession, someone caught red-handed, or an unexpected witness showing up out of nowhere is to keep asking questions. He did not say it but made a note to the effect that the one way to catch Jules would be for him to say something which he could not have known without being involved. Another interesting side note made by the officer though he mentioned he did not say anything to Jules was that the idea of him having a rendezvous in a different canton could be misinterpreted as trying to muddy the waters. It would surely be easier for Officer Marchand to hear from a colleague in the Canton de Geneve than from an officer in the neighboring canton.

Officer Marchand freed Jules to go back to the house in Versoix, in fact, arranging transportation for him. The rationale for releasing Jules once the paperwork he filled out was that the only two things which Jules seemed to ignore were first that somewhat had shot at Marie and that the thief left with Mrs. Edith's favorite artist folder with all the sketches, drawings, and etchings.

Officer Marchand went back to visit Bernard Reinhold, hoping that he would have heard or better yet seen some of the developments the night of the theft. Bernard smiled as Officer Marchand told him of his hopes and simply replied:

"You're in luck officer. I had a terrible night. I heard a lot of commotion."

"Where should we start?"

"Well, I can tell you that a car left the property around 1:00 a.m. It was right after the bell had rung once, though I forced myself to stay awake until the next ring. It would have been 1:00 a.m. if I heard a single ring the next time, as it would then be 1:15 a.m. The problem would be if the bell had rung twice the next time: the single ring I had first heard would be the strike for 15 minutes after the hour."

Officer Marchand was ostensibly a bit annoyed at the length and detail of Bernard's explanations. Yet, he could not push him too hard, as his testimony could be crucial, if not to unveil completely new elements, but at least to corroborate some of the currently available information. He then asked:

"What did you hear next?"

"First, I heard the dog barking and then a gun shot. I know the dog and it sounded quite cross with something or someone. He barked for a minute or two and then I heard a single shot."

"Remember when?"

"I'd guess around 4:00 a.m., maybe a few minutes earlier, but certainly after 3:45 a.m. The bell ring issue again."

Officer Marchand noted that he interrupted the explanation, for fear he would have to go through all the unnecessary details again. He then asked:

"And then."

"The dog certainly stopped barking, though I think I heard him yelp. I was afraid he had been killed and was in death's agony. I was very sorry for him. Such a nice animal. Also, such a beautiful animal. Did you know that both his father and his mother were champions?"

"Didn't. Did you go out to check what was happening?"

"I have a window that opens to the back and from which I can see the front of the garden. So, my first reaction was to look from here after having switched all my lights off. Frankly, I could not see anything. It was pitch black out there."

"I see, and then?"

"Nothing for a few minutes. Maybe five or ten minutes. Then I saw a flashlight coming from the main house and moving toward the gate; remember it's a good 150 feet away from the house. Initially, I thought it had to be Jules or Marie running to take care of the dog. But I wondered why they waited so long."

"Makes sense, though would they not have come from the apartment on top of the garage and not the main house?"

Bernhard nodded but continued his explanation as if the question had not been asked:

"But then I saw the light on the floor above the garage come on, and then the light to the side of the garage as well. The person with the flashlight running toward the gate could not be Jules or Marie. It had to be an intruder. Then I saw someone, probably Marie since the person wore a robe, coming out of the side of the garage. She had her own flashlight and was yelling at the intruder. It's at that point that I was convinced the person that was running was a thief. I was looking for my own gun to run outside when I heard a second shot. I decided to be careful and rather than barging in on the scene I would walk to the other side of our own gate and confront him there. I would have had a much better shot, you know, with the lamps on either side of the gate to give me light. Then I heard a car racing away. I fired my two cartridges in the direction of the car, but it certainly did not stop it."

"That's very helpful. Anything else?"

"Just one. I had my flashlight in the pocket of my jacket. So, I went to look at the tire tracks. You can always see them if there are any in the early morning, with the dew and the fact that I water the flowers and the lawn at the base of the wall just before retiring to my bedroom, usually around 9:00 p.m. to 10:00 p.m. The ground is always wet or at least moist enough. Anyway, bottom line, I would bet that this car was the same as the one on the night of the murder."

Seeing the quizzical look on Officer Marchand's face, Bernard added:

"You are correct, Officer Marchand. As a former police officer, I must amend the statement. I can't say it's the same car, as I did not see the car the first time at least. But I'd say they're the same kind of tires. I am pretty sure they left the same marks."

"Did you hear anything after that?"

"Well, I ran to Marie to see if she needed help. She was not there. I assumed that she went to call you and the vet. She had left the dog by the gate. I went to see him and was happy he was breathing, but there was quite a bit of blood. So, I waited for Marie to come back. She had brought a wheelbarrow to carry the dog back to the house. I told her not to disturb him as we did not know where he had been hit; better wait for the vet. She went back to look for a blanket and returned to place it on the dog. A few minutes later, Marie told me to go back and rest. I had not quite fallen asleep when I heard one, then a second and then a third car. That must be when the vet and you all arrived."

Officer Marchand wrote two paragraphs to summarize the current state of his analysis, all the while being very careful not to go beyond what he knew for sure or had serious reasons to believe.

"The most important new element provided by Bernard Reinhold is the possibility that the cars that brought the murder suspect and the suspected thief to the house could be one and only one vehicle (request outstanding for an analysis of the tire tracks).

Not only would this lend more weight to the hypothesis that both crimes were committed by an intruder rather than by residents on the property, but it would shift the balance of probabilities toward Mrs. Prestat, though not totally. The more one leans toward the belief that the crimes were committed by one or several intruders, the more the hypothesis of a conspiracy must become credible. One could surely argue that both crimes were committed by different persons, however, that would not square with the current hypothesis that the same car was used by both perpetrators to get to and flee from the property, if one excludes the possibility that the car was a taxi, as one does not hail a taxi to go commit a crime, particularly the second one that involved the use of a firearm.

Both Jules and Mrs. Prestat had a possible motive to commit either or both crimes; the opportunity the crime might provide to steal valuable artworks from the deceased and to sell them, to pay debts, create more capital to gamble or both. Jules's deposition following the second crime seems believable and suggested that he is unaware of at least a couple of important elements: there having been more than one shot fired and the nature of the goods that were stolen. His major weakness is that he was absent for the whole period covering the second crime, so far with no witness to corroborate his having been on Place St-François in Lausanne for probably about an hour (request outstanding for any potential witness who would have seen either the car or someone pacing in the middle of the night around Place St. François in Lausanne).

Chapter Twenty-six

2001
NAPLES, FLORIDA

Jim Henderson had asked us to come and visit him when we had returned from the short trip to Switzerland. The day we showed up at his office, just north of Pelican Bay North Road, his mood perfectly matched the weather outside. Bright blue skies, flowers everywhere and the usual late summer humidity. We did not discuss it, but he knew, and we knew that we would almost certainly have our afternoon thunderstorm at some point between 2:00 p.m. and 7:00 p.m. Jim ushered us into a conference room which, facing due west gave us a distant view of the Gulf of Mexico. Unfortunately, the building being only a mid-rise, our view was partially obstructed by the top of palm, royal poinciana or banyan trees which one finds everywhere in southwest Florida.

Jim had considered the Geneva trip a success. All financial assets would be liquidated and paid into an account which he had opened in the name of the Schneider Foundation. As an aside, he mentioned that the total value of the financial assets was more than my estimates, but not by much. He indicated that he had already received a significant sum of money, adding that this would allow "us" as he put it to begin the work with respect to finding a locale for the foundation and its museum. I could not resist asking:

"What do you mean by "us" Jim?

Calmly and with a smile he replied that he would need someone to run the foundation at least on an interim basis and then said that he was hoping that I could help. I jumped up and had to tell him that I was still doing some wealth management consulting for a number of client families and that I was consequently not sure that I would have the time or the energy. That is when Annabelle surprised me. She reminded me, and by the same token Jim, that she had given up all remunerated activities when we moved to Southwest Florida and would thus be able to find the time to help, even if it meant that she had to give up some of what she was currently doing. Jim immediately asked:

"Would you be willing to be the founding CEO, Annabelle?"

"I would, but it should be clear between us three at least that I am not talking of a long-term permanent position. By the way, we had already had this conversation before the trip to Geneva. So, no change in our views. However, Mike and I are committed to reducing our activities to be able to spend more time on other things, such as being good grandparents and generous stewards of the graces we received from God."

I was stunned by her reply, not only because it was right on, but in part because she reminded me right there of the person I married so many years ago, as we were both working out of university. Then, she was assertive, determined, and full of energy; here she was again. I must confess that I had not had too many instances of seeing her interact with other people in a true business context. I had forgotten how forceful she could be when she had to. Jim asked if I would be willing to chair the board, which I fully agreed.

Annabelle was not joking about her duties in her newly minted role. Within a minute of being appointed CEO of the foundation she was fully committed to and involved in the work. She said:

"We need to hire someone who could serve as curator; neither Mike nor I have any experience in how you shape and present an art collection."

Pausing for a second, she added:

"Mike, we should ask Frank Smart . . ."

Jim interrupted asking who Frank Smart was, to which Annabelle simply replied that he was the senior art representative for Sotheby's in the area, adding:

"He helped us get an expert valuation for the first of the paintings we bought at the consignment shop. I'd like to have him on the board, possibly also having Jeff Baker, the impressionist specialist, based in New York."

Always the lawyer, Jim asked:

"Are you not concerned you may be privileging one auction house over the others?"

Annabelle fired right back:

"Why should I? They helped us for free on this very matter. We will not exclude anyone if we are, I mean the foundation is buying or selling, and I would expect Frank and Jim to abstain from voting if the question of using a competitor of theirs arose."

I could only say:

"Boy. You've thought this through!"

She just smiled. Jim then talked of the furniture and artwork and told us that, working with the Geneva Free Port storage arm, he had identified a moving company who would take care of bringing everything into Florida. Yet, he cautioned:

"We will have to say that everything goes to the Foundation otherwise the Florida Government might impose a sales tax on us as the goods come into the State."

I replied that this should not be a problem since it was our intention in the first place anyway. I casually added that one could always consider some form of barter where we could exchange a few of the things we do not need or want for one or another of the things that were in storage which we might wish we had. Jim added:

"The storage arm of Geneva Free Port is taking care of obtaining a valuation for all the goods. However, if that is OK with you, we might invite Sotheby's to provide their own input, for which they would naturally be paid provided it was reasonable. We need these valuations to determine the insurance that we must purchase to cover the goods while in transfer."

I could not resist asking:

"What good would insurance do for us?"

Jim looked quite surprised, though I was happy to see my wife smile. I replied to my own question:

"What would the foundation do with any money they would receive if the goods were lost at sea or stolen?"

Without giving Jim the time to reply and looking straight into Annabelle's eye I answered further my own question:

"Some money which could be used to repair or restore some item damaged in transit would surely be a good thing. But if the container fell into the ocean or burned, the whole reason for the Schneider Foundation would disappear with the collection."

Jim was beginning to understand. He volunteered:

"A bit like parents who take a huge medical insurance when their children travel without them but only have a nominal $1 life insurance . . ."

"Exactly. In the case of an accident, they have enough to afford the best medical care for an injured child, but they would not ever feel that they've made money on the death of the child."

I paused for a second and simply added:

"That's what my parents used to do when my brothers and I used to go on vacation, skiing or at the beach, without them."

Jim whistled his admiration. Bringing us back to the issue of the day, he indicated that our next order of business had to be twofold. Annabelle chimed in, arguing that, first, we had to figure out how much space we would need to present the collection in its best light and second, we needed to find an architect who would translate those needs into reality. I had to ask:

"Are you assuming that we cannot find any space already built? After all, the property debacle we've just been through because of the bursting of the "dot.com bubble" is presenting a few opportunities."

Annabelle replied that she believed that virtually any such plot of land would likely be in a strip mall or some shopping center. She argued:

"I just don't think that space in a strip mall or shopping center, however ritzy, even the Waterside, for instance, would work for us. Most if not all of them are privately owned; the risk that a private owner might at some point decide to redevelop a site is simply not acceptable. Don't you agree?"

Jim suggested that certain spots might in fact work:

"Think of the Waterside. Sure, it's privately owned. But I would have to bet that the foundation that stands behind Pelican Bay would surely have its word to say if a redevelopment of one part or another of the shopping mall was envisaged."

Annabelle fired right back:

"I'll grant you that. But we would not be in control. Should we not first look for some free-standing land on which we can locate our own purpose-built museum?"

Jim agreed that it would be good strategy to try for a free-standing entity first, adding that one could always change one's mind if realities started to conflict with our hypotheses. I could not help interiorly to think that Jim could have been a politician.

As it turned out, our hypotheses were in fact quite reasonable, though the museum ended up not being in Naples. Although the city of Naples was more than willing to help, essentially by giving the foundation a piece of land, we ended up locating the museum in Estero, two suburbs north of Naples. Bonita Springs, the suburb between Naples and Estero, would have loved to help, but there was no suitable piece of land that would simultaneously be readily accessible and not within an existing shopping locale. Estero, that at the time was nothing short of a boom town, still had plenty of land that could be given to the foundation, and they even offered concessions which made construction and future ownership cheaper.

The building was custom-designed and comprised a suite of offices for the staff which we knew would eventually be needed. Interestingly, to the extent that the main regional airport, Fort Myers, is in fact north of Naples, settling in Estero would bring the museum closer to the airport, while still being within easy commute from one of the myriad of hotels in the region catering to all budgets. Jokingly, Annabelle added:

"That's true, though it will be further from Naples Municipal Airport, where most private jets land . . ."

The most significant challenge related to selecting the pieces which would be displayed. Philip Paulsen, the person we hired as founding curator and who, in our opinion, had the width and breadth eventually to take the CEO job if he wanted to, had asked everyone that was involved to write their own short story of the Schneider family. Truth be known, that is why I started to write this, which eventually turned into a book covering the topic in greater depth and including details which did not belong in a museum that honored a family.

Everyone agreed that there were three main themes which deserved to be highlighted. First and foremost, the fact that love for art and support for emerging artists is both a wonderful gift and an opportunity to create a different kind of legacy. The second had to be concerned with the fate of Jews just before, during, and after the second world war, highlighting the need to flee, the challenges involved in the flight, and the strong family ties which the ordeal fostered. The third and final theme had to be dedicated to the birth, initial challenges, growth, and glorious fulfillment of the impressionist movement. Everyone also agreed that, particularly for the second theme, but also maybe for the other two, pictures of the family would be a forceful reminder that the foundation was celebrating a family, not just a random collection of wonderful art. Finally, on the strong impulsion of Annabelle, the group agreed that the careful use of a few pieces of furniture would allow the museum to have the feel of someone's house rather than a cold display hall. She reminded everyone of her love for the Frick Collection in New York or Musée Jacquemart-André in Paris; both museums were built in the respective mansions of two industrial tycoons to display, initially at least, the art they had acquired during their lifetime, leaving the visitor with the real feeling that he or she had been invited to visit someone's house.

Though not crucially important, an anecdote is worth telling here. Because of the desire to make the display halls look like the inside of a house, we were forced to have more than one floor to the museum. For once, I will take the credit for an idea which I believe is a nice touch: rather than using a bank of modern elevators, we elected to have a curved staircase similar to those which one would find in Paris, or even more broadly in France, in buildings of the Haussmann era. Additionally, we placed at the center of the circle created by the staircase an elevator which imitated those found in these buildings there: a body made of metal and wood, with curved glass windows, wrought iron decorations on the windows and surrounding it the cylindric "cage" in which the elevator goes up or down. Additionally, there was a folding black wrought iron curtain as a security at the front of the elevator. Truth be told, we had to cheat and make the elevator larger than those one can still find on the other side of the Atlantic Ocean; their usual capacity of 3 to 4 passengers would surely not suffice in a public location. Mindful of serving all our prospective visitors, we created a second group of elevators at the back of the building: a bank of three modern elevator cabins each holding at least fifteen people.

Chapter Twenty-seven

1948-49, 2002
VERSOIX, SWITZERLAND AND PARIS, FRANCE AND
NAPLES, FLORIDA

Officer Marchand unexpectedly got two important breaks. The first came from the Lausanne Police Department which found an individual who claimed to have seen someone who could have been Jules walk around the Eglise Reformée St-François at about the right time and on the right night. The various descriptions he gave ranging from the physique of the man who was pacing back and forth, as well as around the church and of the car to which the man doing the pacing eventually returned were as correct as any witness statement could be. He even mentioned the fact that the individual turned the car around at some point, though he could not tell when or guess why it happened. Officer Marchand made a note that the deposition strongly confirmed the statements which Jules made, though he added that the fact that Jules was indeed in Lausanne when he said he was did not necessarily mean that he was no longer a suspect, as he could still have ordered the crime, possibly stopping on the way to Lausanne to make a call from a public phone to confirm instructions to the intruder.

The other break involved the discovery that one of the sketches that were in the artist's folder that was stolen from the house in Versoix came up for sale. The element of luck in that case was quite material, as the sketch which was offered for sale first was signed by Renoir and comprised two different views of the two ladies by a pond, a painting which in fact was among those which we bought at the consignment shop. Luck had it that the buyer was an antique dealer at the flea market in Saint Ouen, just north of Paris proper. He happened to be an informer for the French Police and thus had been specifically contacted when Officer Marchand had reached out to Interpol. The combination of having a piece of art that was one of the few that could be readily identifiable and of the piece being offered to someone who effectively agreed to cooperate meant that the French Police were immediately able to arrest the seller. It took less than a couple of hours to find the actual seller, who was none other than Mrs. Prestat.

She claimed that it had been given to her by Mrs. Dumas-Schneider when she visited her in Versoix. Officer Marchand noted that, with Edith dead, there was no way to prove or disprove that Edith had indeed made the gift. Asked whether she had received any other gift, Rose replied that this was the only one that was given to her. Parenthetically, she apparently noted that Edith had at least another couple of dozen drawings, etchings, or sketches, many signed. She bemoaned the fact that she would not offer any additional help. She recalled a conversation which she said had been a bit more heated than usual; an evening when she had told Edith of her serious financial difficulties. She disclosed that she was considering selling her apartment as she claimed she could not afford it. Yet, she said that Edith was adamant that she could not help her financially anymore. She would not part with her art, as she remembered her father advising against it. Apparently, she added that Edith had said that she was sorry that she had given the one sketch in a moment of weakness. Yet, she seemingly promised that she would add Rose as a beneficiary of her estate if she died before her.

Officer Marchand made a note right below that comment that this provided a potentially powerful motive for Rose to have murdered Edith. Additionally, he noted that he would place a call to Edith's estate lawyer to verify whether the new codicil had been added. The next sentence confirmed that the day before her death, Edith had gone to see her estate lawyer in Geneva and bequeathed the full set of drawings to Rose at her death. Officer Marchand's notes suggested that this strengthened any contention that Rose murdered Edith but reduced the credibility of any motive that she might have ordered the theft: why organize to steal something which one was going to get anyway. He added a cryptic comment to the effect that he would rate the odds against Jules to be exactly the opposite; why should he have Edith murdered? However, stealing the artist folder might well help settle any remaining gambling debt.

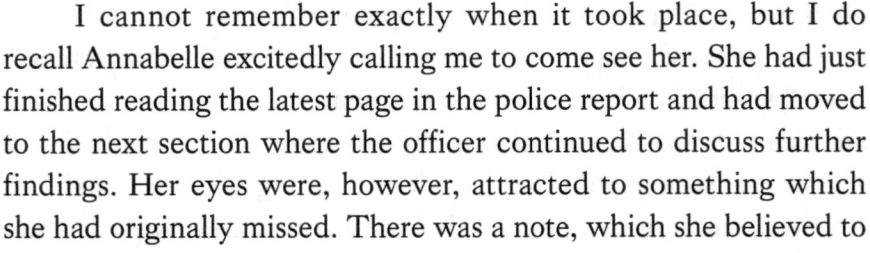

I cannot remember exactly when it took place, but I do recall Annabelle excitedly calling me to come see her. She had just finished reading the latest page in the police report and had moved to the next section where the officer continued to discuss further findings. Her eyes were, however, attracted to something which she had originally missed. There was a note, which she believed to be in Stephane's handwriting, stating that he had sent a message to

Officer Marchand. He wanted to remind him that Jules and Marie would get the beneficial use of the house in Versoix if Edith died, and that she had bought an annuity which would provide them with income to live on and to manage the property.

The next sheet in the police report mentioned Officer Marchand having received Stephane's note and thus concluding that Jules had no motive to steal anything in the house post Edith's dying. The officer wrote a somewhat exasperated note to the effect that the only interest which Jules could have had in having Edith murdered was to speed up a process that was already in place. For that to happen, there would need to be proof that his past had caught up with him and creditors were threatening unless he covered his past debts. He noted that this would likely lower any reason for him to have Edith murdered as her death would not make his financial situation any better to meet debt repayments.

Annabelle and I were surprised to see that the next sheet in the police report was dated a full one year after the prior one, and there was no corresponding tape recording. A second sketch by Renoir had come to the market, though not in France, but in Luxemburg. There were good reasons to believe that the source of the drawing was the stolen folder. First, there were two Renoirs on the list that was found in the E.S. folder; we knew one had already been presented for sale and returned to the family. Second, the theme of the sketch corresponded to one of the paintings that were in storage in Geneva Free Port and had belonged to Edith. The sketch had been confiscated under the Interpol umbrella and would soon be returned to the family as well. The challenge, bemoaned by Officer Marchand, was that there was no direct link to anyone, particularly to either Rose or Jules.

The prior eighteen months had been particularly busy for Annabelle. Planning had seemed to us to be almost interminable as there was a need to construct a building suitable to house the museum; there was the need to bring all the works of art from Switzerland, and most importantly to catalog everything. She had worked with Jim to get all the various permissions and supervised the construction of the foundation building. With my modest help as chairman, she needed to fill up the seats on the Board, which then included the two people from Sotheby's, Jim, Philip Paulsen, our current curator, and a half a dozen local personalities who we hoped would provide useful public relations for the museum, and maybe even contribute to the foundation's substantial endowment. Finally, she worked with Philip Paulsen and our friends at Sotheby's to get all the paintings, including those which we eventually kept for ourselves, cleaned up by professionals; any dirt that had accumulated over the years was removed from the paintings as well as from the frames for those which had original frames.

Though we expected the phase to be simple and non-controversial, the cataloguing of all the various pieces turned out to reserve an interesting surprise to everyone. The list of pieces which we knew belonged to Stephane at his death and were already in the U.S. proved completely correct; everything matched almost perfectly. There were a few hiccups here and there, especially when dealing with the drawings and etchings: however well-described by Stephane, there were still a few hesitations for unsigned pieces, which was the case for most of them, and for pieces which were what we might call "basic." There were indeed drawings that could have been described as "finished" to the extent that they could be viewed as self-standing, signed or not. At the same time, there were several pieces which might better be described as "sketches." In fact, three of them had several drawings on the same piece of paper, representing different perspectives on one element of a painting.

There were also no significant surprises with anything which had been left in France and eventually moved to Switzerland by Stephane, or with anything which used to belong to Edith other than what was held in the artist folder she kept in the house in Versoix. We had found a list of these pieces in the "E.S." folder in the secretary desk which we assumed had been compiled by David Schneider before his death. We also had the list compiled by Stephane Schneider in 1960, therefore after the murder of his sister and after he had inherited Edith's estate. The lists mostly overlapped; however, two pieces were missing from Stephane's list. In many ways, I was quite surprised by the discovery, as I would have expected Stephane to have carried out the comparison himself.

Complications arose with the balance of Edith's artworks, those which were in the house in Versoix. Indeed, though she initially only brought to the house the most valuable paintings she could take from the apartment in Paris, along with the artist folder containing drawings and the like, she eventually moved everything that was in Paris when the apartment was sold. She stayed with her earlier decision that everything that was highly valuable should go into storage at the Geneva Free Port; she thus accepted that she would not have the works by the famous impressionists; she would typically explain that her decision was based on the belief that her stay in Versoix was not permanent. Eventually she would move, probably to join her brother in the U.S., though the timing and exact circumstances never had the time to be finally discussed. The only highly valuable piece of furniture that eventually made its way to Versoix was her own Louis XVI cylinder desk. Unfortunately, nobody took any note of what was where after the move from Paris to Versoix. Furthermore, the house in Versoix was eventually sold in line with the instructions that were found in Edith's will: when the house was no longer needed by her domestic help. Thus, we found double counting in certain instances and items missing in others. Nothing of great value was found to be missing, yet the few items that were raised numerous questions.

On our end, Annabelle and I had to decide what we were going to do with our "treasure," everything we had bought at the consignment house. There was little discussion with respect to the gold, the gems and even the old French Franc notes: we would sell whatever did not fit in our financial asset portfolio. Where things became somewhat more complex was when we focused on the various paintings and other pictural art, on the few table-top bronze statues and on the pieces of furniture.

On the furniture side, we decided not only to keep most of what we had bought, as each piece was stunning. In fact, though I had inherited a few pieces which we had thought were exceptional, we had to concede that aside from one or two of these pieces the items we bought were better ignoring the obvious sentimental value than any inherited item had to have. Furthermore, we decided that we could surely use a few additional pieces of period furniture, particularly the secretary desks, the sloping desks and Edith's cylinder desk. We therefore bartered with the shipment coming from Switzerland, exchanging one of our paintings for those pieces.

There was little doubt in our minds that we surely did not have room, nor would our children have room for all the additional twenty-seven impressionist paintings, those we had bought framed and those we found in the double back of the armoire. The couple of dozen drawings and etchings only added to the problem. We therefore decided to select those paintings which we would have space to display, plus a couple additional ones for each of our four children. We examined the folder with all the drawing, sketches and etchings and made sure that we retained anything which was directly related to any one of the paintings we had selected for ourselves or for the children; they would add to the value of the paintings and would when displayed offer good conversation pieces. We then elected to donate the balance of the paintings and drawings to the foundation and thus to the museum. After all, we had been incredibly lucky to have stumbled on the treasures which we bought at the consignment shop, and it would only be fair for us to share our bounty with all the future visitors to the museum. Annabelle, always the most practical, had simply added:

"And we could not afford the insurance!"

The final sheet in the police report of Officer Marchand hit us like a ton of bricks. It named Rose Prestat as the murderer of Edith and the person who ordered the break-in and the theft a week after her murder. It turned out that she was in much more difficult financial straits than she led Edith to believe. She had had to borrow money to pay her debts and the higher-than-normal interest rates were killing her financially.

She confessed that, though Edith told her that she would never share that detail with her husband, she did occasionally give her some money. As she had told to Officer Marchand the first time he interrogated her, Edith had been particularly generous when Rose's husband died. Though Rose had argued then that she lacked money because of the delay in receiving the insurance on the life of her husband, the truth was that she never had enough, so addicted she was to gambling. She had had a terrible time during the war after Edith had left Paris, as this effectively closed one avenue of finance for her. Yet, truth be told, gambling was not the main preoccupation of most people during the "Occupation"—surviving was. So, she probably missed the fact that she did not have enough money to gamble, though she had fewer opportunities, except in specialized "clubs" run by the underground. She told Officer Marchand that she was delighted when Edith reopened the communications with her after the war, as her vice had resumed consuming her when more genteel and reputable clubs had reopened.

She said that she finally decided that she had to find a way to get some financial help. She discussed her debts with Edith without ever saying that they related to her gambling problem. She blamed them on bad investments made by her banker with her savings and to exceptional expenses to fix things that had broken in her apartment, in part because of the war. She claimed that Edith refused to give her anything she could sell, because she was morally committed to keeping everything that came to her from her father. However, she said that Edith did give her some money, adding that she did so pretty much each time she came to visit her in Switzerland; she also confessed to have stolen in each of her two prior visits small silver pieces which she could slip into her luggage. She further confessed that the last time they discussed money, an evening a couple of days before she was to return to Paris, Edith was very firm and told her that she could not subsidize her any longer. She had to find, she was told, a final solution. Though Edith ostensibly meant for that solution to involve selling the apartment in Paris and moving to a smaller place in a less fashionable district,

Rose immediately thought of what would happen if Edith was no longer around.

She confirmed the information which Officer Marchand had obtained from Erik Sutter, Edith's Swiss attorney, that Edith in a gesture of good will told Rose that she would leave her the artist folder with the drawings at her death. To Rose, this apparently became too much of an invitation. She contacted one of the people to whom she owed money and who she knew was somehow connected to the underworld and asked for help. That was the genesis of the murder which was committed by a hired killer that came from somewhere in the region, though she was never told precisely where. She confessed that she had found an excuse to be outside at the time Jules brought the food to the dog. She had waited until he had returned to the main house and then approached the dog while he was eating. She emptied the contents of a sleeping capsule into his water dish and returned to the house, using the front door. She did also confess that she had asked the murderer to upturn the dog's water dish and make sure it was empty before he returned to his car. Finally, she conceded that just before retiring to bed, she had pretexted that she needed a glass of water to go to the kitchen and unlock the back door which Marie had locked from the outside when she went to join Jules in their apartment.

She said she was surprised that her ploy to load the dice against Marie or Jules was as unsuccessful as it appeared to be. In the end, after Edith's death and just before leaving for Paris a few days after the murder, she managed to get some money out of Edith's money purse, but this was not enough.

That is when she came up with the idea of having someone come to steal the folder in Versoix. Asked by the officer why she needed to steal something which she was going to inherit anyway, she had seemingly replied that she could not wait for her estate to settle. She called again upon the same underworld figure. Her plan worked well to the extent that first the artist's folder was indeed stolen, in addition, since there were coincidental suspicions falling on Jules, Edith's driver, she added that she had composed an anonymous letter asking Jules to drive to Lausanne. However, yet again, she had underestimated the calm and professionalism with which the Geneva police would conduct the process. She thought that she had sufficiently pointed to Jules to be safe, and in fact believed she was out of the woods when she was allowed to return to Paris. Again, the one element which she did not include in her calculations was the fact that she would be signaled to Interpol and that the first sketch she tried to sell would be offered to someone who knew it might be stolen. She was sentenced to life in prison.

Epilogue

NAPLES, FLORIDA

Neither Annabelle nor I will forget the day the Schneider Foundation Museum opened in Estero. The cocktail party that was held was very well-attended, thanks in large part to the public relation work of the local members of the board, and hopefully a bit to the quality of the works on display. We had even arranged for television coverage which was allowed a preview earlier in the afternoon so that they could film a brief clip before anyone was there. They did shoot a few seconds with the crowd to make sure that they showed the success of the opening.

Overall, coverage was very favorable. Philip Paulsen had managed not only to recreate the feeling of a house in a structure which, from the outside, was more like modern office space than someone's home. The use of several furniture pieces that came from Switzerland did the trick. He had mixed with a great deal of success "family history" and family treasures. His most creative idea had been to use the hallways, which one always find in a house, to display photographs as well as selected facsimiles of diary pages (with suitable translations when needed) to ensure that visitors who took the time to look would be able to follow the history of the family from Vilnius to Naples. A chronology of the most important dates was even recreated on one of the walls of the elegant but understated entry hall.

The notion that the Schneider family had been coming to the Naples area for quite a long time was played up, giving Stephane Schneider the credit to have discovered what was eventually called "the Paradise Coast" of Florida. That played very well with the discovery by his father David Schneider of the impressionist movements. That this was in our view at least quite an overstatement as he surely was an early investor in the movement, but not the one who discovered it, was simply credited to natural enthusiasm. To observers like Annabelle and me, though the dates do not really work, this was raising the Schneider family to a level that approached two of the major pioneers in Southwest Florida. Thomas Edison discovered Southwest Florida in 1885 and decided to use it as their winter home which he named "Seminole Lodge," on the banks of the Caloosahatchee River, in Fort Myers, just north of Naples. Henry Ford who had become friends with Thomas Edison first visited him in 1914 and purchased property next door to Seminole Lodge in 1916, naming his estate "The Mangoes." With the Schneider Foundation displaying the exceptional impressionist collection, one could argue that the family's contribution to Southwest Florida though initially much less impressive that those made by Thomas Edison or Henry Ford had now become of equal if not greater importance. Time will tell if the visits to the museum come to equal or exceed those of the Ford and Edison Estates.

The story of the discovery of the treasure by Annabelle and me was also played up, with, I am sure, a sponsorship by the "antique dealers association." What better way to encourage people to go shop and even buy in various antique art shows or antique malls than to point to the fact that one can discover a real treasure? Yet, we made sure that all credit be given both to the great notes and diary entries of Stephane, to the obedience to sons and daughters who did not sell any of the family treasures and to the help received by art specialists, Sotheby's, as well as the professionals who had served the family and their successors.

On our side, the renovation of the house had been finished when the story started and neither Annabelle nor I wanted to make any further structural change to the house. Yet, we were both delighted to be able to have all rooms decorated with period furniture and great art; that our home does not look like a standard house decorated in the best of taste by consultants who want only the best for their clients was but a bonus. We have indeed always bemoaned the fact that too many of our acquaintances do not feel any commitment to what is inside their homes, to the point that a large majority of them would simply sell a house together with its furnishings and decorating items when they moved to the next one. That certain people must do it because they do not have memories attached to anything inside the house is understandable; some people went from zero to something without having the luxury of inheriting or purchasing stuff in their travels; their furnishings were utilitarian with no effort to look for artistic value or even more collectible status. Yet, it saddens us to think that family heirlooms can at times be readily disposed of.

The mystery of who steered the Paris police to the Schneider apartment in 1941 was never satisfactorily resolved. Rose vehemently denied that she had anything to do with the episode. Her logic was supported by a simple question she asked: "how would I benefit from it?" She also argued: "She was my friend," though the rationale was unquestionably weakened by the fact that she did eventually order the murder of "her friend." The clincher in her rationale from everybody's point of view was that, given where she was at that point, confessing that she was responsible would surely not change anything to her prison sentence, or to her relationship, or lack thereof, with the Schneider family. Suspicions shifted to the friends with whom Edith used to conduct her daily shopping during the war, but no proof could ever be uncovered, and no motive identified, other than anti-Semitism or jealousy. With anti-Semitism rejected on the ground that these friends were all Jewish themselves, jealousy would have to be the only possible motive, aside from a possible desire to go into the apartment and steal valuables after the police had left with the occupants.

However, one well-known element was that the French police were constantly hunting any looters, who would try to steal stuff from people whose apartments had been broken into by the police itself or the *Gestapo*. No attempt by any of these friends of Edith was ever reported, though there were a few random situations when outsiders went as far as the front door of the apartment; yet, with the door locked and with the help of Rose, they never went any further. Still, it is sad to have to concede that there were many collaborators in France at that time, and quite a number of them would have done almost anything to get on the Germans' good side and benefit from their favors.

Rose also said she could understand why Edith shut all communications down after the raid and really did not know where she was, confessing that she was not even aware of the property in Switzerland. Rose did confess that she stole a few valuables when she was asked by Edith, after the war, to help move all the contents to Switzerland and sell the apartment. She explained that, at that time, Edith had sent to her via the Post a key to allow her to enter the apartment, the first time she ever had one.

Investigators were surprised that she never expressed remorse for what she did, despite frequently bemoaning the passing of her old friend. Eventually, she was released from prison into a psychiatric hospital's care as it became obvious that she was suffering either from a form of schizophrenia or from a bipolar disfunction. She died there years later, her mental capacities deteriorating further with time to the point that, near the end, she could not recognize anyone.

Officer Marchand wrote a final note to the file to formally explain his decision to exculpate Jules. Ostensibly, Rose's confession was the most important element in the decision, but the full story of Jules's trip to Lausanne shed light on the situation as well. Jules explained that he had believed that the anonymous letter he received was from people in the Paris gambling circles that might have found him and still be after him. He did go to Lausanne though his own instincts told him that was the riskier option. Yet, he felt that calling the police at that time might only provide a short-term help, leaving the long-term problem to fester: he might succeed chasing the "enemy" away for once, but they would come back since the root cause of the problem had not been addressed: the fact that he left Paris owing money to a few unsavory people.

Therefore, he decided and shared the decision with Marie that he would go to Lausanne, though he would take a gun with him. He confirmed that Marie was adamantly opposed to his decision and cried a fair amount when he told her he would go. He said that she understood his logic in her mind but could not get over the personal risk he was taking. His plan was to confront the enemy and do it from a position of strength. He said the lower expenses the couple incurred since they were at Versoix and the fact that his gambling had become more of a side, low-cost activity had allowed him and Marie to accumulate some savings. He then had enough to repay the debts, though he surely did not know what the creditors said the amounts would be because he did not know what interest rate they would apply to a delinquent borrower. Yet, he was ready to repay debts that were still outstanding but made it clear he would not be doing so under duress and was prepared to do it gradually if the terms were reasonable. His plan was to confront any accuser and make a reasonable offer.

Ostensibly, the fact that there was no one awaiting him in Lausanne quickly told Jules that he had been intentionally driven from the property so that the theft could be carried out. Officer Marchand noted the joke as the last line of his report:

"Jules, Mrs. Prestat, and her goons respect you and your ability to defend the property. That may well be the reason why she so strongly tried to lead me toward having you as my main suspect in the murder of Mrs. Edith and to lead you away from the house on the night of the theft."

The underworld figure who murdered Mrs. Edith and then came to steal the artist's folder was ultimately arrested in Paris for a totally different crime. He was eventually connected to the murder and theft in Versoix through the car he was driving when he was arrested. Officer Marchand had ordered plaster prints to be taken from the tire marks that Bernhard Reinhold had noticed. Pictures of these were attached to the Schneider murder files. The criminal was confronted with the fact that the prints from the tires on his car matched those on the file. He initially argued that there could be many cars using the same type and size of tires. He was then shown the testimony of Bernhard Reinhold stating that he had fired twice at the intruder's car; the fact that the suspect had not bothered getting rid of the small impact traces left by the pellets from Bernhard's shotgun took him to the point when he was ultimately forced to confess as he could not provide a good alibi for the time when he committed the crime. Additionally, the gun that he carried when he was arrested fit the two bullets which had been retrieved in Versoix, one in the dog's shoulder and the other on the ground near the servants' cottage. He was sentenced to death.

www.ingramcontent.com/pod-product-compliance
Lightning Source LLC
Chambersburg PA
CBHW051140030726
47504CB00004B/965